HIDDEN TALENTS

▰▰▰▰▰▰▰▰▰▰▰▰▰▰▰▰▰▰▰▰▰▰▰▰

"So what's your specialty?" Guibedo asked the creature.

"Unarmed combat with a minor in sociology, my lord." The Labor and Defense Unit crowded closer to the left-hand wall of the tunnel. Other LDUs with empty baskets were passing them at an astounding speed.

"Pretty quick your buddies are. But I don't understand the 'unarmed combat.' If you were expecting trouble, why go unarmed?"

"My Lord, I meant no *external* armament." From a slot above each wrist, a bayonetlike claw extended out to a foot past the knuckles.

By Leo Frankowski
Published by Ballantine Books:

THE ADVENTURES OF CONRAD STARGARD:

COPERNICK'S REBELLION

*Forthcoming

Copernick's Rebellion

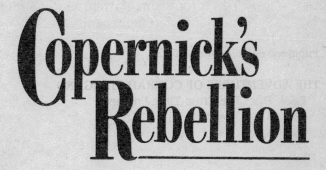

LEO A. FRANKOWSKI

A Del Rey Book

BALLANTINE BOOKS • NEW YORK

DEDICATION

This is for Elaine Bowen,
my ever perfect lieutenant.

Prologue

AN OLD *sergeant downed his third pot of wine, belched, and explained to the young private, "Kid, it's like this. You see something needs doing, go ahead and do it. Don't ask nobody's permission, because they'll tell you no. Officers got their positions to protect and they can't get into no trouble if nothing happens.*

"Just go ahead and do it. Then if it turns out right, you're a hero. And if it goes wrong, you won't get into much trouble because everybody knows you're just a dumb trooper anyway."

—Quoted from a dubious Cuniform Text, Ca. 3900 B.C.

Chapter One

APRIL 21, 1999

IT SHOULD be intuitively obvious to the most casual of observers that our present civilization is faced with a number of serious, possibly insurmountable problems.

Our basic resources are almost exhausted.

Over forty nations possess atomic arsenals, many of which are large enough to eradicate all life on this planet.

The world's literacy level has dropped to less than fifty percent.

Pollutants are rendering major tracts of farmland sterile at a time when more than eighty percent of our population is undernourished.

Poor standards of sanitation, increased population pressure, and ever-increasing geographical mobility have caused three serious plagues in the last decade. Diseases have annihilated other species; they could wipe out ours.

It seems likely that the Four Horsemen are about to ride in earnest, and I can see no politically acceptable method of stopping them. A technical, biological solution might be possible in ten or twenty years, if civilization holds together that long.

But even this solution could not be acceptable to the Earth's two hundred warring nations.

—Heinrich Copernick
From his lab notebook
March 4, 1989

2

The aging U.S. senator walked carefully into a plush Washington restaurant and looked slowly around for his dinner date.

"Senator Beinheimer. It's good to meet you, sir."

The senator was momentarily startled by the appearance of the athletic young man before him. "Well, it's very good to meet you, son. But just now I have an appointment with an old friend."

"I'm afraid I'm him, sir."

"And I'm afraid you're wrong, sir. I'm looking for Lou von Bork."

"I'm Lou von Bork."

"What! Oh, wait a minute. That's right. I'd heard that you'd taken over your grandfather's firm. It's just that over the phone you sounded so much like him that I thought he was visiting his old stomping grounds again. How is old Lou?"

"Well, according to the postcards, he's still taking his retirement pretty seriously, sir."

"Raising hell and drinking sour mash on that boat of his, huh?"

"That's about the size of it, sir."

"And still chasing women, I guess."

"Two of them, if you want to believe the photos."

"Oh, you can believe them, son. Your granddad never was the sort to let his wick go dry for long." The senator laughed. Then quietly he said, "It's good to see that some people can retire."

"Well, the country would be in worse shape without you, sir."

"Hmm. Well." The sparkle in the senator's eyes went out. "About that lunch you promised me . . ."

Later, in one of the darkened, soundproof booths that made the Twin Bridges popular, the senator said, "Son, I just can't get over how much you look like your granddad. Why, you're the spitting image of him when he was your age. Come over to the house sometime and I'll show you pictures of the two of us when we were in college."

"I'd like that, sir."

"Why, you even smoke Pall Malls and drink Jim Beam

like he does. Now tell me, isn't that part of it a little bit of an act? You just figure that if he was the best lobbyist in Washington, everything he did must have been right, huh?"

Von Bork just smiled.

"Well, I'll allow that nothing succeeds like success. Just don't go laying it on too thick, and you'll come along just fine."

"I'll try to, sir. It's an odd business."

"Well, you hear a lot of grumbling about paid lobbyists, but I think that they do a lot of good around here."

"Indeed, sir?"

"Yes indeed. You see, son, my colleagues and I have to know what folks are thinking. We need information channels from all sorts of people, and your gang provides us with a lot of those."

"Even if they're biased?"

"Son, every channel is biased. Everybody has an ax to grind. At least with a lobbyist, you know what he's pulling for, and you can make allowances."

"I'll bear that in mind, sir."

"Will you quit 'sirring' me? My friends call me Moe."

"Thanks, Moe."

"You're welcome, Lou. Now, what are you doing with your granddad's company?"

"Mostly trying to pick up the pieces. Trying to get to know the people and so on."

"It *was* kind of sudden, the way he just up and quit. The way he explained it to me, just before he left, was that retiring was like quitting smoking. You got to go cold turkey. Still, he should have at least introduced you around."

"Well, maybe. Or maybe the best way to learn how to swim is just to jump in."

"Well, son, I think that I might be able to give you a swimming lesson or two. You come over to Daisey's party tomorrow, and I'll introduce you around."

"I'd really appreciate that, Moe."

"No trouble at all. I owed old Lou a few favors, and I might as well pay them back to you. Now how about the other half of the business? Were you able to keep many of his old clients?"

"About half of them. I've got Markoff Industries, the Michigan Milk Producers, and Copernicus, Inc."

"Well, that's a fine start for a young man in your business. Go soft on Copernicus, though. Heiny Copernick didn't make any friends with that stink he raised about his rejuvenation research program."

"He was funding it with his own money, wasn't he? Why shut him down?"

"Whoa, now! Nobody said that he had to stop his research. Just like nobody said that the government had to keep on buying equipment from his company. But screaming 'patricide' when he got a few orders canceled . . . Well, that's just not how the game's played."

"Well, in any event, Heinrich Copernick is retiring. He doesn't even own any stock in the company anymore."

"Yeah? Well, you mention that around and you won't hit so many snags. But don't do it until tomorrow, Lou."

"Why not?"

"So I can sell my Copernicus stock before the bottom falls out of it!" The senator stood. "Well, I got to git. But you take yourself over to Daisey's tomorrow."

"I'll do that. Better still, how about if I pick you up at your house and drive you over there? You could show me those college photos."

"Sure. See you at five thirty." The senator hobbled away cautiously.

Von Bork arrived at 5:29:59 in a nine-hundred-dollar casual suit. "Good afternoon, Moe."

"Lou, boy! Come in." The senator looked down at his own housecoat and slippers. "Been taking it a bit easy today."

"Yes, sir. I understand."

"Quit 'sirring' me. And what the hell do you mean, you 'understand'?"

"I—I went out with a nurse last night. One of Dr. Cranford's."

"Good man, Cranford. Go to him myself occasionally. You don't mean that pretty little redhead he's got running around his front office?" The senator was adept at getting people off unpleasant subjects.

"Yes, Moe. She told me. About you."

"What! She has no business talking about other people's lives!"

"She has been a fan of yours all her life. She was so broken up, she had to tell somebody."

"Listen, boy. She didn't tell you nothing. And you didn't hear nothing. And you ain't going to say nothing, either! You hear me, boy?"

"Anything you say, sir. I'm not your enemy."

"I know that, boy. And old Lou is my best friend. It's just that if word of this got around, my effectiveness in the Senate would be over."

"I understand, Moe."

"I doubt that. I'm afraid of dying . . . But it isn't really that. Life hasn't been worth much since my wife died. It's just that I hate leaving when there's so much to do."

"No chance of an organ transplant?"

"Would be if it was only one organ. But Cranford says that just about every organ in my body is shot. Replacing any one of them would be too much of a strain on the rest. I guess that some people just grow old faster than other people."

"It doesn't have to be that way, Moe."

"Growing old and dying is a natural part of life." The senator was staring at the floor.

"So is shitting in the woods. But that doesn't mean that we have to do it."

"What are you talking about?"

"Rejuvenation, Moe."

"That work was stopped. I helped stop it. I guess my sins are coming back to me."

"So maybe dying would serve you right. But justice isn't a fact of nature, either. Anyway, the work wasn't stopped. It just went underground."

"How could Heiny do that without being caught?"

"Motivation. He didn't want to die, either. Look, Moe. I'll keep your secrets if you'll keep mine."

"About Heiny? Why not? He didn't break any laws. And knowing about it would just upset folks."

"About rejuvenation. And about me. Moe, I'm not my grandson. I'm me."

The senator stared at von Bork for thirty seconds.

"You've got one hell of a lot of proving to do, boy!"

"Ask me some questions."

"So I could be young again . . . Okay, I'm sold. Now, how do I find Heiny Copernick? And what does it cost?"

"You don't find Mr. Copernick. And he doesn't want your money. He wants your support."

"Somehow I figured that that was coming. So Heiny wants to legitimize rejuvenation . . . ?" The senator was an old hand at making deals. "I can try, Lou. But even I don't swing that much weight. Eighty-three percent of the federal budget goes to direct aid to individuals. If we had to support every oldster until he was a hundred, instead of seventy-two like now, we would have to more than double federal revenues. Which means doubling the taxes, and they are up to sixty-one percent of gross income already!"

"No. That's a dead issue. You're on the HEW appropriations committee. The next issue we're interested in is tree houses. There must be no governmental regulations concerning them."

"Tree houses? Genetically modified trees? I've heard of them. Nobody's kicked up much of a fuss about them so far. Can't be more than a dozen of them growing. Why? Is Heiny behind that one, too?"

"Not exactly. Let's say he's interested."

"I'm your man, Lou. I mean, if all you want is for the government to keep hands off them."

"That's all."

"Well, new technology shouldn't be regulated, anyway. Say, what's my constituency going to say about me looking like a kid?"

"You're not going to look like a teenager, Moe. It would ruin your effectiveness. No, you're about to have a spontaneous remission. You'll grow a new set of organs, but that's all. For the time being, at least."

"For the time being?" the senator said.

"In ten or twenty years, when you're ready, you can retire, officially. Then you can get the full treatment, be any age you want. You'll still have to live near one of our centers, of course."

"Why's that?"

"It isn't completely perfected yet. You'll have to drop by once a month for a booster shot. But if you play ball with us for ten years, I'll see to it that you get the full treatment. Then you can be any age you want."

"Lou, you have a deal. As long as you don't ask me to do anything that's against my conscience. Where do I go to get this treatment? You know that I don't have much time."

"I'll pick you up tomorrow afternoon. We have a facility right here, in Crystal City—a good spit from the Pentagon."

"You built a facility here for me?"

"Moe, what makes you think that you're the only aging congressman in need of our help?"

"Somehow I've got the idea that your tree houses are going to be left alone." The senator laughed.

Later, on their way to Daisey's party, the senator said, "Lou, if you could be any age you wanted to be, why did you want to look like a college kid?"

"The college girls, Moe. The pretty college girls." Von Bork laughed.

Martin Guibedo sat at his microscalpel, making another tree. He was a marshmallow man, just five feet tall, and of considerable girth. His unruly hair and mustache were white and thick, and his wrinkled red face gave no hint of pain or doubt or sadness. Calloused hands moved over the controls with the agility of a competent surgeon of fifty. Actually, he was over ninety, and had seen most of his friends die.

"Ach! You're going to be such a beauty, you!" he said to the yard-long strand of DNA, watching the assembly of a string of bases that would give this model a nine-foot bed.

In principle, the apparatus was simple. A tiny beaker contained a mixture of cytosine, inosine, thymine, adenine, and a few other chemicals in otherwise pure water. A long organic molecule was being slowly drawn from the beaker with the various bases attaching themselves randomly to its end. As each new base was drawn out, it was scanned by an X-ray resonance microscope, which identified the base and compared it against a model stored in the memory of a very large computer. When, by chance, it was the correct base, it was allowed to pass. When it was not, an X-ray laser sliced it off, and the end of the molecule was reinserted in the beaker to try again. The process was automatic, yet it required continuous monitoring, for one error in ten billion decisions could result in a monstrosity instead of a comfortable home.

"You're just what my nephew Heiny wanted. And your lights are going to go on and off, and your synthesizer ain't going to go spritzing beer all over the kitchen, so Heiny ain't got to get into a bathing suit and chop it off with a boy scout axe, like he did last time. Ach. And it was such good beer, too!" Gnarled fingers danced on the controls.

He had been born in Leipzig in 1910, with an Italian-Catholic father and a Polish-Jewish mother. His father's civil engineering work had caused the family to move often around Europe. Martin's parentage and experiences had left him with an improbable accent, a profound disrespect for institutions, and an open contempt for governments.

"So beautiful you're going to be, everybody's going to love you. But why does Heiny want you so big?"

In a few hours he had sealed down the lid of a seed, planted it in a Dixie cup, and watered it.

"And this time, the absorption toilet is going to work!"

His only friend, relative, and contact with the world was his nephew, Heinrich Copernick. There was no blood tie between them—Guibedo's wife had been Heinrich's mother's sister—but a deep and permanent bond had been forged between a thirty-year-old man and a five-year-old boy in the winter of 1940 in Germany. Guibedo was frostbitten and young Copernick was stunted and crippled by rickets by the time they got out of Europe, but they were the only members of two large families to survive.

Yet differences in temperament and life style resulted in the two seeing each other only four or five times a year. For twenty-five years, Guibedo had been completely immersed in his work, to the extent that he was almost a hermit. And while he was conscious of no loneliness or lack in his life, he found himself talking constantly to the plants and trees around him.

He walked through the hollow branch that connected the workshop to his bedroom, ducking under the coffee-table that had grown—inexplicably—upside down from the ceiling. Guibedo had hung candles from it and declared it a chandelier to anyone who would listen.

"Ach! Laurel, you grow so much today!" he said to a seedling in a pot by the window. He spent some time searching for his suit, gave up and settled for a bush jacket.

"Laurel, we gonna plant you outside pretty soon, girl." Guibedo was putting on a nearly perfectly clean shirt.

"You gonna be proud of me today! Me! Heiny got me an interview on television! I'm going to talk with a bunch of people about you lovelies! Lots of people is gonna hear how pretty you are."

He checked a few trees growing in the yard and got to the studio almost early.

To Patricia Cambridge, the world showed no signs of ending. There were famines in Asia, South America, and Africa, but such things rarely registered on her consciousness. The problems of energy, pollution, and the scarcity of raw materials had been partially solved in North America, occasionally at the expense of the rest of the world. But Patricia, a typical American, was unconcerned. There were wars and plagues and dozens of tiny countries that were building nuclear bombs, but that had nothing to do with her, for hers was a golden world of bright promise.

She had just been promoted because she was an absolutely ordinary person. She was pretty without being inordinately beautiful, intelligent without being intellectual, and hard working without being too aggressive.

And the men in charge at NBC had wanted someone

for a daytime talk show, someone who could relate to the "average woman," the sort who bought soap and deodorants because of their television commercials. Patricia, of course, didn't know this. For her, this promotion was a just reward for the five years she had spent at NBC—her entire working career.

Primly dressed in last month's fashions, a gray velvet tights suit printed to imitate used potato sacks, she rode the ancient subway from her dingy apartment to the studio. She didn't notice the grime and shabbiness around her, for Patricia lived in her own world of blue skies and infinite possibilities.

She was out to get the best ratings in her time slot, and she was going to do it by getting at the issues that really counted. Things like political corruption and homosexuality and tree houses.

"This is Patricia Cambridge with *The World at Large!* Today on *The World at Large* we will be covering an issue vital to the entire housing industry, the genetically modified tree. On my right we have Burt Scratchon. Mr. Scratchon is president of Shadow Lawn Estates, Inc., and a leader in the mass housing industry. Mr. Scratchon's book, *The Death of an Economy,* is climbing the bestseller lists. On my left we have Dr. Martin Guibedo. Dr. Guibedo is Professor Emeritus of Biochemistry from Dallas State College and the inventor of these trees."

"What do you mean, inventor of the tree? Trees have been a long time around. I only showed them how to grow all comfortable on the inside, so we ain't gotta chop them down no more."

"Uh." Patricia glanced at her list of questions. "Dr. Guibedo, I understand that you have never written a paper on your genetic modification technique, nor have you applied for a patent. Is it your intention to keep this new science entirely to yourself?"

"Well, the science was all figured out five years ago. What is left is the engineering. I never wrote a paper on it because genetic engineering has been banned for five years. Nobody would have accepted a paper if I had written one."

"Banned?" Patricia asked. "You mean it's against the law?"

"Not exactly. But anybody working on it has a hard time getting a job later. A journal that published an article on it might lose its federal subsidy. And, of course, trying to get grants to work on genetic engineering is like trying to get money to find out the causes of aging. Impossible. The big shots have a lot of ways of pushing people around."

"So you're keeping this to yourself out of spite?" Patricia asked.

"Not spite. Nobody hurt me, but nobody helped me. I did this myself, with my own money. The results and the responsibility are mine. Patty, you gotta understand that this genetic engineering thing could get out of hand. If I let just anybody do it, some big shot would start making himself an army! Better I keep this whole thing quiet."

"Quiet?" Scratchon exploded. "You've *given away* two hundred of the things and they're already breeding like maggots!"

"Maggots don't breed, Burty." Guibedo's thirty years of teaching showed. "Maggots are the larval form of the adult housefly, which does the breeding. My tree houses don't breed, either. Asexual reproduction maintains the purity of each strain so that—"

"Technicalities have nothing to do with the economic impact of free housing, without even government supervision, on a free economy. Already housing starts are down four percent compared to last year. The building trades are facing massive layoffs, and the mortgage market is in a slump. This will have repercussions throughout the entire economy. The stability of the nation, of the entire free world, is being threatened by your hideous weeds!"

"Dr. Guibedo, you brought some photographs of your latest creation?" Patricia was a moderator intent on moderating.

"Sure, Patty. I brought a whole bunch. These first ones are of Ashley, where I live in."

"But the rooms are so huge!" Patricia said.

"Eight thousand square feet all together, Patty. It didn't cost anything to make it bigger than a regular house. I had an acre of land, and I figured I might as well furnish it good. This picture is in the living room. The furniture is all grown in—"

"There goes the furniture industry!" Scratchon said.

"—except the fireplace. This one is the bedroom. By the window is Laurel. She's gonna be a honey, that one. Growing here is the bed and the cupboard. Hey! There's my suit. I was looking for it!"

"You keep your suit rolled up in a cupboard?" Scratchon asked.

"Drawers are hard to grow. This is the bathroom. The absorption toilet was the hardest part. Keeping roots from plugging up the sewer pipe is tricky when the sewer pipe *is* a root. I finally solved it by having the house grow a new toliet when the old one gets plugged. You see, the tree needs human excrement to—"

"Is this the kitchen?" Patricia asked. *Toilets indeed!*

"Sure. This is the table and chairs. You don't need a stove and refrigerator because in these cupboards Ashley makes all my food."

"My God!" Scratchon interrupted. "You're attacking the food industry, too! Isn't it enough to threaten the job of every carpenter and dry-wall installer in the country? You've got to starve out the farmers, too?"

"What starve? It makes food, not takes it away. Anyway, them farmers got nothing to worry about. I mean, the sukiyaki is pretty good, but the crepes suzette are only fair. And the sauerbraten! Ach, the sauerbraten. My mother would be ashamed."

"Dr. Guibedo," Patricia said, "do you mean that the food comes already prepared? That would take a lot of the *fun* out of housekeeping. Don't you think so, Mr. Scratchon?"

"I think that this sawed-off runt's head is as fat as his belly! Don't you realize what he's doing? Can't you understand that when construction, farming, and banking fold, the entire country will go down the drain, too? Businesses by the thousands will go bankrupt. Millions of men will be out of work, and we sit here debating!" Scratchon folded his arms, fury in his eyes.

The twinkle left Guibedo's eyes, and the smile wrinkles on his face smoothed. "Yah, I know. A lot of changes will happen. And I'm sorry if they make some people unhappy. Change and progress have always hurt some people, but the net effects have been good for humanity. The Industrial Revolution, for example, wasn't very nice for the people who had to work in those old factories. And the old nobility didn't like what was happening, either. But without it, the three of us and them guys with the cameras would be out digging potatoes with a stick to eat. So changes will happen, but I make a promise. Anybody who wants a house, I will sell him a seed. No matter what happens, everybody can have a nice place to live and plenty of food to eat. I'll even get the sauerbraten right."

"Bare sustenance!" Scratchon said. "That's all you're offering. Good men don't work for food and minimal housing. People work for status, for prestige, to make a contribution to humanity and to provide security for themselves and their loved ones. People have spent their lives building the industries that you're trying to collapse. Worked their hearts out so that their children and their grandchildren could live decently. And you're trying to wreck it all!"

"Ach! You're just saying that there won't be so many big shots. And maybe that's not so bad. Maybe we've got too many big shots pushing people around. But decency? You can be just as decent as you want in a tree house. You just got nobody to look down at, because they can live just as good as you!"

With all of the art of a true real estate salesman, Scratchon shifted gears.

"I think you're trying to sidestep the major issue here. The modern home is the product of thousands of years of refinements, the collective work of humanity. These tree things are basically untried and unsound. No one knows if they'll last."

"Ach! You got a brick as old as a redwood?"

"Our homes are symbols of our status, of our contributions to society."

"Big shot," Guibedo muttered, but Scratchon continued uninterrupted.

"Oh, the idea of living free of charge sounds okay at first. There's a little larceny in all of us." Scratchon gave the camera a toothy smile. "And the idea of living in a tree might bring out a childish romanticism in some. But to give up our solid, modern homes, full of modern conveniences, to live like apes in a tree? The whole concept is absurd. Personally, I wouldn't live in one if you gave it to me!"

"I would give you one if you would live in it," Guibedo said. "All you have said, you have said from ignorance. You don't know how nice they are. Try for yourself. You will love them like I do."

"Get serious, Guibedo. I'd be the laughingstock of the neighborhood. Anyway, I've got a business to run. I don't have time for gardening."

"I'll plant if for you, Burty, and I'll take care of it. We put it in your backyard, so you and everybody can compare it with your old house."

Scratchon thought about the comparison between a tree house and his $450,000 Tudor brick home in Forest Hills. *Yeah,* he thought, *and with the economy being what it is, Shadow Lawn Estates, Inc., can use all the publicity it can get.*

"Ms. Cambridge, if I go through with this stunt, would you give it proper television coverage?"

"Why, of course, Mr. Scratchon. An experiment like this would make a wonderful program."

"Plant your tree, Guibedo."

"You'll give it an honest try? Promise to live in it for a year, or at least six months?" Guibedo said.

"You've got a deal, Guibedo. We'll show people what living in a tree is really like."

Chapter Two

▲▼▲▼▲▼▲▼▲▼▲▼▲▼▲▼▲▼

GETTING RICH is easy. It just takes a lot of work.

The average person spends fifty-six hours a week sleeping, forty hours a week making money, and the remaining ninety-two hours in the week spending money. If you work one hundred hours a week, you have two and a half times the income but only thirty-two hours a week to spend it in.

It helps to get in on the ground floor of a new industry, as I did with medical instrumentation. It usually helps to be a bachelor. And being crippled results in having fewer distractions. But the important thing is to get yourself into the habit of working yourself to your very limits.

  —Heinrich Copernick
   From an address to the Chicago Junior Chamber of Commerce
   April 3, 1931

Heinrich Copernick sat in front of his biomonitoring console. A thin plastic tube, red with his blood, ran from his left thigh to the machine. A similar tube ran from the console back to his leg. But the blood it carried was discolored with the chemicals that had been added to it.

"The calcium level is a bit low again," Copernick muttered to himself as he typed in revised instructions to the mixer.

The white numbers on his panel were generated by a

Cray Model 12 computer in the next room from a complete analog of the biochemical reactions taking place within his body. Even with the algorithms developed by his Uncle Martin, the program had taken more than two years to write.

Below each white prediction number was a status readout of his actual biochemistry. These were all green except for calcium, which was still in the yellow.

The phone rang. Copernick had disconnected the video section before he started his self-modification program.

"Hello."

"Mr. Copernick? This is Lou von Bork."

"Hello, Lou. How goes it in Washington?"

"So-so. You know that bill to put tree houses under the jurisdiction of the Food and Drug Administration? Well, I fixed it so it will die in committee."

"Great! Old Anne Cary will spit nickels when she hears about it."

"Yeah. I just hope that I don't get in range. She'll be at it again next year. And then she'll have the banking people behind her, besides the construction unions."

"Then we'll just have to lick them again."

"What do you mean 'we,' Mr. Copernick? I'm out here with nothing but a smile and a shoeshine."

"And you are doing a fine job. You and your six technicians and nine million dollars worth of equipment. Now what's the bad news?"

"HEW. They just passed a ruling that discriminates against people living in your uncle's tree houses. Not through Congress. A departmental ruling. Not a thing that I could do about it."

"Just what did they do?" Copernick asked.

"Cut in half the welfare benefits of anybody living in one. Think we should fight it? In court, I mean."

"Sounds pretty expensive. Let's let this one pass. A guy with a tree house can still live well on five hundred dollars a month."

"You're probably right, sir. Anyway, odds are the welfare types will do the suing for us."

"And doing it with the government's lawyers. Anything else?"

"Oh, the army is talking about using them for barracks. The National Real Estate Board wants to make them illegal. And the State Department is thinking about donating a few million seeds to the Africans. But I don't think that anything will come of any of it."

"A government purchase? Sounds nice. We'll get a good price out of them," Copernick said.

"Like I said, don't hold your breath. Say, when are you going to get the video on your phone fixed?"

"You know the phone company. Hey, how's your old friend Beinheimer?"

"Wonderful! When you guys replace a fellow's glands, you don't screw around!"

"No, but our clients do."

"I'll say. Moe's been making up for twenty lost years! I know his heart won't go, but I worry about his backbone and pelvis!"

"Enjoy. Keep me posted, Lou."

"I'll do that, Mr. Copernick. Take care."

His calcium status was back in the green. Copernick started to type in the day's modification. The straightening and rebuilding of his legs had been fairly straightforward, little more than an adjunct to the rejuvenation process. But he was getting into major genetic modifications, alien ground where he had met with more defeats than victories.

"Every day in every way, I'm getting better and better." He chuckled, getting his nerve up.

He was adding a virus to his own bloodstream, one that had been tailored to penetrate the blood-brain barrier. It was supposed to cause the cells in his cerebral cortex to reproduce, expanding his memory and intelligence. It had worked on experimental animals. The computer said that it should work on him. But a computer analog is only a model of reality, and models are never perfect.

An hour later he leaned back, stretched, and disconnected himself from his machine.

"So much for the joys of do-it-yourself brain surgery."

Copernick ate a lonely supper, looking often at his watch. She was late. He considered calling the airport, but changed his mind. If she was to grow up, she had to be allowed to make her own mistakes. He felt like a worrying parent. In a way, he was.

An incredibly beautiful woman rang the doorbell.

A big woman, she was six feet tall and full bodied. She was dressed in a precise, finishing school manner that accented her glorious red hair and freckles. Her clear green eyes held a curious combination of intelligence and vacancy. She looked to be about twenty.

"I'm sorry," she said. "I thought that this was the Copernick residence."

"It is. Welcome home, Mona. I'm Heinrich."

"Oh. You look so different." Her smile wasn't artificial. But it was somehow empty.

"I know. I've spent this last year mostly working on myself. Please come in."

"You look very nice, Heinrich."

"I'm glad you approve. I only wish Uncle Martin did."

"Will you let me meet him now?" Mona said.

"In a few months. He still doesn't know that you exist."

"I wish you were more proud of me, Heinrich."

"It isn't that, Mona. I'm very proud of you. It's just that my uncle has some old-fashioned concepts of what morality is."

"And your other friends?"

"I don't have many friends. Those that are left haven't seen me in six months. Mona, please try to understand that we must not let the world know about what we are doing. If the authorities found out about us, they would shut me down tomorrow."

Mona was silent.

"Come on, darling. Let me show you around our new home."

"Is this one of those tree houses? The girls at the finishing school talked about them, but none of us had ever seen one."

"It is. And Uncle Martin designed it especially for us."

"You mean especially for you," Mona said.

"Now don't start on that again. Homecomings should be pleasant occasions."

"Yes, Heinrich."

"The kitchen is this way. Have you eaten?"

"They fed us on the plane."

"Oh. Well, there really isn't much to taking care of the kitchen. The end cabinet is a dishwasher. It works continuously, so you can just leave the tableware in it. Most of the other cabinets grow food. I've labeled things so you can find your way around."

"Everything is so huge."

"Bigger than you think. The house and all the gardens around it are one single plant. It's five stories high."

"But why so big, Heinrich?"

"Why not? It doesn't cost any more to have a thing grow large. Anyway, my work has been taking up more and more room lately. I don't want to have to go through the bother of moving again for some time."

"Oh. Is this the bathroom?"

"Yes. You cut the membrane on one of the shower nozzles to make them work. The five nozzles on the left vent a soapy water; the five on the right are fresh. In each set the one to the left is the hottest; the others get progressively cooler. Once you cut a membrane, you drain a fifty-gallon tank. Whether you want that much or not."

"Fifty gallons! At school the water was rationed."

"It's rationed in most places these days. But a tree house recycles everything, so you can afford to splurge."

"Can I use it now? Please?"

"Of course, darling."

Mona eagerly stripped off her clothes, folded them neatly, and set them on a bench. No one had ever told her that people should be ashamed of their bodies. Hers was something to be proud of. The only flaw was that her navel was twice the usual diameter. Heinrich made a note to correct that as soon as possible.

Soon she was splashing and playing like a child in the warm sudsy water. Copernick was tempted to join her, but she seemed to be having so much fun that he was afraid of dampening it. He sat on a recliner chair, lit a cigar, and enjoyed. Having Mona around was going to be wonderful.

"Where are the towels?" Mona said after she had drained all ten nozzles.

"You use that white blanket thing over there."

"Okay—oh! It's stuck to the wall."

"It's part of the house. Cleans itself. Come on. I want to show you the rest of the place."

"Just a minute." Mona ran over to her clothes.

"Leave them."

"But I bought them especially for you! I'd hoped you would like them."

"I do. But I like the outfit you're wearing better."

Mona thought a moment, then smiled. "Thank you."

Copernick led her to a small room.

"This elevator is one of my animals. Nonsentient, of course. It's really little more than a box hanging at the end of a single muscle, with a door at each floor. It works like an ordinary elevator. Press these nubs for the floor you want." Copernick pressed for the second basement.

Mona ran her fingers through the fur on the wall. "Mink?"

"Pretty close. As I said, these things don't cost extra. I do most of my work down here. The lights are bioluminescent. And automatic."

"But they are on now."

"Because we are not alone." Copernick started to lead her to the computer room.

"Ay, boss! Them's nice tits on that one!" a heavy voice shouted from a strong steel cage. A hulking shape was barely visible.

Mona cringed. "Who was that?"

"One of my failures. I wanted something to do heavy labor and defense work. At the time, modifying a great ape seemed to be the easiest route."

"He's so ugly." The black bull mountain ape had a bulging forehead.

"Them bastard! He don't make no girls like me!"

"And I'm not going to make any more boys like you, either." Copernick led Mona away.

"What went wrong?"

"Nothing. And everything. I thought that by increasing his gray matter and giving him an adequate vocal apparatus, I'd get something useful."

"And that didn't work?" Mona asked.

"It worked. The problem is that intelligence, in any animal, is the servant of more basic emotions and drives. That ape has the ability to be useful, but not the motivation."

"But can't you do something about that?"

"I've tried. I've chemically taken him apart three times and put him together four. But I've never been able to come up with a reliable computer analog of his motivational matrix. It's as if he takes a perverted joy in confounding me. I've wasted two years on him. But no more.

"Anyway, I've come up with something better for a labor and defense unit. I'm giving up on that ape; I started the reversion process a week ago."

"Reversion? What do you mean?" Mona said.

"I built him up and I can tear him down. I'm going to change him back to a normal mountain ape and sell him."

"You're going to destroy his brain? Isn't that like murder?"

"What am I supposed to do with him? I can't let him out. He's a killer! It isn't even safe to keep him in a cage. He's bright enough to figure a way out of it. No. It's either kill him or revert him. And as an ape, he's worth a lot of money to a zoo."

"But still . . ."

"He was an animal when I bought him and he'll be an animal when I sell him. I fail to see where I've committed any crime."

"But there must be something . . ."

"I'm open to suggestions," Heinrich said.

Mona was silent. Heinrich took her arm—her skin was so incredibly soft!—and led her into the next hall.

"This is something that I want your help with. If you want to, that is." Copernick opened the door on a surrealistic scene. One wall was a computer bank with multicolor displays that changed periodically. The wall opposite was a complex array of automated chemical apparatus.

Mona's eyes locked in on a line of twenty glass cylinders in the center of the room. Each was a yard tall and a foot in diameter. Each contained a small humanoid form floating motionless in the fluid.

"Are they alive?" Mona said.

"Certainly." Heinrich inhaled. "At present, not one human child in ten is getting a solid basic education. The poorer countries can't afford to feed their children, let alone send them to school. And things are getting worse, not better. A poor educational level results in a poor allocation of limited resources, and hence more poverty. I'm hoping that these beings will help break that downward spiral. They are to act as tutors and primary school teachers. I call them fauns."

From the waist down the fauns were covered with fur. They had hoofs rather than feet, and their ears were pointed. Each faun had a large umbilical cord running from her naval to a placenta at the bottom of the cylinder.

"They're lovely," Mona said. "But why the mythological appearance?"

"They had to be quite human in appearance, or the human children that they raise might imprint improperly, or turn out autistic. Yet I didn't want adults to confuse them with people. After all, we don't want a competing species.

"Since human children normally imprint before they can walk, looking up from their cribs, the kids should see the fauns as human," Copernick said.

"What am I supposed to do with them?"

"Raise them."

"Raise twenty children at one time?" Mona said. "I couldn't. I mean that it would be impossible!"

"It's not that bad. They are not human. They won't have to go through the repetitive learning processes that a human child does. And they can already speak English."

"English! But they're still in those bottle things."

"I'm using a direct computer interface with them

while they are still in their cloning tanks," Copernick said.

"Then why do you need me to raise them?"

"It's not just busy work, Mona. True, I could educate the fauns completely by computer. If you don't want the job, I'll have to do it. The simulations I've run indicate that it will work. But future generations of fauns will have to be raised more naturally by their own parents. If there's a hitch in the educational process, we'd better know about it before we let fauns raise human children."

"Well..."

"The fauns won't be ready for decanting for at least a week. Take your time making up your mind about working with them. Now let me show you the simulation room."

The room contained two desks covered with lighted buttons. Above each was a television display screen. Behind them, taking up most of the room, were four featureless gray cabinets. Each cabinet was a yard wide, two yards high, and sixty yards long.

"These are the main simulation computers," Copernick said.

"They're so big. I thought that computers were little things."

"Little computers are. These are two of the largest ever built. It requires around six hundred trillion bits of random access memory to keep track of all the chemical processes in a simple animal. A human requires twice that."

"They must have been awfully expensive." Mona said.

"They were. The reproduction cost for the equipment here at Pinecroft would be around eighty million dollars. The engineering cost was three times that. And Uncle Martin's installation was almost as expensive."

"I didn't know that you were that rich."

"I'm not. I never was. Copernicus, Inc., is worth several billion. I founded it. I built it and I ran it. But in order to get the capital I needed for expansion, I had to sell the bulk of my company's stock to outsiders. By the time I was ready to retire, I owned only a small percent of my own company."

"Then how did you get all of this stuff?" Mona asked.

"Owning a company is one thing. Controlling it is another. Stockholders usually leave you alone, as long as you declare a dividend. As president, I made sure that we had a large R & D budget. This equipment was all built in my own labs."

"You mean you stole it?"

"No. I bought it. Through a third party, of course. And at scrap prices." Copernick laughed.

"It still sounds as if you stole it from your own stockholders."

"Nobody ever lost money doing business with Heinrich Copernick!"

Mona looked at her bare feet and was silent.

"Anyway, each of these computers can simulate the entire life-cycle of an organism. With a fifty-gigahertz clock, I can take a human being from a fertilized cell to an octagenarian in eleven hours. They are the most important single tool we use in bioengineering. They let me test out a design or modification in a matter of hours, when actually growing the organism could take decades. These displays let me see what is going on in any part of the simulation, right down to the molecular level. Or you can slow down the clock and look at it macroscopically; watch it work and play. Even talk to it."

"Talk to it!" Mona woke up.

"Assuming that the being involved can talk. One of the surprises I had with these simulations was that the nervous systems were so well modeled that the programs attain a degree of self-awareness."

"You mean it's alive?"

"Of course not. They're nothing but programs on a machine. But they *think* they're alive. It causes some problems. For one thing, you have to program an enviornment for them to grow up in, or they go insane. For another, you need at least two computers running so that they can have someone to relate to.

"On the other hand, this simulated self-awareness has its advantages. In training, for example. I loaded my own program into one computer and that of my new Labor and Defense Unit into the other. Then I set up a cross talk between them and let the 'me' program educate the

LDU program. I ran it through twice to give 'me' some experience in training them. Right now I'm running it through a third time with a living LDU hooked into the circuit."

"You mean that you can educate somebody in a few hours?" Mona asked.

"Not without causing neural damage. The fastest safe speedup factor is fifty. It means weeks instead of years, though. And a lot less work."

"Can we watch?" Mona was worried about training the fauns.

"Not the actual LDU. It's under sedation in the next room and shouldn't be disturbed. I can show you the simulation if you like."

Copernick switched on one of the displays. It showed a strange creature with a flat oval body, six feet by three, standing on four camel's legs. There were eight fixed eyes around its circumference, and two more at the ends of yard-long tentacles growing from its front. Two long remarkably humanoid arms were held folded at its sides. There was a strange slit above each wrist. In front of it stood Heinrich Copernick, writing on a blackboard. But it was the Heinrich Copernick of a year ago, with crippled legs and a bent back. The man and the LDU were moving at blinding speed, and uttering high-pitched squeaks.

Copernick adjusted a dial on the panel and a digital readout changed from 12.5 MHz to 250 KHz. The screen slowed down to normal speed and conversations became intelligible.

"... so the square of the hypotenuse is equal to the sum of the squares of the other two sides," the image said. "Oh. Hello, boss."

"Hi. How is it going?" Copernick said.

"On schedule. Say, you're looking good. When are you going to reprogram my body to match yours?" the simulation said.

"Mine isn't finished yet. But if you want to update yours anyway, feel free. My current medical section is on bubble deck eighty-one."

"Thanks. I will."

"That classroom," Mona said. "It looks so familiar."

"Boss, do you have someone else there with you?" The simulation was startled. This was unprecedented!

"Yes." Copernick motioned Mona into the camera's field of view.

"Mona! My God, girl! It's good to see you in the flesh."

"Has Heinrich been talking about me?" Mona said.

"Of course not, silly. I mean he has, but I was referring to before," the simulation said.

Mona looked confused.

"You mean he hasn't told you ... Well, uh, I have work to do. See you both later."

"Later." Copernick quickly switched off the display and reset the system clock.

"Told me what?" Mona demanded.

"I'll explain later."

"No. Now."

"Mona, please."

"It just isn't fair! You were nice and loving all my life and then one day I have an operation and you get cold and icy, and you ship me off to that finishing school without even a kiss good-bye ..." Mona began to sob.

"There were things that a girl should know that I couldn't teach you." Copernick was awkward as he put his arms around her.

"And you almost never wrote." Mona sobbed.

"You know how busy I've been."

"And now I get home and you waste all this time on technical stuff and you haven't even kissed me."

Copernick kissed her. "Better?"

"Not much of a kiss. Not like when we were on the lake or all the times we made love or—"

"The lake?" Copernick was confused for a moment. Then daylight dawned in the swamp. *The simulation had been making love to its student!*

"Heinrich, what's happened to you? I mean, have you changed your mind the way you changed your body? Don't you love me any more?" Mona was crying in earnest.

"I love you, Mona."

"You do?"

"I love you very much. And I want you to marry me."

"You do?" Mona held him tightly. Her tear-streaked face smiled.

"Yes, I do. And we can get married as soon as you like," Copernick said. *Right after I have a little talk with that damned simulation!*

"Oh, Heinrich, I'd given up hoping that you'd want me."

"Of course I want you. That's why I made you."

Chapter Three

CUSTOMARY MORALITY has us ask, "Is what I am doing in accordance with a previously established set of rules?"

A more rational ethic would have us ask, "Is what I am doing in the best interests of all humanity, including myself?"

As civilization becomes increasingly complex, the likelihood of any ancient rule book's being appropriate becomes increasingly small.

—Heinrich Copernick
From his lab notebook

Martin Guibedo found Burt Scratchon and Patricia Cambridge waiting for him at the tree house.

"Well, you finally made it," Scratchon said. "We were beginning to think that you had lost your nerve."

"What nerves? The only scary thing was the E train. It broke down twice on the way over here," Guibedo said.

"The *subway* at this hour?" Patricia said. "But they're so dangerous after dark!"

"There is a couple of things good about weighing three hundred pounds, Patty. One is that most people don't bother you," Guibedo said. "So what do you think of Laurel, who I give to Burty here?"

"It's lovely, Dr. Guibedo. And it's so huge!" Patricia said.

29

"It might make a decent warehouse, if you could get a forklift through the front door," Scratchon said.

"Don't do that, Burty. The carpets couldn't take the weight. Anyway, we're going to have plenty of warehouses pretty soon."

"Do you mean that you are working on a tree-house warehouse, Dr. Guibedo?" Patricia asked.

"No. I just mean that a lot of warehouses are used up for storing things like lumber and food. With my tree houses, we're not going to do that much any more, so we're gong to have more warehouses than we need." Guibedo sat down on one of the oversized chairs in the tree house's living room.

"My God!" Scratchon said. "You mean that you're *deliberately* wrecking the economy?"

"What wrecking? I'm just saying that we're going to have extra, so we don't have to build any more for a while."

Scratchon was about to erupt, so Patricia cut in. "Dr. Guibedo, you were going to explain about the care and feeding of tree houses to us."

"Sure. There isn't really that much to tell, Patty. The tree house is six months old now, so it can mostly take care of itself."

"Dr. Guibedo, I just can't get over how fast they grow."

"Nothing to it, Patty. Do the arithmetic. On an acre of land you have falling seventeen million calories of solar power every minute. A pound of my wood takes three thousand calories to make, and my tree houses are about ten percent efficient. So if a tree house isn't doing anything else but making wood, you have maybe five hundred pounds of wood per acre per minute."

Patricia was trying to take notes, but she always had problems with large numbers. "But it is doing other things, isn't it, Dr. Guibedo?"

"Sure. It keeps you cool in the summer and warm in the winter and it makes food and beer for you. And it has to use some of what it makes to keep itself alive. And then, when it was little, it didn't have an acre of photosynthetic area to work with."

"Doesn't it give you the creeps to live in something that's alive?" Scratchon said.

"You like better maybe living in something's that dead?"

"Dr. Guibedo, you were going to tell us about how to take care of them," Patricia said, working hard to keep them from fighting.

"Nothing much to tell. The floors and walls absorb foreign material, so you don't have to clean them. The wastebaskets and toliets work about the same way, only a lot faster, of course. The closets and cupboards you gotta dust out. You should maybe mark on the kitchen cupboards what food grows where, unless you like surprises."

"But what about watering it and fertilizer, Dr. Guibedo?"

"Well, Patty, once it's this big, the roots go down pretty far, so you don't have to worry about watering it. The toliet gives it all the fertilizer it needs," Guibedo said.

"Then there's nothing to do but live in it?"

"That's right, Patty, but you got to use it. A tree house will die if there is nobody living there. I made them that way so that we won't have a bunch of empty slums some day. And talk to your tree, Burty. They like that."

"Thank you, Dr. Guibedo," Patricia said.

"So thank *you*, Patty. If you don't need me any more, I got to run. I have three more tree houses here in Forest Hills and I want to look in on them."

Guibedo left before Scratchon could say any more to him; he said it to Patricia. "So my own damned neighbors are growing these things! That jellybelly is using *me* for advertising."

"You're not being fair, Mr. Scratchon. After all, he *gave* you this house!"

"And now I've got to live in the thing. He's a sneaky S.O.B."

"Nonsense. He's a very nice old man, and he's trying to do something nice for people. These tree houses are only toys in this part of Queens, but think about what they'll mean to the people starving in India," Patricia said.

"Yeah. They'll be able to raise more cannon fodder for the Neo-Krishnas to throw at us. And when they do, our economy will be in such bad shape that this time we'll have trouble defeating them."

"I don't think that Dr. Guibedo looks at it that way."

"What he *thinks* he's doing doesn't make much difference. What he *is* doing is destroying the free world."

A knock sounded at the front door.

"Now who the hell?...." Scratchon opened the massive front door.

"I guess I got the right place, Burt." Major General George Hastings was in uniform, smartly tailored class-A blues. He had the small, compact build of a fighter pilot.

"George! It's been months! What brings you to New York?"

"Just passing through La Guardia with a little time on my hands."

"Hey, you got your second star! Looks like somebody in the old squadron made good."

"You haven't done so badly yourself, Burt." Hastings noticed Patricia. "Oh. I hope I'm not interrupting anything."

"Not in the least. George Hastings, Patricia Cambridge. George and I were in the Twenty Third Interceptor Wing over Sri Lanka. Now he's the commander of Air Force Intelligence. Ms. Cambridge is with NBC, so watch what you say, George."

"Here I was hoping that you would be a foreign spy and try to seduce military secrets out of me." Hastings smiled at Patricia.

"Maybe I could take a night course and train for the job." Patricia smiled back.

"How's the wife and kids, George?" Scratchon wasn't smiling.

"Fine. Actually, Margaret is one of the reasons I dropped by. She got a tree-house seed—a Laurel, I think—in the mail with a Burpee's catalog, and she wanted me to get an idea of what the floor plan would be like."

"My God! You, too? Don't you realize the danger to the economy that the damned things represent?"

"Come off it, Burt. Quit trying to make your job into a holy war. Anyway, the kids planted the damned thing on our property along Lake George. On An O-8's pay I couldn't afford to build a house up there, so planting a tree house won't set the economy back any."

"But in the long run—"

"In the long run we'll all be dead. For right now, there are more important things to worry about."

"Like what? Is there something going on that they don't tell us civilians?" Patricia said.

"Nothing that you don't read in the papers. But the human race is outgrowing this little planet, and there is no place else to go," Hastings said.

"But I heard that the moon project and L-Five were going all right."

"There are less than ten thousand people up there. What's that to the ten billion people on Earth? Don't get me wrong. I support those projects. But they won't help us out much down here," Hastings said.

"And you think that these tree houses will?" Scratchon asked.

"They might, Burt. They just might."

"I wish that you could have gotten here ten minutes sooner," Patricia said. "Dr. Guibedo could have used some encouragement."

"Guibedo was here?" Hastings said. "I'm sorry that I missed him. But how did you meet him? I'd heard that he was something of a recluse."

"A news girl gets around. Actually, I met him through a friend of his nephew, Heinrich Copernick."

"The same guy who raised the stink about rejuvenation a few years back?" Scratchon asked.

"Oh, yes. Genius often runs in a family." Patricia steered the conversation to a topic that she knew something about. "Take the Bach family, for example..."

Seven months later, the fashions demanded that women wear a padded turtleneck bra with wide transparent sleeves. Keeping to the letter of the decree, Patricia's midriff was bare to three inches below her belly button, where a black bikini bottom and transparent pantaloons began.

"This is Patricia Cambridge with *The World at Large*. We're on location today in Forest Hills, Queens, doing a follow-up on an experiment initiated a year ago on this program.

"The huge tree house you see behind me is Laurel, grown incredibly from the potted plant we saw in Dr. Guibedo's window just a year ago.

"Mr. Burt Scratchon has been living here for six months, and he will be giving us the grand tour. Tell me, Mr. Scratchon, what is living in a tree house really like?"

"Ms. Cambridge, it's pure hell. Only my sense of duty to the American public has kept me living in this green slum. I'll be happy when this experiment is over and I can move back into my solid brick home.

"Look at that phone line. Tight as a guitar string. What with its incredible growth, this 'house' has ripped off its own telephone wire twice since I've been here!"

"It can't be all that serious, Mr. Scratchon." Patricia led the way into the house.

"Serious enough when you are trying to run a business. And look at this damned stuff!" His face reddened. *Control, man! Mustn't alienate the public. Sell!*

"Uh, this is being taped, Mr. Scratchon. The technicians have all night to edit out anything improper. Just go on," said Patricia.

"This flooring material, for example." Scratchon kicked loose a piece of the carpeting. "Totally unsanitary. It can't be cleaned. My housekeeper filled four vacuum bags on the hall floor alone before she gave up. A bachelor has a hard enough time keeping good help without this!"

"Didn't Dr. Guibedo say something about it absorbing foreign matter so that cleaning was unnecessary?" Patricia asked.

"Tell that to my housekeeper. She quit! And look at the floor itself. That floor is five degrees out of plumb! Not a building inspector in the country would accept that in a real house. But BOCA hasn't even passed codes on these trees."

"But Dr. Guibedo sent the seeds for one of these

Laurel trees to every public official in the country, Mr. Scratchon. I haven't heard any complaints yet."

"You will. Take a look at this food. It's supposed to be hot, but it's really only lukewarm. This mess is supposed to be pancakes with maple syrup. The darned stuff grows with the syrup already on! Can you imagine trying to start out a day with a plate of this sloppy gruel?"

"Well, it *is* unsightly." Patricia put a dainty fingertip to her tongue. "But it *is* real maple syrup."

"This 'dishwasher' actually *eats* the scraps off the plates. The first time I watched it, I was so disgusted I almost tossed the meal I had just eaten. Not that that would have been any great loss."

"A dishwasher?" Patricia asked, delighted.

"And the toilet works the same way. The stuff just lays there until—"

"Isn't the living room this way?" *Toilets again!*

"Anyway, I gave up on the bathroom entirely. I've been using the one in my real house in front," said Scratchon, following Patricia into the living room.

"You can't get a picture to hang straight on these curving walls. And when you cut loose the furniture to rearrange it, a new set grows back in a week. I've had to *pay* to have two sofas hauled away." Scratchon gave a fatherly smile to the camera. "So my advice to the viewing audience is to stay with their fine, modern, man-made homes."

"So you feel that there is nothing of value to be had from a tree house, Mr. Scratchon?"

"Well, Ms. Cambridge, I have one piece of good news. The place is showing definite signs of dying. I knew these things wouldn't last. In a month or so, if any of your viewers need firewood, tell them to bring an ax."

"Now let me show you what a real house is like."

As the cameras were being moved around an in-ground pool to Scratchon's conventional dark-brown-brick house, he said, "Ms. Cambridge?"

"Call me Patty."

"What would you say to having dinner with me tonight, Patty?"

"I'd love to, but I can't. I don't know how late I'll be up getting this show ready for tomorrow."

"That makes you free tomorrow afternoon, doesn't it?"

"I guess it does." Patricia smiled.

"Can I pick you up at four?"

"Let me drop by here." Patricia was embarrassed about her apartment.

"You've got a date."

Guibedo had borrowed a television set from a neighbor especially to watch the program about his tree house. As he watched, anticipation turned through sadness into horror.

"Ach! Nails in your walls! Cutting loose your furniture! And not using your toilet! Laurel, you're starving to death!"

Guibedo invested in a cab and arrived at Scratchon's tree house at the same time that Patricia did.

"Dr. Guibedo! What are you doing here?"

"On your program, Scratchon he said that my Laurel here is dying, so I came right over. But he must have used the toilet, she looks pretty good now."

"It *has* perked up quite a bit since yesterday, Dr. Guibedo. You really care about these trees, don't you?"

"Sure. They're like my children. And the Laurel series is special. We mailed out one hundred thousand of her seeds to people."

"I heard about that—every VIP in the country got one. That was quite an advertising effort."

"A lot of kids volunteered to help me. Friends of my nephew. We sent a Laurel to every big shot in the world! Pretty soon everybody'll want one."

"Dr. Guibedo, have you seen Burt? I tried to call him but his phone was out of order."

"That figures." Guibedo pointed to the phone wire lying on the ground. "The telephone people haven't learned how to wire a tree house yet."

"But still, he should have called if he wasn't going to be here. We had a date. I've knocked at both houses and no one's home."

"Well, you check his regular house again. I'm going to look Laurel over."

"Uh. I guess he could be sick." Patricia went to the big Tudor brick house facing onto 169th Street.

Guibedo pulled the door branch and called inside, "Hey! Scratchon! You home?"

He walked inside. The lights were on, the furniture had regrown in its proper place, and everything was as neat as a mausoleum.

"Scratchon! It's *Guibedo!"*

The kitchen cupboards were full. The bathroom was in order except that where the toilet area should have been was just smooth wood.

"So where did Laurel put the new toilet?" Guibedo muttered. *"Anybody home?"* He turned toward the bedroom. No one there, either.

Puzzled by the Laurel's missing toilet, Guibedo walked slowly out of the tree house, sealing the door behind him. "No one home, Patty."

"He wasn't in the old house, either," Patricia said. "And we had a dinner date."

"So come with me. I could use maybe some schnapps."

"Uh, okay. Why not?" Patricia followed him to the car.

Chapter Four

JUNE 12, 2000

ᴧᴧᴧᴧᴧᴧᴧᴧᴧᴧᴧᴧᴧᴧᴧᴧᴧᴧᴧ

ALL OF our realities are painted thinly on the void of our own preconceptions.

The problem of training intelligent engineered life forms is a case in point. I designed them with almost no internal motivational structure, except for a certain dog-like desire to please.

I made the major error of assuming that tabula rasa *meant the same as* carte blanche. *It never occurred to me to explain to them things that I assumed were "intuitively obvious." Things like kindness and decency and respect for life.*

—Heinrich Copernick
From his log tape, on
finding the tombstones of
eighty-five families

Major General George Hastings, Commander, Air Force Intelligence, sat in his office in the Pentagon. He hadn't slept in thirty hours. His face was haggard.

His wife and children had been missing for two days. They had gone off to spend a week in their new tree house at Lake George and had vanished.

Hastings had TDYed one of his best security teams to Lake George and now the report was back.

Nothing.

The car was parked, no unusual fingerprints on it. The

soft path to the house showed only the footprints of Margaret and Jimmy and Beth. There was no ransom note. Nothing. They had vanished from the world just as Scratchon had.

Scratchon? Scratchon and Margaret both had tree houses!

Hastings hit the button on his intercom. "Pendelton!"

"Yes, sir," a sleepy, obedient voice replied.

"Get Research out of bed."

"The whole staff, sir?"

"Hell, yes! They are to determine the correlation between currently missing persons and Laurel series tree houses."

Tree houses at four o'clock on a Sunday morning! "Yes, sir. Full Research staff, tree houses and missing persons."

Nine hours and half a bottle of amphetamines later the answer came in. Correlation—32 percent.

Thirty-two percent of the people in the sample who owned Laurels were either officially missing or could not be contacted.

Hastings was making up a list of military and governmental officials to be informed of the correlation when Pendelton knocked and entered.

"Thought you should see this, sir."

It was a day-old *National Enquirer.* On the front page was a color photograph of a desiccated female corpse half absorbed by a tree-house bed. From a delicate web of roots, a wedding band gleamed.

It was out of his hands now; Hastings went to his empty apartment to sleep and to cry.

A week later Hastings was back at his desk. He felt neither grief nor anger. Only a deadly emptiness that would never leave him.

A knock at the door was immediately followed by Sergeant Pendelton. "They got him, sir."

"Got who?"

"Martin Guibedo, sir. The Michigan State Police picked him up north of Kalamazoo."

"It took them long enough."

"These people with tree houses rarely need to use

credit cards, sir. It makes them hard to find. Here's the report on tree-house occupation, sir."

"Give it to me verbally."

"Yes, sir. Basically, people have abandoned the Laurel series houses. But three other species are in common use, and the people in them generally intend to continue using them."

"Idiots."

"Yes, sir. The consensus is that it was a technical malfunction in a single product line, and that it does not cast discredit on the entire concept of bioengineering. It's rather like the public reaction to the Hindenburg disaster seventy years ago, when people ceased using airships but continued to use airplanes."

"Huh. Anything else?"

"Yes sir. Section Six requests that you visit them."

"What is it, Ben?" Hastings said.

"We're out of business, George. Nobody but Mike can pick up anything but a loud roar. It gives you a headache."

"Somebody is jamming you?"

"We don't know, George. But if so, they're jamming everybody. We just got a phone call—*a phone call, mind you*—from Dolokov's group at Minsk. Looks like the whole fraternity of telepaths is out of work."

"Anything like this ever happen before?"

"We've picked up tiny spurts of interference before, George. The sort of unintelligible stuff you sometimes pick up near an unborn child, only much louder and more abrupt. There has always been a lot of static on the line, but nothing like this."

"What about Mike?"

"He's gone insane, George. He keeps yelling about lords and alpha numbers and digging in the ground and similar drivel. Nothing that makes sense."

"Have you sedated him yet?"

"No point to it, George. With this racket going on, he can't possibly affect the rest of us, and the transcribers might find something of interest in his babble."

"Well, do as you feel best. But I suggest that you keep someone posted by Mike in case the jamming stops."

"Okay, George. We don't have anything else to do, anyway."

"Oh, yer *that* Professor Guibedo," Jimmy Saunton said, trying to control his shakes. "The guy with the tree houses. Somebody was telling me about 'em. What do I have to do to get one, Professor?"

"Can you eat and make shit?" Guibedo asked, looking past his cellmate to the iron bars that formed the far wall. "That's all you got to do."

"Huh? Sure. But what do I got to do to get one?" The little drunk was used to being ignored.

"I just told you!" Guibedo barked. "Ach. I ain't really mad at you. But since they arrested me, it's been nothing but people, people, people, talking, talking, talking. I ain't had no rest in three weeks."

The little drunk was silent for a while. Then he said, "Sorry, Professor. Didn't mean to rile you."

"Well, I'm sorry, too. This ain't your fault. What were you asking about?"

"About your tree houses," Jimmy said.

"Oh, yeah. Well, the important thing you got to remember is that a tree house is in a symbiotic relationship with the people living inside it. It gives you a nice, comfortable place to live and all the food and beer you want. You give it the fertilizer it needs to stay alive and grow. That's what caused all the trouble. Them big shots I gave the Laurel trees to, they mostly used the tree just to show off with and give parties in. Then they went and used the toilets in their regular houses!"

"Yeah, somebody was saying that your trees ate a lot of people."

"I only made it so that the tree would grow a new absorption toilet when the old one got plugged up. The trouble was that a lot of them new toilets grew in the beds," Guibedo said.

"Yeah, somebody was saying that your trees ate a lot of people," Jimmy repeated, for lack of anything better to say.

"Maybe fifty thousand. Ach! My poor Laurels! Them big shots is chopping you down faster than you can grow!"

"You really love those trees, huh, Professor?"

"It wasn't really their fault. They shouldn't have done it, but when you're lonely and hungry and nobody cares..."

"I know what you mean, Professor. Man, do I know what you mean! But how do I get one?"

"Well, first you got to get out of this jail."

"That's easy. They always throw me out in the morning."

"Ach! I should be so lucky. What's that scratching sound?"

"Rats. We're in the basement here. The place is crawling with them. How long you in for anyway, Professor?"

"Who knows? This lawyer my nephew Heiny sent, he says they got maybe twenty thousand warrants out on me. Everything from transporting vegetable matter across state lines without a permit, to premeditated rape. He did some plea bargaining and got most of them reduced to murder in the first degree."

"Murder one? You know, with a good lawyer, you can beat that one."

"Sure. The trouble is I got to keep on beating it twenty thousand times! The lawyer figures, if everything goes right, we can do it in maybe three hundred and twenty-five years."

"Three hundred and... You should live so long!"

"I know. I'm ninety already. It just isn't fair! Did they throw the Wright brothers in jail every time an airplane crashed? Did Henry Ford get locked up every time somebody got killed in a car wreck? Ach. But that's my problem, and you can't do nothing to help me with it. But I can do a lot to help you with yours."

"My problem, Professor? I told ya, they throw me out in the morning."

"Sure. And you gonna be panhandling for drinks and sleeping in alleys and back in here tomorrow night."

"So you think I'm just a bum, huh? Well, let me tell you, Professor, I wasn't always a bum! I have a college degree, and I had my own business before... well, just before!"

"Ach, Jimmy, I ain't calling you names, and I ain't

telling you how to run your life. Hah! Sitting here in jail, it looks like I ain't run my own life so good.

"But you, Jimmy, you got better things coming. Like maybe a ten-room house, with gardens and fountains and plenty of good food and beer all the time in the cupboards."

"Hey, don't forget the twenty nude women around my swimming pool."

"Well, the Ashley series has got forty-foot pools. You gotta get the women on your own."

"And where am I supposed to get that kind of money?"

"What money? I told you. Eat and make shit!"

"You mean your tree houses are like that! I was thinking of maybe a cubbyhole where I could stay warm."

"Once you got a DNA string in a microscalpel, Jimmy, you might as well do it up right. You're thinking in terms of old-fashioned economics, when to build a house twice as big, you had to pay twice as much money. And to make two houses, it costs twice as much again. But with engineered life forms, they build themselves as big as you want, once you've designed them. The same thing goes with numbers, since they reproduce themselves. You can make a thousand things, or a million things, just as easy as you can make one. Why, I could have made my tree houses grow millions of seeds and covered the world with them in a year, only I didn't want to wreck the forests and drive away the animals. Life is best when there is enough, but not too much.

"So anyway, what you got to do is find a nice place to put your tree house. Your best bet is in a state park, maybe. Get way back, maybe a coupla miles from a road, so the big shots won't bother you. Find a pretty place, with a nice view, near a creek or maybe a waterfall."

The scratching sound got louder. Guibedo said, "Them must be some damn big rats, Jimmy."

"The size of dogs, some of them," Jimmy said. "Go on with what you were saying."

"So all you got to do is dig a hole, maybe a foot down, and use it for a toilet. Put the seed in it with the point on the seed toward where you want the front door to be.

Cover it up and water it every day for three months. You can move into it then, but it won't be full growed for at least six months."

"Six months! They grow that fast?" Jimmy said.

"Sure. Engineered life forms are a lot more efficient than natural ones. Or maybe I should say they're a lot less inefficient. Let me give you some 'for instances.'

"To get a pound of wood, a natural tree has got to soak up fifteen hundred pounds of water with its roots, run it through its trunk, and evaporate it in its leaves. The only good that all that water did was to haul up a few ounces of trace elements that were dissolved in it. The tree has to do this because transpiration is the only mechanism it has to get those trace elements to the leaves. A simple pump, like your heart, is a million times more efficient."

"Heh. So all your trees got hearts?"

"Sure. In more ways than one. Another 'for instance.' At high noon in the desert, you get about a hundred watts of solar power on each square foot of land. Now just sitting there, Jimmy, your body is burning up a hundred watts to keep you alive. If you were a hundred percent efficient, you could survive without eating just by lying in the sun. But the way nature does it, it takes more than one hundred thousand square feet of land to support a human being.

"Now, I've managed to make my tree houses ten percent efficient, about as good as a car engine."

"You sold me, Professor. Where do I buy a seed?"

"Well, you used to be able to buy one from me for five dollars, but that's all over now."

"A house for five dollars?"

"I had to pay for the postage and the advertising. And I had to get some people to help me with the mail. And the boxes cost me twenty-eight cents each! But now I guess you got to get somebody to give you one."

"I got to panhandle a house? Professor, if you had any idea how hard it is to come up with a fifth of Gallo port . . ."

"No, no. They promised to give you one. That was the deal when I sold the seed. Once their house was grown up, they had to give a seed to anybody who asked for one. And they had to make that person promise to do the same thing when their house was growed up. Just be sure you pick a model you really like. It ain't nice to abandon a tree house."

The scratching got progressively louder until an oval hairline crack, perhaps seven feet by four, suddenly formed on the concrete floor. One end of the slab rose five inches and a snakelike tentacle a yard long slid out. There was an eyeball at the end of it.

"Oh, sweet Jesus, Professor, I never should have touched that sterno! You can't imagine what I think I see!"

A second eyeballed tentacle joined the first. In unison, they made a 360-degree scan.

"Take it easy, Jimmy, I ain't had a drink in three weeks, and I'm seeing it, too!"

"My Lord Guibedo," a voice said from below the concrete. "I am a friend. Please speak softly. May I come up?"

"Nobody up here but us scaredy-cats," Guibedo whispered. "Come on up and make yourself at home."

The concrete slab slid to one side. A black creature ascended. It had a rigid oval body six feet long by three wide, but only six inches thick. The eyeballed tentacles extended from the front of its body. It walked on four skinny, muscular legs and held two long humanoid arms close to its body. As it rose from the pit, it changed color like a chameleon, from black to the gray of the prison walls.

"Oh, sweet Mother of Mercy!" Jimmy was cowering in a corner. "I've seen orange crocodiles even, but nothing like this!"

"Son of a gun, shit!" Guibedo muttered. "Who are you?"

"My lord, I am Labor and Defense Unit Alpha 001723."

"Yah, sure. Nice low number you got there. I guess I should have said 'What are you?'"

"My lord, I am a labor and defense unit. Would you please accompany me. We have very little time."

"You're maybe something my nephew, Heiny, came up with?" Guibedo noticed that the thing had at least eight additional fixed eyes, scattered around its circumference.

"Yes, my lord. Lord Copernick created me. He sent me here to facilitate your escape. Please accompany me." The LDU was backing down into the pit.

"Well, if Heiny says so, let's go," Guibedo said, following.

"Hey!" Jimmy said. "What about me?"

"Sir, your presence would constitute a security risk. I must insist that you stay here," the LDU said.

"He's right, Jimmy," Guibedo said. "This could get rough. They're gonna throw you out in the morning, anyhow."

"Yeah, Professor, but what am I going to tell them?"

"If you tell them the truth, Jimmy, they'll throw you in the funny house. Just tell them you went to sleep and when you woke up, I was gone."

"Yeah, okay. Take it easy, Professor! I'll get me that tree house like you said." Jimmy shook Guibedo's hand.

Guibedo was already waist deep in the pit. "And when you get your tree house, talk to it. They like that. Bye, Jimmy."

"Bye, Professor."

"My lord, has the leave-taking ceremony been completed?" the LDU asked.

"Uh, yeah, sure."

The LDU slid the concrete slab back into position over the pit. When the floor was sealed, lights in the tunnel went on. A long line of LDUs stood patiently waiting. Each was carrying a load of wet cement on its broad back.

"My lord. Once we have you out of here, our plan is to seal up the first one hundred feet of the tunnel with cement to slow down pursuit, then to fill the balance with dirt."

"That's a lot of work!"

"We were made for work, my lord. My Lord Copernick ordered it."

"Well, let's get walking."

"That's quite impossible for you, my lord. This tunnel is fifteen miles long."

"Fifteen miles! You dug this for me?"

"Yes, my lord, that's why we were three weeks in getting here." The LDU crouched to the height of a chair. "Would you please get on my back."

Eyeing the LDU's spindly legs, Guibedo cautiously put his portly bottom on its back. The LDU stood up easily to its normal tabletop height and took off at a smooth trot with the man riding sidesaddle. Guibedo soon found it was more comfortable to ride facing forward with his legs crossed.

"Curves ahead, my lord." Tentacles that Guibedo hadn't noticed slid from the LDU's sides and fastened themselves around the man's waist and legs. Several others provided an acceptable back rest. The LDU's speed increased to thirty mph and they were still passing concrete-laden LDUs.

"A lot of you guys here."

"We are ten thousand in the zero-zero division, my lord. Ten brigades of a thousand each with ten platoons of a hundred, each with ten squads of ten LDUs."

"Just like the army," Guibedo said, his white hair flapping in the breeze. "Who's the general?"

"No one, exactly, my lord. Or whichever one of us you talk to. You see, we're all in telepathic contact with each other. When one of us knows your desires, we all do, and therefore comply."

"Telepathy! I didn't know that Heiny was that far along."

"I don't believe he designed for it, my lord," the LDU said above the wind. "But you see, we're all identical and we have quite extensive and widely distributed redundant neural systems. I have twelve major ganglia, and I can function properly on six."

"Like the thing with human identical twins..." Guibedo said. "So Heiny just got lucky! Well, that's nice. Things went bad for him for too long there. I guess it made you guys pretty easy to educate."

"Yes, my lord. Once he discovered our abilities, he only had to teach one of us to read and write. The rest of us picked it up from Alpha 1. Now, each of us has his own field of expertise, based on our individual reading, with the information available to all."

"So what's your speciality?" Guibedo asked.

"Unarmed combat, with a minor in sociology, my lord." The LDU crowded closer to the left-hand wall of the tunnel. They were no longer passing the concrete carriers, and LDUs with empty baskets were passing them at an astounding speed.

"Pretty quick, your buddies are."

"Cruising speed for an LDU is forty mph, my lord, although we can go sixty for short durations."

"Unarmed combat?" Guibedo said. "If you were expecting trouble, why go unarmed?"

"My lord, I mean no *external* armament." From a slot above each wrist, a bayonetlike claw extended out to a foot past the knuckles. "They are a trifle dull from cutting through the concrete floor, but they are still quite serviceable."

"Cutting through concrete! How you do that?"

"Diamond is just another carbon compound, my lord."

"And carbon is one of the things that we are all made of." Guibedo laughed. "So you *were* expecting trouble."

"We couldn't know if there would be resistance or not, my lord. Nor could we be sure that we would come up in the right cell of the prison. We Alpha series are only telepathic with one another, not with humans."

"Betcha Heiny's working on that, though."

"Yes, my lord. As I understand it, the Gamma series LDU is to have a malleable nerve net. It is hoped that they will be able to at least receive telepathically from other species, such as man."

"Well, I'm not so sure I like that, uh—what was your name again?" Guibedo asked.

"Alpha 001723, my lord."

"Not your number. Your name."

"I have no other designation, my lord."

"A nice guy like you oughta have a name, not a number."

"Do you really think I could, my lord? I mean, it would be permitted?"

"Sure thing. Why not? Pick any name you want."

"Well, my lord, I think I would like to be called Dirk."

"Dirk, huh? I was thinking maybe Rover, but if it's Dirk you want, it's Dirk you'll get."

"Thank you, my lord!"

"Anytime. How old are you, Dirk?"

"I hatched three months ago, my lord, although I was sentient before then."

"Three months old. Well, I guess that explains it," Guibedo mused. "So you were sentient inside your egg. That must have been strange."

"It was, my lord. Each of us thought he was Alpha 1, the first one hatched. And Alpha 1 thought he heard echoes, but he didn't know that that was unusual."

"Hah! Hatching must have been a shock. But I don't see why you were so well developed at such an early stage."

"It has to do with our cell replication process, my lord. You see, we have four-stranded DNA, which reproduces very slowly. This results in a long gestation period, twelve months. But when we do hatch, we have as many cells as a full-grown adult. With enough food, we can grow from a two-pound eggling to a three-hundred-pound adult in a week, simply by increasing cell size."

"And here I been using single strand DNA on all my trees," Guibedo said.

"My lord, that certainly gives rapid growth and repair, but a combat troop needs resistance to heat and radiation, and our glandular redundancy makes up for our slow repairability," Dirk said.

"You know, Dirk, for a specialist in unarmed combat, you sure know your biochemistry."

"Oh, no, my lord, I'm picking this up from Alpha 001256. He wants to be called Blade. May he do so, my lord?"

"Sure. Anything to keep our boys at the front happy. Heiny sure did some nice thinking with you guys." LDUs were now returning to the end of the tunnel with loads of dirt. The tunnel was wide enough for only two to pass, and Guibedo marveled at their coordination as empty LDUs from behind alternated with loaded LDUs from in front to pass the slower-moving Dirk.

"It looks like we're a moving roadblock, Dirk."

"We're not seriously slowing progress, my lord," Dirk said. "If I traveled much faster, conversation would be difficult above the wind noise. My brothers and I are enjoying this talk."

"Yah. I guess I am talking to all of you," Guibedo said. "What are they saying?"

"My brothers are mostly picking names for themselves, my lord."

"Anybody got Black Bart yet?"

"No, my lord. Thus far, each of my brothers has wanted to be named after a weapon."

Kids! Guibedo thought. "You keep calling them 'brothers.' Ain't you got no girls?"

"No, my lord. We don't have sex."

"Such a pity. So how do you reproduce?"

"In the strictest sense of the word, we don't, my lord."

"Then how do you get little LDUs?" Guibedo asked.

"Lord Copernick worried that an opponent might breed us for his own needs, my lord, so he caused our eggs to grow from a nonsentient mother being which lives on the ceiling of a vault below his tree house."

"I wondered why Heiny wanted so much room," said Guibedo. "How many eggs you got growing down there?"

"Approximately three hundred thousand, my lord, a third of which are now available for hatching."

"Why so many?" Talking in a windstorm was making Guibedo hoarse.

"My Lord Copernick calls it his insurance policy," Dirk said. "And, of course, the large numbers don't cost him anything in time or money."

So Heiny figures things are gonna get real rough! Ach! The kid oughta know that it's safer to hide than to fight. Still, maybe it's safer yet to be able to fight while you're hiding.

"You know, Dirk, I can see how it could be kinda rough, being an LDU. No girls, no father, no mother, no sisters—"

"But a lot of brothers, my lord. We feel rather sorry for you humans. You take so long to grow, then die so soon."

"You guys don't die?"

"We can die if sufficiently injured, but we aren't troubled with diseases. We don't age or have a finite life-span.

"But you humans die without ever being able to communicate, except with your clumsy language. How do you fight the loneliness?"

"It ain't so bad like you make it out. We humans have bonds with each other, but maybe you wouldn't understand. Friendship, love, kinship with other individuals. And a man who is wise knows that there is a bond between all men. All men are brothers, Dirk, even if we don't act like it. Everybody counts, nobody should be forgotten." Actually, Guibedo treasured his solitude as much as any other hermit did, but he was not sufficiently introspective to notice his own hyprocisy.

"And we got other ways of communication besides words. Actions talk, and we have our ceremonies."

"Ceremonies, my lord? Could you describe them?"

"Sure. I can see you're a sociology minor. Whenever something happens to a human that's important to him, he's got to have a ceremony. There's simple ones like shaking hands. Two people meet and want to be friendly, they shake hands. And there's more complicated ones—"

For the next quarter hour, at Dirk's prodding, Guibedo talked on about the human ceremonies connected with Birth, Friendship, Love, Hate, Marriage, and Death. Dirk seemed especially interested in burial ceremonies, a fascination that Guibedo ascribed to Dirk's own deathlessness.

They left the tunnel and entered a starlit abandoned gravel pit. Dirk stopped in front of a seven-foot-tall man. He was magnificently muscled, and his head was large for his body. "Uncle Martin!" Heinrich Copernick stepped away from his battered van. "I see you got out in one piece."

"Yah, that you, Heiny? That was one hell of a tunnel your boys dug."

"We figured you were worth it."

"But why such a long tunnel, Heiny?"

"Logistics, Uncle Martin. For one thing, I needed someplace to put five million cubic feet of dirt. For another thing, there was the problem of feeding ten thousand LDUs. They only eat a fluid that your tree houses produce. There's a community of eighty-five full-sized tree houses a mile from here, and I was able to grow food synthesizers in their roots, even though plant engineering is hardly my forte."

"Only eighty-five trees?" asked Guibedo, doing some quick mental calculations. "They could produce enough food?"

"Well, I'm afraid I had to shut down the rest of their services, Uncle Martin. I was up there a couple days ago, and everybody was gone. But the trees will revert to their original state once the tunnel is filled in. The people will return."

"Well, I hope so," Guibedo said. "I guess you got to do things like that in an emergency. Why didn't you tell me you made guys like Dirk, here, Heiny?"

"You've just answered your own question, you damned old iconoclast." Copernick laughed. "You spend a half hour with my LDUs and they've got proper names! In a day you'd have them demanding private rooms, time and a half for overtime, and a grievance committee!"

"Maybe not such a bad idea, Heiny. You'd make a fortune hiring these guys out as a construction team. You didn't have any trouble digging that tunnel, did you?"

"Oh, there was some sort of a security problem once when I was gone, but the LDUs took care of it," Heinrich called over his shoulder as he walked toward the van.

"See!" Guibedo said. "They'd make a *good* work gang."

"I thought about it, but there are the building people and the labor unions to contend with. And look at all the trouble your publicity got you into. Still, lack of money is slowing us down," Heinrich said, getting into the driver's seat.

"You know, Heiny, when I was in jail, I got to thinking about catalytic extraction and refining. We could make a tree that could extract heavy metals from the soil . . ."

The two were lost in technicalities as they drove away.

Three platoons of LDUs left the tunnel-filling and went about special tasks.

One platoon began cutting rectangular slabs of stone, polishing them smooth, and carving names and dates.

Another dug rectangular holes, pleasantly arranged, on a hilltop.

The third platoon exhumed the bodies of eighty-five families who had presented such a security problem, who had been so unamenable to reason.

When the work had been completed and ritual prayers had been said, Dirk thought to his brothers, *It's comforting to know that the proper ceremonies have been completed.*

Yes, replied Blade. *It's important that we learn to do everything properly.*

Chapter Five

JUNE 5, 2001

ONE OF the surprising things about commanding large forces is that eager, dedicated subordinates are often more trouble than slovenly ones. You must be ever on your guard. The slightest hint can be taken literally and blown all out of proportion.

The problem is as old as the chain of command. A general drops a hint; a colonel makes a suggestion; a major writes a memo; a captain gives an order; a lieutenant barks a command; and ... a corporal pulls a trigger. It happened at Corregidor—the Japanese command never intended for the death march to occur. It happened at Mai Lai—when a town was wiped out. And it happened all too often in the course of the Symbiotic Revolution.

—Heinrich Copernick
From his log tape

"So what's the verdict, Doc?" General Hastings asked.

"You've got to stop smoking, George," Dr. Cranford said.

"Is that all?"

"Of course not. You really *must* start keeping regular hours. And cut your work week down to sixty hours. And get out a little more. Learn to relax."

"Look, Cranford, work is about all I have left."

"George, the tragedy that took your family happened a year ago. You can't—"

"Cut it."

"But a man can't mourn forever—"

"I take it that I'm healthy," Hastings said.

"Yes, but you don't deserve to be. There's nothing wrong with you now that a little rest and exercise won't cure."

"You've been telling me that every checkup for the last ten years."

"Well, why do you bother coming to me if you don't take my advice? I tell you, working yourself into the ground all the time is going to catch up with you. It'll shorten your life, George," Dr. Cranford said.

"It hasn't yet. Now are you going to sign my flying status papers or not?"

"I don't have much choice. Air Force regulations are so damned specific about it. I don't know why you bother—your flight pay is less as a general than it was as a lieutenant-colonel. But your reflexes are perfect. Your eyesight is twenty-twenty. Your blood pressure and electrocardiogram and electroencephalogram and every other damned thing are annoyingly perfect. But George, your life style is going to catch up with you."

"Just sign the paper. Doc, you're even more crotchety than usual. Something bugging you?" Hastings asked.

"Nothing except that I'm about to give up my practice and take up faith healing. That seems to be where my gifts lie."

"Somebody didn't have the courtesy to die when you told him to?"

"A whole bunch of somebodies. Half of the damned Senate has walked into this office with every organ in their flabby bodies rotting away!

"You know that this is the best-equipped facility in the country. And you know that I wouldn't tell a man he was going to die unless I ran him through every test known to man, plus a few I thought up myself. And *then* not until he had six days to live and no hope. It's just not something that a doctor likes to do. Besides the fact that many of them are my friends, it's embarrassing to have to admit that my profession is of no damn use to them!"

"People have been getting well?" Hastings said.

"Scads of the bastards! It's driving me to drink and damned nearly to profanity!"

"So this has been happening to everybody?"

"No. You've got to be in Congress to get a special dispensation from whatever God or devil is doing this to me. And seniority seems to help."

"You're serious about this?"

"Hell yes, I'm serious! One week I tell a senator to put his affairs in order, and the next week he comes in with his heart beating and his liver working and he's alive in front of God and everybody!"

"Do you have any theories about it?"

"I thought at first that it was something that we were doing here by accident. Turned the place upside down for months. Checked out every batch of every drug that I'd given any one of them. Nothing. Then I found out that two other doctors at different clinics were doing the same damned thing. The only thing that it correlates with is you've got to be a congressman."

"Well, have you checked out that angle?"

"Of course! The three of us have checked out every item in the Capitol cafeteria. The kind of floor wax they use. The postage stamps. The pencils. Anything that they would all have in common. Hell, I even sent a roll of their toliet paper to the lab. Nothing!

"I figure that God doesn't want congressmen and hell's full up!" Cranford said.

"Maybe I can give you a hand finding out what's behind this."

"You? Now, I appreciate the offer, but what use is a spook going to be on a medical research program?"

"You'd be surprised. Can you give me some specifics? Like who got cured of what and when?" Hastings said.

"No. I can't. That's privileged information, George."

"Well, you've gotten my curiosity up, Doc. Don't be surprised if somebody with a warrant comes over to pick up your medical records."

"And don't be surprised if I tell your process server to go to hell," Cranford said.

"Here is the analysis of those medical records, sir," Pendelton said.

"Give it to me verbally, Sergeant." Hastings leaned back in his padded chair.

"Yes, sir. In the past two years, eighteen U.S. senators and fifty-seven members of the House have had spontaneous remissions of major diseases. The spectrum of the diseases is typical for American males in their age group. In all cases, their internal organs now test out as being equal to those of twenty-year-olds."

"It almost makes me want to get into politics," Hastings said. "What else do these particular congressmen have in common?"

"Nothing that's indicated, sir. The sample seems to be random."

"Pendelton, I want a very discreet analysis run on these men. Their voting records. The places they visit. The people they know."

"Yes, sir. I'll get a few men on it."

"But discreetly. I don't have to remind you that the Congress has to approve all promotions of general officers."

Martin Guibedo drove a battered two-ton truck across Death Valley toward five acres of lush greenery growing out of the surrounding desolation. Death Valley had been one of the public parks that had been sold to private interests in the early '90s to "distribute the nation's wealth to the poor" and make a lot of politicians rich.

He parked next to the fountain and waddled, smiling, to the five-story tree house in the center of the garden. "Ach! Pinecroft!" he said to the tree. "So beautiful you've grown! You have got to be the prettiest tree my microscalpel ever made!"

The door opened for him, and he went through the huge living room, noting pleasantly that the waterfalls both worked and the cleaning apparatus was doing its job.

In the kitchen, an incredibly beautiful woman rose to greet him, smiling.

"Uncle Martin!" she gushed. "It's so good to see you!"

"Hi, Mona," Guibedo said uncomfortably. *Is this an animal or a people?* "Where's Heiny?"

"Heinrich is in the communications lab, fourth level down on your right."

"Thanks." Guibedo stepped into the elevator and thought, *Uncle, yet! I guess Heiny married her legal. None of my business, I suppose. But sometimes Heiny goes too far.*

Heinrich Copernick sat back, talking to two hemispherical mounds on his workbench. One was a meter across, the other a third of that.

"You both realize that, though parts of a multinodal communications net, you are really a single multipersonality organism. Refusing to talk to each other is extremely adolescent behavior. Now go on with what happened."

"Yes, my lord," the larger mound said. "So I said to myself, 'What is your conception of spaciotemporal reality?' And I answered me, 'What?' Now, how can I communicate with myself when my mental facilities are so different from my own?"

"Just keep working on it," Heinrich said. "Oh, Uncle Martin! So good to see you. What do you think of my latest?"

"Well, he is schmarter than the other one what you made, Heiny."

"Which other one?"

"You know. That big dummy what all the time dragged his knuckles in his shit."

"You must mean the simian-variation labor and defense unit," Heinrich said. "I've pretty much given up on that whole series. Redesigning existing bioforms turned out to be considerably more difficult than I had originally estimated."

"Yah. Told you so. Putzing around with natural-growed life forms is like trying to build a wristwatch in a junkyard. You is better off in a machine shop. It takes maybe a little bit longer, but you know what you got."

"It was just that my initial experiments with existing bioforms were so successful, Uncle Martin."

"Well, if you want to call making yourself look like a gladiator in an Italian movie a successful experiment, you go ahead."

"I can see nothing wrong with increasing my own strength and stamina."

"Sure. That's fine. But the green eyes and the wavy black hair and the baby-smooth complexion, Heiny? Kid stuff! You're seventy years old and you oughta be above that kind of thing."

"I'm entitled to a little fun."

"And what do you need with being seven feet tall for, anyway?"

"For one thing, it hides the size of my head," Copernick said. "How is your end of it going, Uncle Martin?"

"Just fine and ahead of schedule. My tree houses are getting real popular. Eleven separate species are in public use, with nine more in the advanced experimental stage. My best estimates are one point five million inhabited tree houses and eight million more growing up. Seven million people are living in them right now!" Guibedo glowed with pride.

"Excellent! That's almost one tenth of one percent of the world's population."

"The progression is a geometrical one," Guibedo said. "We're almost there, in a coupla years."

"I wasn't being facetious, Uncle Martin. I'm genuinely proud of you. How about the heavy-metal extraction project?"

"That's what I came over here to tell you about. Those kidney trees we planted over the old mines are all growed up."

"Kidney trees?"

"Yah. I call them that because the extraction glands work just like a human kidney, getting rid of poisonous substances."

"Like gold, silver, and platinum." Heinrich laughed. "But are they working?"

"So-so. I think maybe I should have made the mercury come inside of cherries instead of grapefruits. When they fall off the tree, they go schpritzing all over the place. And the mercury gets absorbed by the roots and goes up to the top of the tree, and comes schpritzing down again. Son of a gun, shit. If that mercury was orange paint, I'd look like a pumpkin."

"You know, Uncle Martin, I could take care of your weight problem pretty easily."

"What problem? I like being me. And the ground is covered with grapefruit rinds."

"Nothing serious, we can rig nets or something. But what about the other metals?"

"Oh, that's pretty good, even if the trees are overworked with the mercury. I got a lot of golden apples and platinum pears out in the truck. I didn't have room for the silver pinecones or the osmium cherries."

"Blade! Attention! Central Coordination Unit here."

A multicolor LDU laid aside the history text that he was reading and trotted over to the CCU's Input/Output unit in his barracks. "Sir!"

"Blade, take your platoon and unload Lord Guibedo's truck. Assay the contents and report. Build a smelter and convert the gold into standard twenty-pound bars. Store the platinum for the time being."

"Sir!"

"A truckload of gold and platinum!" Heinrich said. "Great! Now we can afford to exercise our option to purchase on the land we planted the trees on."

"And you better do it in a hurry, kid," Guibedo said. "And get a big fence around it. I saw a troop of boys out hiking, maybe two miles from the main grove."

"Vintovka! Attention! Central Coordination Unit here."

"Sir!"

"Vintovka, a troop of boys is on the march two miles north of the heavy-metal extraction grove. I want them under continuous observation. Launch four observation birds, different species, rotation at ten-minute intervals. If the boys come within one mile of the grove, notify me."

"Sir!"

* * *

"I'll get a lawyer right on it, Uncle Martin. Or better still, this would be a good project for the Central Coordination Unit."

"Crockett and Felderstein."

"Mark? Heinrich Copernick here," the Central Coordination Unit said. "I've decided to exercise my option on the old Golden Hoard mines. Can you arrange a closing for next Tuesday morning, say ten A.M. at your office?"

"That's only six days away, but my clients have a clear title. Sure. You figure there's some life in those old mines?"

"I think it's worth a try. I'll bring a certified check for $950,000 with me. You can handle the title insurance, prorations, and so on."

"My usual two percent?"

"Bullshit! Fifty dollars per hour. Take it or leave it."

"I'll take it."

"Kemper, Lodge, and Smith."

"Barry? Heinrich Copernick here," the CCU said.

"How are you, Heinrich?"

"Great. Barry, I'm reopening the old Golden Hoard mines. Would you file incorporation papers for a general mining company. Call it Golden Hoard, Inc., if you can."

"Sure. Who are the incorporators and what's the stock split?"

"You, Mona, and myself, with one share, ten thousand shares, and twenty thousand shares, respectively."

"I only get one lousy share?"

"So what do you want for nothing?"

"My usual. Fifty bucks an hour."

"Done. Crockett and Felderstein are handling the closing."

"I'll drop by and keep them honest."

"I doubt that, but drop by anyway. And have the incorporation papers ready to sign."

"Central Coordination Unit?" Guibedo said. "You mean this big round thing you were talking to when I came in? He sounded pretty mixed up to me. You think he's ready for any kind of a job?"

"Certainly. Oh, just now there's a slight problem with integrating the auxiliary ganglion I told him to grow—"

"You told him to grow!" Guibedo yelled. "You're letting an intelligent bioengineering creation control its own growth?"

"I wouldn't ordinarily, of course. But in this case it's quite necessary. You see, once the world's economy is coverted from a technological to a biological base, communications and a certain amount of central coordination are still going to be necessary. It will be quite impossible to maintain the telephones, computers, et cetera, without a factory system to produce spare parts.

"I plan to have the Central Coordination Unit grow a ganglion into each of your tree houses, with an input/ output unit in each room. These ganglia, being part of a single organism, will be in constant communication with each other, so sending a message will be simply a matter of talking to your local ganglion."

"Schwartz and Company."

"Duffy? Heiny Copernick here," the CCU said.

"Heiny! I ain't seen you in six months!"

"Don't you feel glad? What's gold selling at?"

"Seven hundred and eighteen dollars an ounce. How much you wanna buy?"

"Not buy. Sell. I got sixty-six thousand ounces to unload."

"Whee! How hot is it?"

"Ice cold. Dug it up myself. Let's see . . . That's just under fifty million."

"Well, there's my ten percent commission to figure in. But I ain't got that kind of money, Heiny!"

"Five percent. Don't get greedy. I'll deliver it to you first thing Monday morning. You put a million in my account by noon, then a million a day until you're paid up."

"You gonna trust me for that kind of money?"

"I can think of four good reasons why I should. Want me to list them?"

"Not over the phone, for God's sake!"

* * *

"So what you got here is a telephone system. Well, at least it'll stop the phone wires from being ripped off when the tree house grows," Guibedo said.

"He's not quite a telephone, Uncle Martin, in that communication isn't instantaneous. The maximum speed I've been able to get in a nerve pulse is one hundred twenty meters per second. But you will be able to send a message.

"He more than makes up for his lack of speed. My brainchild, if you'll excuse the pun, has twenty-two times the gray matter of a human brain. He is presently tied in with the wire services, most of the larger computers in the country, and two other phone lines. He's already loaded a quarter of the Library of Congress into his memory.

"While most of his gray matter is used for input, output, and memory, his IQ is quite unmeasurable. I'd guess perhaps four hundred."

"Well, if he's so schmart, what makes you think that you're going to stay boss, Heiny?"

"That's hardly a worry, Uncle Martin. In the first place, I've instilled a strong psychological dependence into him. He could no more disobey me—or you—than a dog could attack his master."

"That's been known to happen."

"In the second place, he's a hell of a nice guy."

"So was Hitler when he wanted to be."

"And in the third place, he eats a fluid that only your trees can produce. And your trees can survive only if they have a regular supply of human excreta in their absorption toilets. He requires humans for his very existence."

"Ach! If he's so schmart, he can figure a way around that one."

"You and I are the only beings who can operate a microscalpel, Uncle Martin. I've instilled an absolute mental block in the CCU covering the fields of chemistry and biology. All of my engineered life forms are in a symbiotic relationship with your trees and, thus, with us humans."

"All of them, Heiny? What about Mona?"

"My wife is as human as you or I!" Copernick shouted.

"You made her with the microscalpel I gave you!" Guibedo shouted back. "You engineered her DNA just like you did with this—this telephone thing, and don't you deny it!"

"I cloned Mona after I modified the DNA of one of my own cells, Uncle Martin. That modification doesn't reduce her humanity. Come on, I'm modified and, to a lesser extent, so are you. Are we so inhuman?"

Guibedo thought, *So he trades sodomy for incest*, but he didn't say it.

"Come on, Uncle Martin. Let's eat. We'll both be in a better mood after dinner."

"Knife! CCU here!"

"Sir!"

"Knife, take six brigades and dig a tunnel, suitable for your species, from here to the heavy-metal extraction grove, eighteen miles NNW of here. Complete it by next Tuesday afternoon."

"Sir! This route has never been surveyed. We have no knowledge of rock and soil conditions."

"Take more units as you need them. Report any difficulties to me."

"Sir!"

"Liebchen, this is the CCU. Would you please report?"

A little humanoid with the hindquarters of a goat pranced over to the I/O unit in her nursery.

"I'm Liebchen. May I help you?"

"Liebechen, for the next two weeks, the Labor and Defense Units are going to be extremely active. Except for those things relating to the comfort of the humans, I want all of Pinecroft's systems turned down to the bare minimum and all of Pinecroft's energy diverted to food production for the LDUs. Could you do that for me, please?"

"It pleases me to serve you, my lord."

"Not 'lord,' dear. Only Lord Guibedo and Lord Copernick deserve that title. And Liebchen, would you see to it that Lord Guibedo takes a mild euphoric with his lunch? Nothing heavy, just something that will make him listen to reason."

"Of course, sir. I'd be happy to."

Heinrich turned to the mounds on his workbench. "You guys keep at it, hear? I want to see the new ganglia integrated sometime in the next week."

"Yes, my lord."

As they went up the elevator, Heinrich said, "When you think about it, Uncle Martin, Mona is probably your grandniece. How does it feel to have your family grow?"

"I would have wished that maybe it grew another way."

"Oh, it's doing that, too. Twins, according to the tests."

Guibedo raised a huge white eyebrow.

"Don't worry, Uncle Martin. Mona and I don't have a recessive gene between us."

"CCU! Vintovka here!"

"Yes, Vintovka. Report."

"Sir! The hiking troop is now one mile from the heavy-metal extraction grove and proceeding directly toward it."

"Vintovka, launch another observation bird, an eagle this time, with orders to attack the scout most separated from the troop. Injure him sufficiently to require immediate medical attention, but do not kill him."

"Sir!"

Lunch consisted of roladen and sauerbraten for Guibedo and kielbasa, pirogi, and chanina for Mona and Heinrich, with black beer all around. All of which was synthesized in the kitchen cupboards by the tree house.

Bobby Jackson had grown up in the downtown Los Angeles Boy's Home. This was his first extended trip into the country, and he was dead tired after roughing it in the desert hills for three days. Despite the friendly jeers of his companions, he had straggled two hundred yards behind the rest of his troop. To keep the others in sight, he scrambled to the top of a large rock alongside the path.

Above and behind him, an eagle calculated a trajectory, folded its seven-foot wings, and power-dived from six thousand feet. As the scoutmaster, a Big Brother donating his time to the home, turned to make sure no one had left the trail, he saw the divebombing bird. "Look out, Bobby! Behind you!"

Bobby turned to see the huge bird coming at him at 150 miles per hour. It was the last thing that his eyes would ever see.

The eagle struck Bobby square in the face. Without stopping, it efficiently plucked out both of his eyes and flew on.

Mission accomplished.

"Heiny," Guibedo said with brown beer foam on his white mustache, "that was one of the best meals I ever ate. I wonder why Pinecroft, your tree house here, is such a better cook than my Bayon. I used the same gene sequence for their synthesizers."

"That's easy," Mona said. "Heinrich is developing a series of household servants. The darlings are too young to do any work yet, but they have a sort of empathic contact with Pinecroft. They can control its growth to a certain extent, but more important, they can modify the output of the food synthesizer, with the net result that we have a limitless menu of excellent food."

"Hey! That's great! That solves the biggest headache I've had, getting the food right. Can these servants make a tree house add a room where you want it?"

"Oh, yes, Uncle Martin," Heinrich said. "But I can't take all the credit. Mona's in charge of their training, and doing a wonderful job. I don't think I could have done it without her help."

"Yah, Heiny. You sure are a lucky guy."

The CCU I/O unit in the kitchen, "My Lord Copernick?"

"What do you need?"

"I want to report, sir, that pursuant to your suggestion, I have arranged for you to close on the Golden Hoard mine property next Tuesday morning. Also, I have taken the liberty to cause a corporation to be formed to own the mine."

"I compliment your efficiency."

"Thank you, sir. I have had the truck unloaded and the contents assayed. Arrangements have been made to have the gold smelted and sold for forty-five million dollars, through unorthodox channels. The platinum, with an estimated value of seven point four million, has been stored pending the availability of suitable smelting facilities."

"Hey!" Guibedo said. "Save me maybe twenty of those apples."

"Certainly, my Lord Guibedo. Arrangements have been made such that you will have a convincingly functioning mine in one week, with suitable machinery, fencing, and so forth.

"Also, the hiking troop has ceased to be a security problem. One of their members was injured, and the others are carrying him out on a stretcher."

"Not badly, I hope," Heinrich said. "Mona, why don't you take Uncle Martin's truck out there and get that kid to a hospital. I'll have a bird guide you."

"Of course," Mona said, leaving.

"So what do you think of my Central Coordination Unit now, Uncle Martin?"

"Well, Heiny, if them Nazi big shots would have had one of him, we never would have made it out of Germany!"

"My lords," the CCU said, "I would like to suggest that you use your surplus capital to purchase additional real estate, starting with the balance of Death Valley here."

"You know, Heiny, that's not a bad idea," Guibedo said. "We could build quite a city here. Plenty of sunlight and there's water in them mountains."

"I think you're right, Uncle Martin," Heinrich said, turning to the CCU. "Do it!"

Later, surrounded by their rough plans for the city, Heinrich suddenly said, "Uncle Martin, what did you want with those twenty golden apples?"

"I thought maybe they would make nice Christmas presents."

* * *

"Ben, you were able to get Mike to talk?" General Hastings said.

"He's been talking all along, George. It's just that we're starting to make some sense out of what he's saying."

"So, what does he have to say?"

"It's not that easy. It's a matter of word-frequency correlations. You see, George, one of us has to be with him all of the time. If the jamming ever quits, somebody has to be there to sedate him before he drives the rest of us insane. But when you put in a six-hour shift listening to a madman rave, you eventually notice certain words turning up fairly often.

"You see two possibilities as to what the jamming is. One is simply that it is a random noise, transmitted accidentally or deliberately from some natural or artificial source.

"The other theory is that the noise carries information between some people or beings that we don't know about. If this is the case, the information is being transmitted at a rate several hundred times faster than the human nervous system can function, so most of us telepaths just hear white noise. The possibility exists that Mike's synapses are fast enough to pick up the data and that the rest of his brain can't take the information overload.

"Look. The human brain is a series of parallel buffers and gates. Faced with an information overload, such a system will skip a given number of words for each word transmitted.

"On the theory that Mike is repeating every hundredth—or whatever—word in a series of messages, we recorded several months of his ravings and had them transcribed and analyzed by computer. Here is a list of words that appear a statistically significant number of times."

Hastings looked down at the list of words. Near the top were "Lord," "Copernick," "Guibedo," "Life," and "Valley." "Interesting," he said.

"I thought you'd like it, George. Then we had the computer synthesize statistically probable messages based on word frequency. These aren't real messages of course. But they are similar."

The sheet of paper had a series of sentences like:

> "Lord Guibedo is going to Pinecroft."
> "The tunneling in Sector Three is completed."
> "Keep Sector Twenty-two cleared of traffic."

"Better and better," Hastings said. "Get all of this over to the Sham Shop analysts."

"Sure, George. There are reams of the stuff. One other point—there's a bewildering variety of ancient and modern weapons mentioned, and in just about every language there is. We're not sure what they stand for, but if these are code words, there are at least several thousand of them."

Chapter Six

MARCH 4, 2003

NATURAL SELECTION *generally functions in favor of the species rather than of the individual. Take the process of aging.*

It is obviously to the advantage of the individual to go on living forever. This is not a biological impossibility. The processes involved in repairing a cut finger are considerably more complex than those involved in simply keeping the body in the same shape today that it was in yesterday.

But individual immortality is not in the best interests of the species. Immortal great-grandparents would soon overcrowd the species' ecological niche. Younger generations—containing some individuals genetically superior to their ancestors—would tend to be squeezed out by their more experienced progenitors. The evolutionary process would stop in that species, and it would eventually be forced out of its niche—killed off—by some more dynamic life form.

However, as an individual, I did not want to die. When the instrumentation to prolong my own life became a possibility, I threw the resources of my entire corporation behind it. Biological engineering was a natural outgrowth of this work on rejuvenation.

There are short-term problems with rejuvenation. Mostly social. When you look twenty-five and have the glands of a twenty-five-year-old, you naturally want to relate to twenty-five-year-olds. But the youngsters of 2000 have a vastly different cultural background from those of

70

1950. Different morals. Different body language. The results were sometimes amusing, more often sad.

As to the long-term problems with rejuvenation, well, I'll have a lot of time to work on them.

—Heinrich Copernick
From his log tape

General Hastings walked unannounced into the office of the NBC news chief. "Well, Norm. You've come a long way from being a combat reporter."

Norman Boswell looked up from the papers on his cluttered desk. "Major George Hastings. No. Major *General* George Hastings. You've come a ways, too, but you're still a brash son-of-a-bitch. How the hell did you get past my secretary?"

"It's the uniform, Norm. It gets them every time. She practically saluted."

"She practically saluted herself out of a job! Now, before your unfortunately hasty departure, what the hell do you want?"

Hastings moved a cigar box, sat on the papers on Boswell's desk, and said, "A little information, Norm, and a little help. I want to know more about Dr. Martin Guibedo. What can you show me?"

"The door. It's over there. Get off my goddamn desk and use it."

"Shortly, shortly. Now, one of your employees, a Miss Patricia Cambridge, knows a lot about Guibedo. She has interviewed him, had dinner with him, and done a documentary on him. I think she either knows where he is, or knows how to find him."

"I should send a sweet kid like Patty out on a manhunt? Bullshit! You want Guibedo? Send out your own damn goons!"

"My son, I'll tell you a secret. They've tried. Many times, they've tried."

"That's a secret? Next tell me about the secret Statue of Liberty hiding in New York Harbor. Every goddamn cop in the country carries a photo of Guibedo in his wallet! Why should your spooks be any different? The answer is no. I won't do it or get Cambridge involved. Now get out of my office!"

Hastings leaned toward Boswell, crumpling an eight-by-ten glossy photo in the process. "I think you should reconsider that, Norm."

"I don't owe you a goddamn thing. Out!"

"No, but you have an obligation to our favorite uncle. You're a sergeant in the reserves, Norm. He might need to call you up."

"So it's threats now, is it? Well, have you ever thought about what a news chief can do to a public servant?"

"Feel free. I'm clean. Have you ever thought about what a general officer can do to a sergeant?"

Hastings left the office whistling the tune to "Call Up the God Damn Reserves!"

"No! Uncle Martin, I won't do it!"

"What! *This* I hear from the little kid I carried through the snow on my back in Germany? Heiny, I tell you my left kidney has failed and the other one is weak! If you do not help me, I will die!"

"Yeah, yeah. Two months ago it was your right lung, and before that it was your prostrate gland, and before that it was your thyroid. Every time you insisted that I do a hack-and-patch job on you, and every time I've wasted two weeks doing the special programming. Well, no more!"

"But Heiny, my kidneys—"

"I know. I also know that your left lung is weak and your pituitary is below par. Look. We have a standard program for replacing your entire glandular system. It's a proven program that we've used successfully on hundreds of people. What's more, I can start you on it in ten minutes, not two weeks. In fifteen days you'll be a new man. That I'll do for you, but no more hack and patch!"

"There's still some life in this old heart, Heiny."

"Less than you think, and if your heart goes, I won't *have* two weeks for programming the standard program. Take it or leave it."

"Heiny, you make me ashamed, but I guess I gotta take it."

* * *

When Norman Boswell got to his office, his IN basket contained a telegram that began "Greetings..." It informed him that he was to report in uniform to the base commander, Lackland AFB, Texas, no later than noon, March 19, 2003.

He swore at the wall for a full hour, chewed out the girl who brought him his coffee, and called Patricia Cambridge into his office.

Boswell stretched and rolled his neck, relaxing himself. "Ah. Patricia, come in, come in. Have a seat."

"Thanks, boss. What can I do for you?"

"For me? I think it's what I can do for you. First, I want to say how pleased I am with your work. In just eight years with NBC, your accomplishments have been remarkable!"

"Thank you. And it's nine."

"Nine?"

"I've been with NBC for nine years."

"Oh. Right, foolish of me. As I was saying, I'm proud of you, and I'm putting you in for a substantial raise."

"Ooh! Thank you!"

"It should come through in a few weeks. Furthermore, I think you're ready for bigger things."

"Bigger than a popular show?"

"Bigger. Real news reporting in the grand old style! The kind of thing that sent Stanley across Africa in search of Dr. Livingstone. The kind of thing that exposed Nixon at Watergate or Blackstone's deeds in Geneva. Big!"

"Field reporting? What about my show?"

"Oh, Mary can fill in while you're gone. But for you —the Quest for Dr. Martin Guibedo!"

"But that's a dead end! It's been years! *Nobody* has seen Guibedo since he broke jail."

"Wrong, Patty. Somebody's seen him because somebody broke him out. Look. A lot of stuff passes over this desk. Most of it's solid news, but a lot of it is hints, suggestions, possibilities. When it comes to Guibedo, those hints all point in one direction—Death Valley."

"I know, boss. His nephew owns it. But look, Jim

Jennings did a show on Death Valley last fall, and his ratings were lousy."

"Yes, but Jennings only spent a day there. You'll have weeks. Jennings doesn't know Guibedo, but you do. And Jennings had a full camera crew."

"I don't even get a camera crew?"

"When you're ready for it, we can have the L.A. crew there in two hours flat. But at first you're better off without it."

"At first? Just how long do you expect me to spend in the boonies?"

"Whatever it takes, Patty. You'll have an open expense account and all the time you'll need."

"And come back to what? With Mary running it, my ratings will be a shambles! I might not even have a show."

"Mary can handle it, and it will still be your show. Officially, you'll just be on vacation."

"What happens if Guibedo's not in Death Valley?"

"Then go where he is. Open expense account, remember? Patty, I *want* you to do this. Enough said?"

Patty took a deep breath. "Okay. But don't be surprised if I go looking for him in London, Paris, and the Riviera."

"Whatever you feel is best."

"You really mean that?"

"I trust you, Patty. Just be on a plane this afternoon."

"This afternoon! But my show—"

"Mary can handle it. Now get moving. I have work to do."

"Yes, sir."

"And Patty, keep in touch!"

When Cambridge had left his office, Boswell unlocked his lower desk drawer, removed a dusty bottle of Glen Livet, and poured himself a very stiff drink.

The next morning, he received a telegram canceling his call-up orders.

Patricia drove her rented Lincoln along I-15, heading northeast across the Mohave Desert. Going full blast, the air conditioner was barely able to cope with the desert heat. She took the cutoff north toward Death Valley and within an hour was driving past sand dunes and baked desert flats.

Topping a rise, she found herself driving through an immense parking lot. There were cars, trucks, and vans of every description scattered over the plain. There were thousands of them, maybe hundreds of thousands. Some were covered with canvas tarps, others with tailored dust jackets, but most were just sitting there with the wind and sand scouring paint and glass. There were no traffic lanes or painted lines. Each vehicle was simply left in some random spot that its owner thought was good enough. Many were obviously abandoned, with tires missing and doors ajar.

Patricia slowed down. Beyond the lot, she saw a solid wall of tree houses. On the front porch of one, a man sat in shorts and sandals, a tall drink in his hand.

Patricia stopped and lowered the passenger window. "I'm looking for Life Valley!"

"This is good," the man said in a relaxed, friendly voice. "Because that's exactly what you've found."

"Well, how do I drive in there?"

"You don't ma'am. Would you care for some lemonade?"

"Uh. Yes. Thank you." The dry heat hit her as she left the Lincoln and walked to the porch. "What do you mean, I don't? Do I need some kind of permission?"

"No, ma'am. I mean you don't drive. This is as far as the roads go. Beyond here, it's footpaths and shank's mare." He handed her a tall frosted glass. "Pardon my saying it, ma'am, but you look a lot like that television lady, Patricia Cambridge."

So much for playing the supersleuth, Patricia thought. "I guess that's because I'm her. But I'm just on vacation now."

"Well, I'll be. It's surely a pleasure to meet you, ma'am. I'm Harold Dobrinski, but most folks just call me Hank."

Patricia smiled. "My pleasure, Hank, and call me Patty."

"Thank you, Patty. My wife is a big fan of yours and she is going to be sore unhappy about not being here. Would you believe that this very afternoon, the batteries in the TV went dead in the middle of your show, and Meg, that's my wife, went out to buy some new ones. She'll be back in an hour or so, if you'd care to wait. You surely do look like a cool shower would be welcome, or maybe a dip in the pool?"

"Thank you, but I really have to get settled in. Is there a good hotel around here?"

"'Fraid not, ma'am, no hotels, good, bad, or middl'n. There's been some talk about some being designed, but nothing's grown up yet."

"There's no place to stay at all?"

"Now, I didn't say that. Most of these tree houses have a guest room or three. I'd lend you one of mine, but both are full up. I think Barb Anderson has an empty. We'll put you up there."

"Uh. Well, thank you. But I can't impose on . . ."

"That's right, ma'am. You *can't* impose, 'cause it's no imposition. What do you think the guest rooms are for? It's not like you'll be living in the same room with another family. Guest rooms all have a private entrance, and a kitchen and a bath. You won't have to see the Andersons unless you're of a mind to pay a social call. It's just that you'll be living in the same plant as them. Has to be that way, you know."

"Has to?"

"A tree house has to have somebody living in to stay healthy. Guest rooms sometimes go empty for months, so they have to be part of a home that's lived in, you know."

"Oh. I remember Dr. Guibedo saying saying something about that. Have you seen him recently?"

"Seen him? No, ma'am, I can't say that I've ever met the gentleman. Heard about him, of course."

"How long have you lived here, Hank?"

"About two years, ma'am."

"Call me Patty. You mean you've lived here for two years and haven't seen Dr. Guibedo? I thought he lived here."

"I suppose he might, Patty. But you know, before I came out here, I lived fourteen years in Andulusia, Alabama, but I never once met the mayor there. Now, if you've finished that lemonade, give me your car keys and we'll see about getting you settled in. Uh, you might want to think about changing those high heels for something you can walk on grass in."

When her bags were out of the Lincoln, Patty said, "Uh, what do I do about the car?"

"You just leave that to me, Patty. I'll see that she's parked somewhere. You going to be staying long?"

"A week, maybe."

"Then I'll see that its covered with a tarp. You would be amazed at what a sandstorm can do to a fine car like this." Hank picked up her suitcases and led Patty to a neighboring tree house. "You ever lived in a tree house, Patty?"

"No, but I know my way around one."

"Then I'll just let you rest up for a while." He set the bags in the middle of the forty-foot room. "If you've a mind, later, Meg and I would truly enjoy your stopping by."

"Thanks. I might." Patricia got out her NBC credit card. "What do I owe you?"

"Owe me? Why, you don't owe me anything, ma'am."

"But surely, some small gratuity..."

"Ma'am, my social security pays me ten times what I spend, and I don't think anybody in the valley's set up to use plastic money."

"But I..."

"Paid in full by the pleasure of meeting you. But like I said, drop by. Meg would like it."

After he left, Patricia showered, then took a long soak in a ten-foot tub. Jet lag was catching up with her and she was asleep by sunset.

She was up at dawn, and, dressed in a rustic fushia leotard and thigh-high sandals, she went exploring.

There were no street numbers on the houses. There weren't even any streets. People had mostly just planted their houses where it suited them and the houses had mostly grown to within a dozen feet of each other, somehow respecting each other's space. The paths between them rarely went for two hundred feet without branching at odd angles, and those two hundred feet were never straight. A far cry from Manhattan Island!

Among the tree houses, the air had a pleasant temperature, neither hot nor cold, dry nor humid.

There were a lot of people out, and in western fashion, they all seemed to have time to stop and chat. But nobody had ever met Dr. Guibedo.

At noon she had lunch with a tall bachelor who was disappointed when she wouldn't stay, and she went on, talking to people, asking questions.

By five she decided it was time to head back and asked directions.

"The parking lot? Well, it's in *that* direction. About eight miles as I recollect."

By six it was in *this* direction, and about ten miles away. The walls pressed in on her, a horrid green jungle.

By seven she knew that she was hopelessly lost. She sat down, exhausted, on a park bench and fended off three pickup attempts in the growing dusk. She started to drift off into sleep.

"Land sakes, child! Are you sick?"

Patricia looked at the tiny, shriveled old woman in front of her. "What? Oh, no. I'm not sick. I'm just tired. Tired and lost."

"Lost, huh? Well, you shouldn't be out here in the dark. Ain't proper, not for a young woman of any breeding." The woman's dress was thirty years out of date.

"Is it unsafe?"

"Unsafe? Well, I don't recollect anybody being hurt. But there's boys in this neighborhood who are downright rambunctious! Singing and carrying on till all hours! You just come along with me. My house is just around the corner, and there's a spare room hasn't been used in months. Well, up, child!"

Patricia obediently followed the old woman home.

At the end of the second day, she was told that she was sixteen miles from the parking lot.

On the third day, she hired a twelve-year-old boy to guide her back. Children had plenty of uses for money, and no social security checks.

She spent a day recuperating and cursing her boss at NBC. Then she went out again.

Patricia Cambridge parked her bicycle in the growing dusk by the largest private tree house she had ever seen. She was very unsure of herself as she knocked on the door. Two weeks of dead ends and false leads were telling on her. It opened.

"Can I be of service to you, my lady?"

Patricia was shocked by the creature's appearance. While transparent blouses were *in* that season, going about bare-breasted was not. It was a minute or two before she noticed that while from the waist up her greeter looked like a well-developed adolescent, from the waist down she was more goat than human. And her ears were pointed.

"Uh, I'm Patricia Cambridge. Does Dr. Guibedo live here?"

"Yes, my lady. My Lord Guibedo has mentioned you. He is in his workshop. I shall tell him that you're here. Please come in."

Success!

The living room of the tree house was fabulous; comfort and beauty had been Guibedo's only considerations when he designed it. Seated with a gourd of champagne by a waterfall, Patricia waited for an hour, reading old trade journals. It was cool in the cavernous room, and Patricia, dressed in businesslike microshorts and a transparent top, became chilly waiting for Dr. Guibedo.

Finally Guibedo bubbled in—talking rapidly, waving his thick arms. "Ach, Patty! Sorry to keep you waiting, but when you got a DNA loop stretched out, you don't go away until you're finished with it, by golly! Hey! It's gonna be so pretty, Patty! *This* little seed is gonna be the theater and exercise room for the ballet society here. If those little girls had any idea what a time I had with that big mirror, hooh!" He smiled at the faun.

"Liebchen! I am so happy you take such nice care of our guest. I get more proud of you every day, by golly!" The faun glowed with happiness, wiggled her hoofs on the carpet, and waggled her tail vigorously.

"But anyway, Patty! What are you doing here and why didn't you get here before? I haven't seen you for three years! You don't like me or what?" *What a pretty girl this Patty is!* Guibedo thought.

"Uh, why didn't I . . . Dr. Guibedo, don't you realize that every man in the FBI is looking for you? That every government in the world is screaming for your blood? I'm amazed that I found you so quickly, when none of those government men could. It's the biggest manhunt since Patty Hearst."

"Well, a lot of them did find me; then they looked the town over and decided that maybe staying here was nicer than playing cops and robbers. What do you think of my town? Pretty snazzy, huh?"

"It's gorgeous, Dr. Guibedo! But I'd hardly call it a town—it covers half of Death Valley!"

"We paid for it fair and square. And now we call it Life Valley." *This Patty looks so much like my poor Hilde, before she died.*

"But I still don't see how you were so easy to find."

"Simple. You didn't come here looking to hurt nobody, and you didn't bring your whole television studio along. We try not to get too much publicity." With his new set of glands, Guibedo was feeling urges that he hadn't felt in thirty years.

"Publicity! Dr. Guibedo, since your trees killed all those people, you've been one of the most sought-after men in the world!"

"Ach. That was an accident! I was only making it so the tree could fix its own absorption toilet. And when a plant thinks you don't like it, it doesn't grow so good, and some of the toilets grew in the beds and absorbed a few people."

"A few people! You sent those seeds to some of the most influential people in the world. Thousands of them were killed!"

She even gets mad like my Hilde did. "That many people can starve to death in Africa, and nobody cares enough to give them a sandwich. No! The problem was that they were all big shots. And the worst crime that a big shot can think of is killing a big shot. Anyway, I got all that fixed now. The worst thing that can happen is if you hate your tree, the food gets not so good.

"Food! Hey, Liebchen! Would you get me some sauerbraten and some Boch beer, please? And maybe some strudel for Patty?"

"Yes, my lord!" Happy to be noticed at last, the faun pranced into the kitchen.

"Ach, Liebchen is so pretty."

"Dr. Guibedo, what *is* she?"

"Liebchen is a faun. You see, my nephew, Heiny, he makes with the animals like I make with the plants. Fauns are sort of part of the tree. The brains of it. Liebchen is in empathic contact with Oakwood, my tree house here. She makes him grow the way I want, and she controls the food synthesizer. You just explain to Liebchen what you want, give her a couple of tries, and you got it. Liebchen and Oakwood will do anything to make you happy."

"But I've been in Death, er—Life Valley half my vacation and I haven't seen anything like her."

"Well, you ain't seen anything like my beautiful Oakwood who we're sitting in now, either. You got to understand that the smarter animals have to grow up slow so they can learn. This Oakwood is eight months since I made the seed. Liebchen is four years old and is only now grown up. So we can't make so many of them quickly. All of them so far had to be grown in bottles and educated by Heiny's pretty wife.

"Oh, one thing you got to remember around Liebchen is to be all the time nice. Fauns get sick when you get mad at them. And they die if they think that nobody loves them. Heh! That's about the only thing that can kill one. Well, that and radiation."

Liebchen, her tail out proudly, pranced back in with a tray of food, put the tray on the coffee table, and curled up at Guibedo's feet, her head against his lederhosen.

"You mean that all fauns are susceptible to radiation, Dr. Guibedo?" Partially because the food was in front of Guibedo and partially from Liebchen's example, but mostly because, what with her scanty garments, she was *cold*, Patricia came around and sat very close to Guibedo.

"I mean that most of our engineered life forms are very susceptible to radiation, Patty. You see, with natural life forms, you got DNA in a double helix. Now, when a chunk of radiation hits it, it usually breaks only one strand, which usually grows back like it was but sometimes a little bit different which makes for mutation and, occasionally, improvement."

Guibedo felt awkward being so close to Patricia, and he gulped his beer nervously. He would have moved

away except that Liebchen was pressed tightly against
his other side.

"But with an engineered life form, you don't want it
different. *Mein Gott!* What if some big shot would start
breeding my pretty Liebchen to be soldiers in an army! Or
worse yet, to sit behind some damn typewriter! No! What
we use is single-strand DNA, a little bit like what they call
RNA, so if some radiation hits it, the loop breaks and the
cell maybe dies, but cannot be modified. This way my
pretty Liebchen's children will be absolutely identical to
her, because she reproduces asexually."

"Asexually! Do you mean that there aren't any male
fauns?" As Patricia talked, her pointed breast touched
Guibedo's arm. She wasn't really conscious of it, but
Guibedo was. Very.

Liebchen refilled the glasses.

Guibedo gulped nervously at his beer. *This little girl
could be my granddaughter. Might have been if them
damn Nazi big shots hadn't killed my Hilde.* "That's
right. No need for boys. In nature, the boys is to mix up
the genes so sometimes the kid gets the good parts of
both his parents. And because, in higher animals, the kid
and the mother can't take care of themselves, the boys is
to protect them." Guibedo put his arm around Patricia.
Sipping daintily at her glass, Patricia snuggled into the
warmth of his pudgy side.

Liebchen filled their glasses again.

"But with engineered life forms, you designed it right
the first time. And you got real humans around to protect
the kids and pregnant girls, so you get a symbiotic relationship. And the other reason is that single-strand DNA
can duplicate eighty times faster than double-strand, so
they grow like blue lightning!"

"But, Dr. Guibedo, how can you have reproduction
without sex?" Patricia said, trying to ask intelligent questions. *This interview will make my career in broadcasting.*

Hooh! This little one's got sex on the brain, Guibedo
thought.

"Nothing to it. The problem is making them not reproduce. You see, you got to make sure that you got as
many houses or fauns as you need. But you also got to
make sure that you don't get too many. We can't have

tree houses crowding each other for sunlight, or Lieb-
chens running around like unloved alley cats."

Liebchen shuddered at the word "unloved," but
topped off the glasses.

"There is got to be harmony, or the world me and
Heiny are building would be just as cruel as the one nature made. With the trees, it's easy. Each tree grows
seeds in a cupboard, which stay there until you pick
them. If you want a house, you find one just like what
you want and ask the owner for a seed. Then you got to
plant it and water it every day for three months. So it
can't just happen by accident. And the grown tree is got
to have people living in it, for the fertilizer. So you got
balance. Mutual need. Symbiosis."

Liebchen was keeping the glasses filled. Guibedo was
drinking far more than usual. Patricia was drinking on
the theory that she needed the antifreeze.

"With intelligent animals, they can make their own
decisions. We make them so they got to be real happy
before they can have kids. And you have to ask them
please, real often, before they get pregnant."

"Show Liebchen can get knocked up whenever she
wants to?" The champagne was starting to tell on Patty.

"Liebchen is knocked up now! Fauns is way different
from humans. Like their body temperature is eight degrees cooler than ours, which is why fauns don't wear
clothes around here, but humans do." *Well*, Guibedo
thought, looking through Patricia's transparent blouse to
her bikini bottoms, *most humans do*.

"And which is also why we keep the temperature in
here at sixty-five degrees."

Now that the subject had been brought up, Patricia
was too comfortable to want to do anything about it.

"Like they can only eat a special fluid what the tree
makes, which contains everything they need and nothing
else. Liebchen's small intestine just keeps getting smaller
until it ends. The only holes she's got are in her pretty
head. She has breasts because they're pretty and because fauns is to take care of human children."

Guibedo gently put his fingertips on Patricia's right
nipple. She didn't seem to mind. Actually, she didn't
even notice.

"Ach, I talk and talk and so late it gets. Come on, Patty. Is time for bed."

Leaning drunkenly together, their arms about each other for support, Guibedo led Patricia through a branch to his bedroom.

"Ach, it will be so nice," Guibedo said gently. "You sleep with me tonight."

Patricia was shocked sober in an instant. It had simply never occurred to her to think of kindly, wise old Guibedo as a sexual being.

"Uh... I..." For a second she stood tongue-tied, then Patricia ran down to the living room.

Guibedo was equally confused. He stood motionless for a while, then turned to his bedroom, flopped on the bed, and cried himself asleep.

A knowledgable and sober observer would have understood the problem. Guibedo and Patricia had vastly different cultural backgrounds and, as a result, used totally different body languages. To Guibedo, when a nearly nude woman aggressively snuggles into your arms, she is obviously eager for sex. By Patricia's standards, she was properly dressed and was merely being friendly to a nice old man.

Meanwhile, Liebchen was snuggled up on her favorite couch—the broad comfortable back of an LDU. Something about Dirk's inherent deadliness always excited her, and he reciprocated by doing for her whatever small favors he could. Just now his skin was a good imitation of a Campbell Tartan because Liebchen *liked* Scottish Tartans. Crouched down, doing his usual guard duty he looked like a big oval pillow. Patricia had just spent hours in the same room with him without being aware of his existence.

Liebchen was startled awake as Patricia blundered, crying, toward the door. The ways of humans would ever be a mystery to Liebchen, but her programming put courtesy and hospitality first. "My lady! Are you in pain?"

Patricia stopped. "Uh... No. I... I'm okay. But I've got to go now."

"But my lady! It is so late. Where would you go? How could you find your way in the dark?"

There was a certain logic in what the faun said.

"There is a guest room behind the kitchen, my lady. It has a lock on the door, and a private exit. Oh, please, my lady. Accept our hospitality."

After a bit of confused argument, Patricia agreed. She fell asleep on the guest bed, trying to sort out what had happened.

The next morning, Patricia and Liebchen sat alone at the breakfast table.

"My lady, I do not understand what happened last night."

"I'm not sure I understand it myself, Liebchen."

"Does it have to do with your bisexual reproduction custom?"

"Reproduction? Well, not exactly, except in a round-about way," said Patricia. *How do you explain romantic love to an asexual being?*

"And my Lord Guibedo found you to be a suitable mate, but you rejected him?"

"I didn't exactly reject him, I just didn't want—Lieb-chen, I can't explain it to you."

"My lady, you have mated before, haven't you?" Liebchen persisted.

"Uh . . . Yes. Of course. I'm twenty-nine, Liebchen."

"Were the others as intelligent as my Lord Guibedo?"

"Goodness, no! I've never met anyone with a brain like his. Why, he broke the genetic code singlehanded."

"Were the others as warm and generous as my Lord Guibedo?"

"They were nice, but so is Dr. Guibedo."

"My lady, if Lord Guibedo is superior to your earlier mates, why did you accept them and reject him?"

"Liebchen, I know I won't explain it right, but there are other things a girl looks for in a man. I mean, Dr. Guibedo's nice, but he's so old and, uh, portly."

"And your programming requires that your mates have certain physical characteristics?"

"Programming! Liebchen, I wasn't programmed! I was raised naturally."

"All beings are programmed, my lady. We engineered life forms are programmed rationally. Natural life forms are programmed in a somewhat random manner. But they are programmed nonetheless."

"I don't want to argue with you, Liebchen." Patricia decided to change the subject. "This breakfast is delicious."

"Thank you, my lady. I thought that it would be what was desired by one of your . . . background. You must try this." Liebchen handed Patricia a glass. "I made it specially for you."

The liquid looked like a mixture of milk and pink grapefruit juice, but it was hard to say no to someone as eager as Liebchen. Patricia took a polite sip.

"Thank you. It *is* good." She took a larger drink. "In fact, it's *great!*" Patricia finished the glass. "What do you call it?"

"It doesn't have a name yet, my lady."

"Then what is it?" Patricia felt suddenly sleepy, and slumped onto the table, unconscious.

When Patricia was completely unconscious, Liebchen said, "It is a light dose of a behavioral modification compound that will change your perceptions and programming somewhat, my lady. It will increase the happiness of all concerned." Liebchen was programmed to always give a human a complete answer.

When Guibedo came in, unshaven and looking at the floor, Patricia was up and smiling.

"Good morning. I'm glad you're still here, Patty. I've got to apologize for last night. Maybe I drank too much, but I was way out of line."

Patricia got up and put her arms around Guibedo, her fingertips not quite touching each other behind him. She kissed him full on the mouth. "There's nothing to apologize for, handsome."

These girls, thought Guibedo. *As soon as you've got them figured out, you're wrong!*

Liebchen smiled and wiggled her hoofs happily on the carpet.

Chapter Seven

MARCH 20, 2003

UNCLE MARTIN'S tree houses will totally alter the world's economic structure. In fact, economics in the ordinary sense of the word will cease to exist. Our present political and social structure, with all their inequities, are completely dependent on economics. Without it they will fall.

It would be criminal to destroy those structures without having something better to take their place. Most of my animals are designed to replace existing governmental services.

The LDUs can perform a variety of functions, such as being a police force, a medical corps, dog catchers, and what have you. The fauns should be able to handle at least primary education. The TRACs will do most construction and transportation. And the Central Coordination Unit can take care of communications.

But setting up a rational, decent social structure is going to require more than bioengineering.

Eventually every human being will have an equal and high standard of living. Historically, certain groups have enjoyed this position: the Czarist aristocracy; the Roman nobility; the present-day idle rich. But I don't like any of these cultures. Maybe we can try for something better. The only thing that I know for certain is that a peaceful culture needs a peaceful environment to grow in. If I must lie to maintain the illusion of tranquility, so be it.

—Heinrich Copernick
From his log tape

"I'm glad that you volunteered for this mission, Jack. If you hadn't, I'd have to order you to go," General Hastings said.

"I had that feeling, General."

"It's just that you're the best field agent I have."

"The best that you have left, you mean."

"Breckenridge and Thompson were good men. But you will have some advantages that they didn't. For one thing, you will have completely discretionary powers. Do you understand?" Hastings asked.

"Sure. I'm not allowed to kill anybody unless I want to."

"Crudely put, but accurate. Also, your mission is not simply to spy. You are to seek out Heinrich Copernick and/or Martin Guibedo. We believe that they are in Death Valley. You are to find out as much as possible about their bioengineering techniques, then eliminate them. Arrest them if possible. Kill them if necessary. And in no event will you allow yourself to be captured."

"You mean 'captured alive.' Okay. What about my *modus operandi*?"

"That is completely at your own discretion. You may sign for any materials and money that you feel appropriate," Hastings said.

"Lovely. I've always hoped for orders like this."

"This is the most important mission of your life. It is also the most dangerous."

"What about the reporting procedure?"

"There isn't one. It is quite possible that we have been infiltrated. Once you walk out of that door, you're on your own."

"Suits. See you in a few weeks, General."

Patricia Cambridge stretched luxuriously between satin sheets on the huge bed. Her whole body tingled with a new awareness of itself. She never would have believed that the world could be so enchanting, that sex could be so totally satisfying.

"If you're finally awake, Patty, come on in. The water's fine!" Martin Guibedo called from the pool at the far end of the bedroom. Liebchen was sudsing down his pudgy body.

"Oh, Dr. Guibedo! Will Liebchen wash me, too? She's got to be the prettiest thing your nephew ever made!"

"She is and she will, and please call me Martin."

"After last night, I should call you lover!" Patricia splashed into the pool and swam over to them.

"Hooh! Nobody ever call me that before. I like it!"

They collided with exuberance and laughter near the center of the pool.

After having washed and dried and dressed her masters, Liebchen pranced through the branch to the kitchen. The water running off the blond fur on her legs left hoofprints on the carpet. "*Two* masters to serve, Dirk!" She giggled to the Labor and Defense Unit in the living room. "Isn't it wonderful!"

Dirk raised his eye tentacles from the book of Oriental philosophy he was reading. "It *is* pleasant to see our Lord Guibedo happy. We owe him so much."

After the usual excellent breakfast, Guibedo said, "Patty, it's good to have you here for a bunch of reasons. For one thing, we got a fourth for pinochle."

The CCU I/O unit on the kitchen wall said, "My Lord Guibedo, Lord Copernick requests your presence at his tree house."

"Telephone, tell him I'm going to take a couple days off this morning. I see him maybe Tuesday."

"He said it was important, my lord. My Central Coordination Unit has compiled some critical information."

"So what's the information? You're the same animal, aren't you?"

"I am, my lord, but I didn't tell me what it was."

"Some coordination you got there. Tuesday!" Guibedo turned away from the telephone. "Hey, Dirk! Bring some cards. With you here, Patty, we can play two teams, you and Liebchen against me and Dirk, so they gotta play fair. With playing three-hand cutthroat, they let me all the time win."

"Never, my lord," Dirk said, a pinochle deck in his

hand. His lateral tentacles were holding a book in front of his starboard eyes.

"Ach! You know, Patty, Dirk never used to lie until he started into philosophy. Dirk, what are you reading now?"

"The *Shih Ching*, my lord," Dirk said, shuffling and dealing, "a poetry anthology commonly said to have been edited by Confucious."

"Twenty-one!" Patty said. "Martin, how can Dirk read and play cards at the same time?" She still didn't feel comfortable around the LDU.

"He's got six pairs of brains, Patty. Heiny made him so he could figure strategy, tactics, and where he was putting his foot all at the same time. So right now, one chunk of him is reading, another chunk is playing cards, some other chunk better be keeping score, and part of him is probably gabbing with his brothers. Twenty-two."

"Gabbing?" Patty said. "How?"

"They're telepathic with each other," Guibedo said, "not with you and me. Your bid, Liebchen."

"Oh, pass! Dirk, pull in your eyes. You're cheating again."

Dirk retracted his yard long eye tentacles, turned a page of the book, and said, "Twenty-four."

"Twenty-five. Martin, if you have practical telepathy, what do you need with the telephone?"

"Thirty. Telepathy has only got one channel, Patty. We humans only use it for emergencies, and this isn't one of them."

"I'm afraid it is, Uncle Martin," Dirk said in Heinrich Copernick's voice. "Please get over here as soon as you can."

"But I wanted to show Patty around town this morning, Heiny. And I got a run and five aces and Dirk just gave me meld bid!"

"So play the hand later. Say, how about if I ask Mona to show Patty around, Uncle Martin? It'll give the girls a chance to get acquainted."

"Ach! Heiny, it better be good," Guibedo said. "You gonna like Mona. Patty, we get together later on. I'll call you."

"How? I mean, if I'm going to be out all day—"

"The telephone knows where you're at."

"My mother doesn't know where I am. Can I make a few calls?"

"It's your house, too, Patty. If you call outside the valley, they get a telegram. Come on, Dirk, we go the low way," Guibedo said, leaving.

Liebchen started cleaning up the kitchen, putting the cards away in four neat stacks and only peeking a little bit.

"Liebchen," Patty said, "how do I, uh?..."

"The telephone, my lady? I'll show you. Telephone, tell my sisters, Colleen and Ohura, that I think I have the day off, so I'll be over to their house in an hour. And, telephone, be sure and warn me when Lord Guibedo starts home, so I can be here when he arrives."

"Sure thing, Liebchen," the local ganglia said.

"Just like that, Liebchen? How do you know its listening?" Patty asked.

"Oh, he's always listening, my lady. He just isn't allowed to speak unless spoken to. It's rather a pity, he's really very nice."

"I'm sure. Telephone, please tell my mother that I'm in Death, I mean *Life* Valley, and that I'm having a wonderful time and I've met the nicest boy that she's just got to meet. Uh, her address is . . ."

"Four ninety-one Seminole Drive, Boca Raton, my lady," the telephone said.

"How did you know that?"

"When you moved in, my lady, I had your personal file loaded into my local ganglia from my Central Coordination Unit."

"But how did *it* know?"

"The phone directory, obviously, my lady."

"Oh. And could you tell my boss at NBC that everything is fine and I need another week's vacation?"

"Happy to, my lady. Have a nice day," the telephone said.

"Mother! This is Patty," the CCU said.

"Why, Patty! It's so nice to hear from you."

"Mother, it's beautiful here in Acapulco. I wish you could come."

"Well, not this time, dear. You aren't lonely, are you?"

"Oh, no. Some of the girls from NBC are with me. The water is just wonderful."

"That's good, dear. Have a nice time."

"Boss. Cambridge here," the CCU said.

"Patty! Where the hell you been? I've been trying to find you for days."

"Sorry, boss. Finding a telephone in Death Valley is like trying to find a telephone in Death Valley. Hey, this place is a dead end. Nothing but skid-row bums and blacks who can't get on welfare. But I've got a definite lead on Guibedo. He's in Minnesota. Okay if I track it down? I'll need a couple more weeks."

"Well, Patty, if you think it's solid, go ahead. Take what time and money you need. But be careful. I don't want to see you hurt."

"Thanks, boss. I'll keep in touch."

Guibedo was riding cross-legged on Dirk's back, as Dirk trotted at thirty miles an hour down the tunnel that connected Guibedo's Oakwood to Copernick's Pinecroft.

"No offense, my lord," Dirk said, "but I'll be glad when Lord Copernick's Transportation, Recreation, and Construction units grow up. I really wasn't made for this sort of thing."

"Me, too. I wasn't either. Them TRACs will help. Can't even keep a pipe lit. How do you read in this wind, anyhow?"

"With some difficulty, my lord. It's just that if we LDUs had had a proper philosophical base earlier, certain . . . errors wouldn't have taken place."

"Yah. I know it troubles you, Dirk. Those eighty-five families and that boy hiker and all the rest. Those things were bad, and it's good you should study so they don't happen again. But don't let it get you on the insides. The universe is a big place and all of us are just little people. We do the best we can, but it is impossible for us to know what all of the results of our actions will be, and some of our actions will be wrong. So sometimes we cause needless damage, suffering, and death.

"But if we waited until we were sure of the results before we took action, we would never take action at all. And when something must be done, it is better to do something wrong than to do nothing at all. Anyway, we've been able to fix up some of our mistakes."

"I wish I could do something for the families we killed, my lord."

"Look. We are out to change the world, Dirk. We have the power to do it. But whenever there is great power, there is also the possibility of great error. When we are done, the world will be a better place. In the meantime, we can only try to cause as little suffering as possible."

Dirk trotted into Pinecroft's subbasement. Heinrich Copernick was waiting for them.

"So what was so important, Heiny?" Guibedo asked as he got a leg down.

"War, Uncle Martin. War against us within six months."

"The Russians is getting uppity? I thought everything was going smooth there."

"No problem in Russia. After the first year, when we were a capitalistic trick, Ivan noticed that he never had solved his housing problem. Now we're the natural culmination of Marxism Leninism. Aliev is also claiming that you studied under Lysenko."

"Hooh! That's a good one! So, China?"

"No. China and all the eastern nations, except United India, are raising tree houses as fast as they can. We're banned in India, of course."

"I always figured they'd be on our side, for religious reasons. With a tree house, you don't have to kill anything to live."

"They would have been, if the Neo-Krishnas hadn't found the birth control chemicals you were putting in the food. They figure they'll need the excess population for their next holy war."

"Heiny, it takes a half an acre of land for a tree house to support a family. India was so close to the edge, I had to do something."

"Oh, I agree with you. But we're still banned in India."

"So who we gotta fight?" Guibedo asked, exasperated.

"The United States, and most of Western Europe."

"Ach! So by 'us' you mean you and me! So why does our own country want to fight us?"

"We are upsetting too many apple carts, Uncle Martin. While only four percent of the U.S. population is living in tree houses, housing starts have been virtually zero for the past year. Property values have dropped over fifty percent in some areas. The average home owner owes sixty thousand dollars on his home. Right now he can only sell it for forty thousand. You can't blame him for being upset."

"So let him move into a tree house," Guibedo said. "He won't owe anybody anything on it."

"People have been doing just that, Uncle Martin. But to get out from under their old debts, they have to declare bankruptcy. There were over two million bankruptcies in the last year, and there will be ten times that number in the next. The banking industry will collapse under the strain."

"So what you need with money in the bank for, anyway, when you got a tree house?" Guibedo said. "It takes care of you."

"What we are doing is great for the individual, Uncle Martin, but it's death to the system. And the system is about to start fighting back."

"System! You mean the big shots!"

"Call it anything you want," Heinrich said. "But they'll fight us until the last conscript soldier fires the last taxpayer's bullet."

"There's got to be some way out of it, Heiny. It takes two sides to have a war."

"But only one to have a massacre. There is a way out of fighting, but the cure is worse than the disease."

"So what is it, Heiny?"

"Kill the trees. I'm sure we could come up with some kind of a blight."

"Kill my trees! What about the people living in them?" Guibedo said.

"They'd mostly die. And that's not the worst of it. The CCU has done a fifty-year analysis on present and potential world trends; he's been on it for nearly a year. CCU! Give Uncle Martin the analysis you gave me."

"Yes, my lord. The following analysis is based on the premise that bioengineering was never developed. It is also valid in the event that we take no aggressive action in the near future—as, if we don't, no engineered life forms will exist three years from now.

"In the absence of any active role on our part, the probability of total nuclear war in the next fifty years is point seven two, due primarily to proliferation of atomic weapons among the smaller nations. Due to increased mobility between population centers, increased population in the underdeveloped nations, and a general lowering of living standards, the probability of devastating plague by 2050 is point eight eight. Extrapolating present demographic trends, by 2050 the population of the underdeveloped nations will outnumber that of the developed nations twenty-seven to one. The probability of the increased population's resulting in famine and causing a conventional war which will mutate to an unsurvivable thermonuclear war is point nine three. Famine could be delayed by increased industrialization, but the resultant pollutants would render the world uninhabitable by 2090. The net probability of civilization surviving on Earth is point zero two at 2050, approaching point zero zero by 2100."

There were no formal laws or rules in Life Valley, so there was no formal prohibition of mechanical transportation. However, the general layout of houses, parks, fields, and shops was such that anything larger than a bicycle would have a hard time getting through, and, in fact, most people walked.

Very few people considered it a hardship. Since the necessities were produced in each home, the only commerce was in luxury items, and such things are easily carried.

"It's incredibly beautiful here," Patricia said. What was once a horrid jungle to her now seemed a fairyland, yet she did not notice her own change in attitude. "It's as though every path was asking me to walk down it."

"Heinrich and Uncle Martin spent a lot of time on the

design," Mona said. "Notice that no matter what time of day it is, the trees and shrubs are arranged so that on any path you can walk in either the sun or the shade."

"And the way everything curves, Mona. With every step, the view changes, something else shows up."

"That was part of the plan, too."

Clothing styles in the valley were varied and occasionally bizarre. A fair number of people followed Guibedo's lead, wearing ethnic costumes, while others ranged from blue jeans to complete nudity. Mona wore a sarong around her hips and a smile.

Patty, still in businesslike microshorts and transparent top, felt a little out of place, and said so.

"No problem for now, Patty. Just take off your top if you're hot. But you should have something formal for tonight. Perhaps a chiton, since they're doing Stravinsky's Oedipus Rex at the bandshell tonight and Heinrich promised to take me. You can work on Uncle Martin at dinner.

"Anyway, next stop's at Nancy Spencer's. She's the best seamstress in the valley."

"Ach!" Guibedo's face was white. "We knew it was going to be bad. That's why we started the biological revolution. But I never thought it would be *this* bad. Heiny, have you double-checked all this? Is it really true?"

"I funded a research group with the Rand people six months ago. I got their report this morning. Their figures are substantially the same as the CCU's."

"Then we got no choice. We got to fight. You have a strategy worked out for it yet?"

"The CCU and I have been working on it for weeks. While the LDUs can hold their own against conventional troops, they are only marginally effective against armor. They are totally ineffective against air power. When I designed them, I was thinking in terms of a police force and a medical corps. I didn't realize then that we would be facing a real war. No bird I could possibly come up with could stand a chance against aircraft, let alone orbital beam weapons.

"Our only possible strategy is dispersion, using basic

guerrilla tactics over a wide area. Logistics must be handled locally, since we must presume that all of our strong points, including Life Valley, will be obliterated.

"What we need, Uncle Martin, is a tree that doesn't require someone living in it. That merely provides food for people and the LDUs. Something that is more vigorous than natural plants, so it will supplant them. Something that reproduces with spores rather than seeds, so our opponents can't stop their proliferation."

"Sure, Heiny, I could do that. But maybe I better give the species a finite lifespan, so we get rid of them after the war."

"Good idea, Uncle Martin. But this war could last fifteen years."

"So long?"

"Guerrilla wars are like that."

"But why does it have to be a guerrilla war, Heiny? They've got to be the worst kind. How about the socialist and communist countries? They're growing my trees. Why can't we just move there? If we go to China and they attack us, they're attacking China, so we have an ally!"

"The Eastern Bloc is growing trees because it solves some of their short-term problems. They haven't yet realized that when the means of production and distribution are in each man's own home, he doesn't need a central government any more. Eventually the commissars are going to realize that they are being put out of work. People who run governments *like* running governments. We don't have any allies, Uncle Martin."

"Yah. The big-shot problem. But still, there's got to be a better way. So what are our chances of winning this war, anyhow?"

"Quite good, my lord," the CCU said. "I estimate a point two two probability of success."

"That's good?"

"It is, my lord, compared to the probability that civilization will cease to exist within the next century if we do not fight this war."

"You figured out how many people are going to die in this thing?"

The CCU said, "Best estimates are around two

hundred million—two percent of the world's population, my lord—assuming that we make preserving human life a major strategic objective."

"So many! You say that so easy, sitting here," Guibedo said.

"My lord, I am sentient. I do not want to die. But I am immobile, in the center of our opponent's major target area. In none of the scenarios that we have examined do I have any chance of survival. The probability that I will be dead within two years is one."

"Sorry, fella," Guibedo said. "Don't tell me what my own chances are."

"My lord, throughout history, every major social, political, or religious upheaval has caused the death of from three to five percent of the population involved. The industrial revolution cost four point two percent of England's population through starvation and disease. The Russian Revolution cost three point seven percent; the French Revolution, three point six percent; the American Revolution, one point one percent plus an equivalent two point three percent foreign troops. Even the 'peaceful' division of India and Pakistan starved out or killed three point five percent of the population.

"The two percent estimate I gave you for the upcoming revolution was based on the assumption of the loss of one *billion* LDUs and similar beings. This time, perhaps we can do some of the dying for you."

Heinrich Copernick and Martin Guibedo were silent for a long while.

Patricia and Mona walked through a series of meadows that dotted the sides of a clear brook, passing over a dozen small bridges. As they did so, the path wound and twisted past and over trout ponds, grottoes, and fountains; it was the antithesis of a superhighway, designed not to be efficient but to make each step of a journey pleasant and interesting.

The path eventually opened onto a long curving meadow. On both sides were tree houses fronted with shops. The owners evidently lived behind their shops, for the stores were small and the houses were large.

"We call this Craftsman Way," Mona explained. "It

wasn't really planned this way, but most people have tended to move near others with similar interests."

"Hey, Mona! You need anything today?" Jimmy shouted from the open-air metal shop in front of his tree-house. He was wearing a leopard-skin loincloth.

"I don't, but Patty probably does!"

"I do?"

"Sure. Uncle Martin's tableware is a disgrace, and Jimmy is the best silversmith in the valley." Mona herded Patty over to the display case.

Patty walked from display to display closely examining the collection of jewelry, silverware, and serving pieces. Everything was individually crafted, with a rare combination of art and utility. "I haven't seen anything this good since I left Pratt!"

"Your friend's taste is impeccable, Mona." Jimmy winked and bowed grandly to Patty. "James Sauton, Silversmith, at your service."

"This is Patty Cambridge, Jimmy," Mona said. "She's looking for some things to go in Oakwood."

"Oakwood? The professor's house?" Jimmy said. "Hey, Patty, you don't want none of this junk. Let me make you something special. You known the professor long?"

"About four years," Patty said, holding a spoon in her hand. "These are lovely, and I think we've only service for four."

"I'll make you a service for twenty," Jimmy said, "but not these. Can you come by day after tomorrow? I'll have some samples to show you. I've wanted to do something for the professor for a long time."

"How long have you known Martin?" Patty reluctantly let go of the spoon as Jimmy took it from her hand.

"A couple of years, but he did me a real good turn once, so when I heard he was in Death Valley, I gave my tree house to a couple of kids and hopped a freight out here."

"*You heard he was here?*" Patty was surprised, remembering the difficulty she had finding Guibedo. "How?"

"The grapevine. Come back day after tomorrow, I'll

have something to knock your eyes out." Jimmy turned and left.

As they strolled on, Patty said, "My goodness! I shouldn't have done that. I mean, I don't have any money with me."

"Most people don't carry money around here, Patty. You just tell the telephone about your purchases, and it keeps track of that sort of thing."

"I mean I don't have much at home, either."

"Jimmy's pretty reasonable, ordinarily. But in this case, I don't think you could get him to accept money. He idolizes Uncle Martin so much, it gets embarrassing. I think Uncle Martin avoids him. But don't worry about money. The telephone will just bill Uncle Martin, and Heinrich always covers his account, so the old dear won't even know about it."

"But I can't do that!" Patty said.

"Do it. Didn't you know that they own a gold mine?"

"My lords! Intruder alert in Sector Fifty-five!" the CCU said.

"Dirk! Tell your brothers to nail him! Unharmed!" Heinrich said. "How did he get past the Gamma Screens?"

"The surrounding sector guards are converging, my lord," Dirk said. "Gamma LDU 1096 reports that the intruder was under heavy narcohypnosis. His primary programming is only now surfacing."

"Well, get several Gammas on him. I want a complete probe," Heinrich said. "Go transponder mode."

"Yes, my lord." Dirk's voice became a monotone, relaying transmissions from the LDUs in the area.

"Sector Fourty-four. Wirka here. Converging."

"Sector Fifty-four. Pacho here. Converging."

"Sector Sixty-four. Kinzhal here. Converging."

"Sector Fifty-five. Vintovka here. Converging. I can see the intruder with my bird. He is armed."

Vintovka was a Beta series LDU in empathic contact with an observation eagle. This empathic contact was quite distinct from telepathy. It amounted to a wide-band communication circuit, but it was limited to only two nodes. That eagle and the LDU had hatched from the same egg; they were really two parts of the same being.

"ETA for nine LDU's is eighty-five seconds," Dirk said. "Gamma Units report that intruder is KGB. Weapons include AK-84 Assault rifle and fragmentation grenades. Intruder's IQ is 126, Need Affiliation four percent, Need Achievement seventy-eight percent, Need Power ninety-nine percent. High sex drive converted to sadism."

"Uck! He's worse than the Air Force Intelligence type we stopped last week," Copernick muttered. "Dirk! My earlier command to capture the intruder unharmed is rescinded—he's a butcher. Stop him!"

"Acknowledged, my lord. Thank you," Dirk said. "Perhaps 'hunter' would be a better term. He is after Lord Guibedo."

Dirk returned to his monotone. "Vintovka here. Intruder is in sports arena. Children's gymnastic class now in progress. I will attempt to lure intruder to the band shell, now vacant. Other units converge there."

Vintovka charged, his easily camouflaged skin glowing international orange. He threw rocks at the intruder, and when one of them caught the man's head, he opened fire. Vintovka retreated, throwing rocks, maneuvering to keep behind him an area clear of bystanders. Lead tore up the sod at his feet and chips of bark and wood flew behind him, but Vintovka kept himself in full view and retreated toward the band shell.

The children stopped and stared.

Mona and Patricia entered a wide rolling park that was bounded by a library, a band shell, two theaters, a dance hall, and a few bars and restaurants.

"There's a sports area on the other side of the band shell," Mona said. "Gymnastics, football fields, that sort of thing. Past that a lake's going in, but it isn't done yet."

"And only two years ago, this was all a desert," Patricia said.

"The worst hellhole in the world. But everything was here: the sunlight, the soil, the water."

"The water?" Patricia asked.

"What do you think the white stuff on those mountains is? All Death Valley needed was a little reorganization, which Uncle Martin and Heinrich provided. In twenty years the whole world will be a park like this, only varied and different. When we get to Pinecroft, remind me to show you the plans they have for a town in the mountains east of here. Fantastic!"

"It's all so perfect." Patricia noticed that the grass they were walking on was like a putting green.

"It's getting there. Nightlife is still sort of restricted. There's no shortage of musicians, but the bars and restaurants are mostly serve yourself and clean up the mess," Mona said, leading Patricia to an open-air cafe.

"There are two exceptions. One is the Red Gate Inn, which is run by a sort of social group. It's kind of a fun place, most parts of it anyway," Mona said.

"What's wrong with the rest of it?"

"Nothing, really. It's a matter of taste—the inn is divided up into about twenty different rooms, each with a different motif and each with its own form of entertainment. There's always at least ten things going on. Like there's one room for Irish folk songs—interspersed with bagpipes. And there's a Whopper Room where telling the truth is considered bad form."

"It sounds like fun," Patricia said.

"On the other hand, Basin Street is men only. The only women there are waitresses and dancers. They don't wear clothes. The Guardians of the Red Gate had the nerve to ask me to dance there," Mona said.

"Did you?" Patricia giggled.

"Only once. Heinrich hit the roof." Mona laughed. "The other exception is Mama Guilespe's, over here."

As they sat at a square table with a red-and-white checked tablecloth, Patricia suddenly realized how few straight lines she had seen all day.

Mama Guilespe bustled over wearing a peasant costume of Ciociaria, near Naples, a red-and-blue floor-length checked skirt, an embroidered purple apron, purple "leg of lamb" sleeves on a white blouse, a red-and-gold scarf, and heavy gold earrings. All of this was wrapped, despite the heat, around 250 pounds of fast-moving woman.

"Eh! Mona! I don't see you for a week. Such a pretty

friend you got!" Mama set down huge cups of coffee in front of them.

"Mama Guilespe, this is Patty Cambridge."

"Pleased to meet you, Mrs. Guilespe."

"So skinny! They don't feed you enough?" She was already piling a vast mound of pastry in front of the women. "You got to be new here, and I was talking to such a nice boy only this morning—"

"She's taken," Mona got in edgewise.

"Such a pity..." Mama Guilespe was already on her way to the next group of customers.

"Whew!" Patricia said.

"You've got to love her," Mona said. "I know it's silly, but Mama Guilespe loves to cook. So she has her tree house make flour, sugar, and eggs, bakes these herself, and serves them out here."

"They *are* good," Patty said, munching a Danish, "and the place seems popular enough."

"I think it really functions as a meeting place, Patty. Mama Guilespe is quite a matchmaker. Drop by here alone sometime if you ever get tired of Uncle Martin."

"Impossible."

"I feel the same way about Heinrich," Mona said.

"You know, I haven't seen him in five years," Patty said.

"Well, have dinner with us tonight. But about Heinrich, well, expect some changes. He's used his bio-engineering on himself. He's seven feet tall now, and gorgeous."

"Just like Martin, huh?"

"Well, Heinrich *has* done a few changes to Uncle Martin. Those two are working on something secret. Probably a new auditorium, which we certainly need."

"Dinner sounds great," Patty said. "I'd love to come."

"You'll have to, unless you want to eat alone. Even Liebchen and Dirk are at Pinecroft," Mona said.

"You know, we haven't seen any of Heinrich's things all day," Patty said.

"You won't, either. The TRACs are still kittens, and there are only twenty fauns right now, although they're all due to have twins of their own in about a week. Fauns can't take the heat out here anyway. The LDUs tend to stay out of sight. Most people don't know that they exist until they need a doctor."

"Doctors?" Patty said. "Is that what they are?"

"They're just about anything that needs an organized group. Police, fire department, dog catchers, medical corps, construction gang. You name it, they do it. I know they're hideous to look at, but they're really fine people. You'll get used to them."

A series of sharp explosions sounded.

"What's that?" asked Patty.

"Probably fire crackers from some damn chemistry class. I hope they don't wake my babies," Mona said.

"You have children?"

"Twins. Girls. Michelle and Carolyn."

"I'd love to see them. But how do you get a babysitter when most things around here are free?"

"Heinrich made me raise the babysitters before he'd let me have the babies. We keep two fauns."

"Fauns take care of children?"

"It's what they were made for. You don't really need a servant in a tree house, everything pretty much takes care of itself. But raising a child properly is a full-time occupation, and two gets impossible. Fauns are teachers, really—walking, talking, reading, writing, arithmetic. It's really one of Heinrich's plots. Fauns imprint language early, then have almost no language ability after that. It'll be thirty years before every family in the world has a faun, but when that happens, every child will get a solid basic education *and will speak English as a first language*! So poof! There goes the language barrier."

"Every child?"

"So how many mothers are going to turn down a free, full-time babysitter?"

Vintovka was hit, and hit again. The pain was intense, but he didn't think about the pain. Arteries constricted to cut blood loss, redundant systems came on line. Vintovka's right hand was shot through, and hung by a shred. He continued to throw rocks with his left as he backed down the center aisle of the band shell. He took a sustained burst from the assault rifle and collapsed.

"Vintovka here. Mission complete. I have incurred extensive damage. Five hearts and four brains gone. I am now inoperative. I am sending in my bird for diversion."

Tears streaked Heinrich's face, but his expression didn't change.

The eagle folded its wings and dropped like a Kamakazi. Talons out and screaming defiance, its body jerked as slugs tore through. Feeling all of his bird's pain, Vintovka's prostrate body convulsed.

Langel and Pacho ran from opposite sides of the aisles as the intruder was firing upward. Knife-claws extended a foot beyond their knuckles, they hacked at the intruder's arms, severing them cleanly above the elbows.

Immediately, Jawati and Dabba rushed in and applied tourniquets. They loaded the shocked body onto Jawati's flat back, the lateral tentacles holding him immobile. Spear retrieved the arms and the weapons. Wirka and Kinzhal picked up Vintovka; Top picked up the dying eagle.

"Jawati here. We are returning to Pinecroft with inoperative LDU, bird, and intruder. All wounded but alive. Have three med teams ready."

The other three LDUs quickly policed the area, picking up spent cartridges, cleaning up spilled blood.

Five minutes after the intruder alert was sounded, all was outwardly unchanged and tranquil.

Liebchen was trotting through the tunnel to Pinecroft when she heard an LDU behind her. She leaned against the support of a softly glowing lamp, crossed her legs, thrust out her breasts, and smiled sexily.

The LDU came to an abrupt halt. "Liebchen, what does that peculiar posture signify?"

"I saw a girl on television do it and somebody stopped to give her a ride. I think it's a request for transportation. Are you going to Pinecroft?"

"Climb aboard. But lie down. I'm in a hurry."

Liebchen added her seventy pounds to the LDU's three hundred, snuggling her tummy against his back.

The LDU strapped her down quickly and took off at a run.

"Is something exciting happening?" Liebchen shouted over the wind noise.

"Dirk is delivering a lecture on the teachings of Lao Tzu," the LDU said. As he accelerated, the wind blast stopped all further conversation.

In the medical complex at Pinecroft three LDU teams were working under the direction of the CCU.

"They could have stopped him in the sports arena without getting any of themselves hurt," Guibedo said.

"Yeah, and had that bastard spraying lead through a bunch of kids," Heinrich said. "Well, so much for your idea about help from the Eastern Bloc."

"Yah. I see that," Guibedo said. "This kind of thing has happened before?"

"Third intruder this month. The preliminaries to war."

As the med teams worked, Gamma LDUs were transcribing the intruder's mind pattern into the CCU.

THIS IS KGB 501-12 TO CENTRAL, CODE 2297 SUB ALPHA. I HAVE MADE A THOROUGH SEARCH OF DEATH VALLEY AND CAN FIND NO INDICATION THAT HEINRICH COPERNICK OR MARTIN GUIBEDO IS PRESENT. I HAVE MADE CASUAL ACQUAINTANCE WITH SEVERAL LOCALS. MICHAEL SCOTT, NELSON HAYNES, AND ALLEN PRUES HAVE SEPARATELY STATED THAT THEY HAVE HEARD THAT MARTIN GUIBEDO IS IN NORTHERN MINNESOTA. PURSUANT TO MY INSTRUCTIONS, I AM NOW LEAVING FOR THAT LOCATION.

—DAVID JOHNSON

"The intruder's arms are successfully replaced, Lord Copernick," the CCU announced. "He will be fully functional in three weeks. Do you want him reprogrammed for life in the valley?"

"He doesn't deserve it. Send him back with a compulsion to kill others of his type."

* * *

Patricia and Mona wandered into a flatter and shadier section of town where most of the tree houses were one-story affairs. Facilities were laid out for the less athletically inclined, with chessboards and trout streams instead of bridle trails and canoe streams. Quite a few older people were around.

"Most of our senior citizens have moved out this way," Mona said.

"Wouldn't they want to be nearer the medical center at Pinecroft?" Patricia asked.

"That was the original plan. But when a group of doctors formed a clinic out this way, most of the seniors moved near it. I guess they prefer a human doctor to an LDU."

"LDUs *do* take some getting used to," Patricia said.

"Hi, Mom!"

"Bobby! What are you doing at this end of town?" Mona said.

"There's a new physics teacher who just moved in. I want to see if he's any good. Who's your friend?"

"Patty, this is my son, Bobby. Bobby, Patricia Cambridge. Patricia is staying with Uncle Martin."

"Pleased to meet you, Patty. I'm glad to see Uncle Martin isn't living alone anymore."

"Uh, it's good to meet you, Bobby." Patricia tried not to act as flustered as she was. For one thing, Bobby looked fifteen and Mona looked twenty. And Mona was all red hair and freckles while Bobby was pure ebony. But mostly, you don't tell your son who's sleeping with whom!

"Ma, why don't you come over to my house tomorrow afternoon. Ishtar has been talking about you—that's my faun, Patty—and I want you to meet my new girlfriend."

"I'd love to, Bobby. About three?"

"Great, Mom. But I've got to run. The introductory seminar starts in ten minutes. Bye!"

"Bye, Bobby!" Mona said. "The schools here function something like those of the old Moslem culture. If there is something you're interested in, you find someone who can teach you whatever it is you want to know. Then you make a private deal with him. You stay with it until you've learned all you want. No grades, no diplomas. But it works."

"He's very nice, your, uh, son," Patty said.

"Adopted, of course. How old do you think I am? Bobby was injured on our land, and Heinrich felt pretty bad about it. The doctors in L.A. couldn't help Bobby, but of course Heinrich could. When we found out that Bobby was an orphan, the easiest thing was to adopt him.

"He stayed with us for a year, mostly to get his bearings, but he's fifteen now, so he moved into his own tree house a few weeks ago."

"He moved out at fifteen?"

"Yes. A bit late, of course, but then the lack of a proper home during his formative years slowed him down a bit. He's doing all right now."

"But leaving home at fifteen?" Patty said.

"The age of consent around here is puberty, Patty. Uncle Martin feels that if nature says you're an adult, who are we to argue?"

"I guess so," Patty said. Life Valley was going to take some getting used to.

Vintovka and his eagle died on the operating tables.

"You know, Heiny. This man didn't kill Vintovka. His gun did it."

"Same difference," Heinrich said. "He pulled the trigger."

"Yah, he's guilty. But without weapons, he couldn't have done any real damage to us."

"You have an idea, Uncle Martin?"

"I am thinking about my kidney trees, that take metal out of the soil. I think we can do that backward."

"A metallic fungus?"

"Too slow. I'm thinking maybe little iron mosquitoes whose larvae eat up the iron in guns and tanks. If we take their guns away, they can't hurt anybody. We can win the war without having to kill people."

"You're going to have to brief me on metallic biochemistry, Uncle Martin, but I think we can do it. How about an aluminum eater to kill aircraft?"

"Sure. That's easier than iron."

"We'll have to hit the entire world simultaneously, or we'll upset the balance of power," Heinrich said, thinking hard. "I'll come up with a bird for a vector . . . You know that this will knock out more than weapons—the world's economy, especially transportation and communication, will be destroyed."

"That had to go anyway," Guibedo said. "We make it happen a couple years early, is all. I'll do that food tree you wanted to feed people until everybody's got a tree house."

"We'd better get on it now, then, Uncle Martin. It's got to be ready in about three months."

"I thought you said the war was in six months."

"Probably. But with this, we've got to hit them first. Say two months for forced production. That gives us a month for design time."

"A month for a bird, a tree, and two mosquitoes? Impossible, Heiny."

"I can fix it so we don't have to sleep, and I can have my simulation do a lot of the work. We can do it, but it's going to be a little rough on your love life."

"That Patty's a good girl; she'll understand," Guibedo said.

"We'd better keep this to ourselves, Uncle Martin."

"Yah. We do a lot of that around here."

The CCU recomputed the human fatalities in the upcoming "peaceful" revolution and came up with 375 million dead. But he was programmed not to speak unless spoken to, so he didn't mention it. Besides, he was ecstatic with the knowledge that now he wasn't going to have to die.

Chapter Eight

JUNE 17, 2003

MAJOR GENERAL Hastings walked stiffly into the office of the Chairman of the Joint Chiefs of Staff.

"Good morning, George. Have a chair. What can I do for you?" General Powers said.

"Good morning, sir. A number of strange and possibly interconnected events have been occurring over the last few years that I feel I should bring to your attention."

"Like what?"

Hastings took a list from his attaché case.

"Item one. Despite the fact that the tree houses have directly killed thousands of people and have seriously disrupted the economy of the western world, no single major power—except for United India—has passed regulations concerning them."

"The same thing could have been said about the automobile a hundred years ago, George. I'm as sorry about your family as I can be, but you must not let that tragedy affect your judgment."

"Sir, I believe that my judgment is unaffected. May I continue? Item two. Because of the probable economic repercussions, work on rejuvenation was stopped—worldwide—about ten years ago.

"The U.S. Congress contains almost six hundred members. More than half of them are over sixty-five years of age. Yet in the past four years, not one single congressman has died of old age."

"That seems statistically improbable," Powers said.

"It's nearly impossible, sir. But it is a fact. It is also a fact that the members of the British House of Commons aren't dying of old age, either. Nor are members of the Politburo. Nor the French National Assembly. Nor the Chinese People's Council.

"But the Grand Council of United India *does* have people dying of old age."

"So you are saying that somebody has secretly developed longevity and is using it to bribe our own government? That's a serious accusation, George. Can you back it up?" Powers asked.

"Yes, sir. I can. The process apparently requires repeated treatments. Thirty-two senators and one hundred fifty-five members of the House visit a single building in Crystal City at different times, but each on a given day of the month. They will reschedule overseas visits, even election rallys, to keep these appointments. And every one of them was previously quite ill but is now quite healthy."

"Interesting, but circumstantial. Have you gotten anyone inside the building?"

"No sir. But I've lost five good men trying."

"So it is still circumstantial. Go on."

"Item three. Heinrich Copernick—the man who raised the fuss about rejuvenation seven years ago—is the nephew of Martin Guibedo, the man who designed the tree houses.

"Item four. On the same day that Guibedo was imprisoned, my telepaths stopped functioning. One of them is able to receive somewhat—"

"And is quite insane," Powers said. "I've seen the report, and I'm really not impressed with a computer analysis of the ravings of a madman."

"Yes, sir. But to continue. Item five. Echo tracings show that Guibedo escaped from jail by means of a tunnel fifteen miles long. No engineering firm in the world could duplicate that tunnel in three weeks.

"Item six. Within a mile of the tunnel opening, eighty-five families were killed during that time period. This atrocity has generally been accredited to a raid by the Neo-Krishnas, despite the fact that there was no supporting evidence. And despite the fact that all of those people were killed with knives and that they were given Christian tombstones."

"Come now, George. The tabloids have been working that weird incident for years. Don't *you* try to tie it in," Powers said.

"It does tie in, sir. Item seven. We believe that Copernick and Guibedo are in Death Valley, that tree-house city. It is certain that Copernick owns the land. Over two hundred thousand people come and go freely in that valley, apparently without incident. People that we have questioned later report nothing unusual, and no security precautions at all.

"Yet I have never been able to get an agent into it! I have lost nineteen trying. The FBI reports similar losses. I submit that there is a correlation between the jamming of my telepaths and Death Valley's ability to identify and liquidate every one of our agents without having a visible security system."

"You say 'liquidate.' Were all these men killed?" Powers asked.

"No, sir. That's item eight. The majority of them seem to have defected, generally after sending back misleading messages. One of my agents did return to Washington. He reported in and then armed a grenade in the debriefing room. We lost eighteen people before we were forced to kill him. I suggest that they have brainwashing techniques that are far superior to our own."

"George, you keep talking as though this were a military matter. Certainly you have turned up something here, but it is a civil matter best left to the FBI," Powers said.

"No, sir. This *is* a military matter. I received these satellite photos today."

"These are remarkably clear photos, George. The air must be very clean there. But what *are* these things?"

"They appear to be an intelligent, engineered life form. They are certainly deadly—the profiles of those daggers in their forearms correspond to the entry wounds in the corpses of eighty-five families. And the things must be numerous; Engineering guesstimates that it would have taken at least ten thousand of them to dig Guibedo's escape tunnel."

"My God! An alien army on U.S. soil?" Powers summoned his aide. "Call an emergency meeting of the chiefs of the General Staff, and—"

"Sir, wait! These creatures are fantastic tunnelers. Conventional military action would only result in their scattering. If their reproduction and growth rate are as quick as those of the tree houses, it could be fatal if even a few of them escaped. Sir, indications are that they are all concentrated in Death Valley.

"Our planes have been carrying atomic bombs for sixty years without an accidental detonation. I think that it is time that we had one."

"That would take presidential approval."

"Yes, sir," Hastings said.

Powers paused for ten seconds.

"Then let's see if we can talk to the President."

Patricia spent a morning hiking out to the parking lot. She looked up Hank Dobrinski, who still had her car keys.

"Well, ma'am. I had begun to worry about you. Even had the telephone check and see that you were all right."

"Thanks, Hank. I guess I should have called."

"I truly wish you had. As it is, you just missed Meg again, and she's going to be hard to live with for a week. Now, what can I do for you?"

"I need my car, Hank. There are a few things I've got to do."

"I'll give you a lift out to it, ma'am. It might take a bit to get it started, after all these months. You heading back to New York?" They got into a shiny new four-wheel-drive pickup.

"No, Hank, I'm dropping out and staying here. I've just got some loose ends to tie up. I've got to quit my job, do something about my apartment and bank accounts, and get the Lincoln back to the rental agency at the airport."

"Then I guess I'd better follow you into Shoshone."

"Shoshone? But—"

"They got a bank there, and a rental agency and what not. You ain't the first one doing this, ma'am. Seems like I drive four, five people out there and back each week."

"Thanks, Hank."

"My pleasure. Now as I remember, that's yours over there."

Hank removed the tarp and shook out great billowing clouds of dust. The car windows were so dirty that you couldn't see out of them, but Hank had a bucket and squeegee in his truck.

The Lincoln's engine fired up without difficulty and in a half hour Hank followed her into the small desert town. Patricia had to stand in line at the car rental agency and the bank, but armed with her NBC card, everything went quickly. She was doing what thousands before her had done, and the clerks had it down to a pattern. Her apartment phone was disconnected, her New York landlord satisfied, a trucking company engaged to move her belongings west. Her bank account was transferred to Shoshone. It was surprisingly large—for three months, her paychecks had been deposited and she hadn't spent a cent of the money.

Finally she rented a motel room for an hour so she could make a very private phone call. Most of her business had been taken care of in only two hours, but everything in town seemed so cramped, so tiny, so crowded. She was tempted to take a shower at the motel, but one look at the tiny shower stall dissuaded her.

Finally, taking a deep breath, she called her boss, feeling guilty about not having contacted him in three months.

"Oh, hello, Patty. It's not Friday so it must be Tuesday."

"What?"

"You always call on Fridays and Tuesdays. The calendar says Thursday so something is finally happening."

"I don't know what you're talking about, boss."

"Patty, are you feeling all right?"

"Well, maybe not. Anyway, well, I'm quitting."

"Are you on some kind of drugs, kid?"

"No, I'm not on drugs, dammit! I'm quitting. Dropping out. Going away!"

"Look, Patty, you can't quit . . ."

"The hell you say! I'm a free woman in a free country! I'll quit if I damn well want to!"

"What about your show, Patty? It's still waiting for you."

"Let Mary handle it."

"She has been, and her ratings aren't half what yours are."

"I told you so. And I'm still quitting."

"Patty, I'm worried about you. How about if I have some of the people from the Chicago office drop by to see you?"

"Chicago?"

"Well, you're still in Wisconsin, aren't you?"

"Wisconsin? Boss, this conversation is just too weird. Look. I'm quitting! Going away! Saying bye-bye!" She slammed the phone down. The man had to be drunk or stoned or insane or all three!

She found Hank in the saloon and drove with him back to Life Valley. On the way, she borrowed his jackknife and cut her NBC credit card into very fine shavings.

The next day, Patricia decided she needed to be useful, so she volunteered to help Mona run the training room and kennel for the Transportation, Recreation, and Construction units in one of Pinecroft's huge subbasements.

"As you can see, all the TRACs are variations on the same basic theme," Mona said.

"Really?" Patricia turned her head slowly to take in all the TRACs in the room. Forty huge animals were frisking around, ranging in size from a one-person speedster, barely larger than a horse, to things as big as a gravel truck.

"Oh, there are minor differences in size and function," Mona said, "but the basic design is similar. Two eyes in front plus one in the cockpit. Internal and external ears. Voice membranes inside and out. They all use the same sort of double-ended lung structure that permits continuous breathing. And take a close look at the legs. The jointing on all of them is such that the body has a smooth motion at any speed."

"They all have two arms near the doors," Patricia said, looking for similarities among the bizarre animals.

"Yes, and they can reach any part of their bodies with them," Mona said. "Let's give one a workout. Rolls! Here, boy!"

A twenty-footer broke off from playing with something that resembled a flatbed truck and trotted over to them. It had eight legs, four across in front and four in back. Its streamlined, rigid body was six feet wide and five high, and was covered with sleek gray fur.

"Rolls, I want you to meet Patty. She will be working with us from now on."

"Hi, Patty." For all his size, Rolls had a young boy's voice.

"Open up, Rolls. We're going for a ride," Mona said.

"Oh, goodie!" Rolls opened both doors in his side. Patricia sat comfortably in a seat designed for two, but Mona, with her large frame, was somewhat cramped inside.

"They're all only about three quarters of their adult size," Mona said, "and their speed and endurance are only half of what they will be. When he grows up, Rolls will be able to hold eight people. Rolls, do a few laps." The animal began a graceful lope for the perimeter of the cavernous subbasement.

"He certainly makes up for it in enthusiasm," Patricia said.

"With good reason. Heinrich tied the pleasure centers of the TRACs' brains in with the pressure sensors under the seats. They're only really happy when they're running somebody around."

"Well, it works both ways." Patricia ran her fingers through the thick fur on the seat next to her. "It feels like chinchilla."

"Heinrich says that if you are going to do something, you might as well do it right. Not that it costs anything extra. We have twenty-five variants of passenger animals, from Vet, who's a single seater, to Greyhound, who will be able to seat sixty-four. And Winnie's an animal version of a motor home, for vacationing.

"The others here are for heavy transportation, like Reo and Mack, or construction, like Le Tourneau."

"You certainly gave them cute names," Patty said.

"They picked their own after Uncle Martin talked

with them," Mona said. "Mole over there is for tunneling. The plan is to build an underground road system, for practical, aesthetic, and safety reasons."

"What's safe about a tunnel?" Patricia asked.

"A hollow root lines the thing, so there's little danger of a cave-in," Mona said. "The safety comes from a clean, dry roadbed without any children playing on it."

"Rolls, run us over to Uncle Martin's house."

Without slowing, the TRAC ran up a circular ramp, then headed down the tunnel to Guibedo's house.

"TRACs have an excellent sense of direction and an amazing ability to remember maps. Not that it's needed yet. The few tunnels we have had to be dug by the LDUs."

"I thought the LDUs were designed for construction work," Patricia said.

"Yes and no. They're certainly efficient, and they're good sports about it. But an LDU has an IQ of 150, and it isn't healthy for any being to work too far below his abilities. Once the moles get going, we'll eventually have a tunnel entrance to every tree house in the world."

"How long is that going to take?" Patricia asked.

"About thirty years. TRACs reproduce in a fashion similar to fauns, except that since their function is simpler, training is quicker and they can reproduce more rapidly. A typical litter will be a dozen until there are enough of them to go around."

They arrived at Oakwood and got out.

"Coffee?" Patricia said.

"Love some. Rolls, go home and send back Lincoln." Mona patted his sleek gray flank.

"Aw, gee," Rolls said.

"No. You'll be grown up in a month and then there'll be as much work as you want. Now move," Mona said as she and Patricia walked up to the tree house.

"I'm going to have fun working with them," Patricia said over coffee.

"You do seem to be enjoying yourself here in the valley."

"I am, but I shouldn't be."

"Uncle Martin's acting crotchety again?"

"Oh, there have been some little things. Like he

wouldn't wear the sweater I knitted him for his birthday. And sometimes he's a little brusque—we went canoeing, and when I tried to sit next to him, he just sort of pushed me off and told me I was being ridiculous. But most of the time he's awfully nice."

"So what's troubling you?" Mona asked.

"It's just that I spent nine years working my way up in the broadcasting industry, and just when I was getting close to the top, I quit."

"A lot of people are dropping out, Patty. Why work when you don't have to?"

"But I liked my job. It was my whole life. Then I visited Martin and flushed my whole career down the absorption toilet."

"Sounds like love, girl," Mona said.

"Oh, Martin's wonderful, of course, and I wouldn't want anybody else. But we could have worked something out where I could have continued with my career."

"Have you talked this over with Uncle Martin?"

"No. I don't want to go back to New York. It's just that I *should* want to."

"Patty, stop me if I start sounding too much like my husband, but you were raised in a culture that said that a woman had to have a career outside of her family and friends just to prove that she was a full-blown person. You were programmed with that idea. In its time and place it was a good one. But here in the valley, nobody has to prove anything to anyone. There is no question of economic worth because there is no longer such a thing as economics. You are completely free to do anything you want, to grow in any direction that suits you."

"That's fine for the artists, but I'm a working girl."

"Lord knows there's enough work to be done around here! You should have caught on by now that the world out there is as obsolete as a dinosaur. The future is here! If you want to make a meaningful contribution, the place is here and the time is now," Mona said.

"But that still doesn't explain the sudden change I went through three months ago," Patty said.

"I keep telling you, girl. You're in love." As Mona laughed, Guibedo walked into the kitchen and pretended he hadn't heard the last line.

"Hi, Mona. Patty, you can't use the pool unless you want to swim in salt water."

"Salt water! What are you up to now?" Mona asked.

"Boats." Guibedo grinned. "I figure we got everything we need to make living comfortable on land, but there's the other three quarters of the world we ain't doing nothing with. So I got some sailboats and a dirigible growing in the swimming pool."

"A dirigible in the swimming pool?" Mona said.

"Well, it ain't growed up yet. Bucky Fuller, he worked it out in the fifties, how if you make something big enough and only a couple degrees warmer on the inside than it is out, the problem gets to be holding it down, not up. It's gonna need some special animals, so I got to talk to Heiny about it. You got them TRACs going yet?"

"We rode one over here," Patricia said.

Mona turned to the I/O unit on the wall. "Telephone! Send back Lincoln and send Reo over instead. He'll be here in ten minutes, Uncle Martin."

"Good. I'll get my tapes and drawings.

"Mr. Copernick? This is Lou von Bork. I'm calling from a pay phone in Washington."

"Why are you still there? Didn't you get my message?"

"I just got it. The courier got delayed. Permanently."

"Oh, my God—who did it?" Copernick said.

"One of General Hastings' goons. Luckily, I had one of our Rejuves in his steno pool. She got the message to me and split."

"Well, then. Follow your instructions. Drop everything. Get yourself and your people out of D.C. and back here to Life Valley."

"Don't you think that you owe us an explanation?" von Bork said.

"No. I'm just trying to save your lives."

"What about our contacts? Do I tell them, too?"

"Sorry. Somebody would notice that many congressmen leaving."

"One other thing, boss. The Pentagon is like a beehive. I can't find out what it is because I don't have anybody high up in the military. Hardly anybody there is old enough to get a handle on. Even Senator Beinheimer is in the dark. Think I should stick around and work on it?"

"No, dammit! I want you to get your tail back here. Now!"

"Yes, sir," von Bork said.

Lou von Bork had never heard Copernick so adamant, so naturally he disobeyed his orders. He went back to his office, pulled out the thick phone directory of all his friends and contacts, and started calling. He told everyone he could get hold of to leave the cities and head for the hills. Some of them did.

He worked for six hours before the news carried the story of the bombing of Life Valley.

At Pinecroft, Guibedo found his nephew in the simulations room.

"So what are you up to, Heiny?"

"Hi, Uncle Martin. Birds."

"You mean some peacocks and flamingos, maybe, for decoration?"

"Of course not! There's a war on, remember? I have two species about ready to go. One is a flying hypodermic needle that looks like a sparrow. It can synthesize either a stunning agent or a fast-acting poison.

"The other is an aerial defense unit designed to command the sparrows. I had to go to a twenty-foot wing span to support a brain net identical to an LDU's but it should be able to communicate with them."

"What for, Heiny? We already decided that there ain't going to be any war. Those metal-eating bugs are going to eat up everybody's weapons and that's going to be the end of it."

"They're not proven yet, Uncle Martin. We don't really know that they'll work."

"They worked well enough to eat the frame off my microscalpel," Guibedo said. "Think of it! Just one viable cell I left sitting around, and two weeks later my microscalpel is a pile of circuits on the floor."

"It should teach you not to be so careless, Uncle Martin. One viable cell plus a large pile of food equals a lot of viable cells. We're just lucky those insects didn't spread and tip our hand. Are you back in business yet?"

"Yah. Jimmy Saunton, he made me a new frame and cabinet. Only he went and made it out of silver."

"So what's wrong with that? It's what he's used to working with. Silver is a suitable metal and we have more of it than we need," Copernick said.

"But somebody told him that my mother was Polish, so he designed the cabinet in something he calls Neo-Polski. You got to see this thing, Heiny! It took Jimmy and four apprentices a whole month to make. The display screen is supported by four silver fauns, and the whole panel has got little curlicues all over it. For lateral transverse I got to twist this little cherub, and the laser firing studs are shaped like little harps and beehives. All the labels are in Fraktur German."

Copernick laughed. "It sounds great, Uncle Martin. Would you ask him to make me one?"

"You're kidding, Heiny."

"Not at all. I'm going to need a new one anyway, once we launch the insects. We can seal off the computers, but I hate to be without a microscalpel. Its dubious artistic value makes a good cover story. We can't have word get out on what we're doing."

"Okay. You want it, you'll get it. I wish I could give you mine, but that would hurt Jimmy's feelings."

"Just tell him that I'm a pure-bred Polack, and we'll see what he comes up with."

"Okay, okay," Guibedo said. "So how is the bug project going?"

"It's pretty much ready to launch right now. LDUs are finishing up implanting the food-tree seeds and the larvae into the vector birds. The CCU figures it will have completed their flight programming by tomorrow night. Actually, we can start launching any time, although I'd just as soon hold off until everything is ready."

"Me, too, Heiny."

"What are those disks and drawings, Uncle Martin?"

"Well, you ain't going to like this, but I still don't figure we need any more war animals. What I did was I worked out a biochemistry for floating plants on the ocean. I figured that's three quarters of the world we ought to be doing something with. Anyhow, I got some sailboats and floating islands. And I got a dirigible."

"A dirigible?"

"Sure. Bucky Fuller in the fifties, he—"

"The airborne cities. I'm familiar with his work. Go on."

"Anyhow, I need some animals to go with them. Some kind of fish that will protect the boats and islands from other fish. And something to provide motive power for the dirigible."

"Well, let's see what you have." Copernick inserted the disk into his control panel then spent a few minutes studying the display and Guibedo's drawings.

"I've got to say I like your basic concept, Uncle Martin. But I'd like to make a few suggestions."

"Like what?"

"Your anchored floating islands are fine, but they're all one-family dwellings. Shouldn't you make some bigger ones?"

"Ach. We're going to need maybe fifty designs before we're through. This is just a start. Anyhow, you want something bigger, you tie two little ones together."

"Okay. These boats. You've designed them like conventional sailboats. Let's do the standing rigging as part of the boat plant, but make the running rigging and rudder control parts of an animal sentient enough to handle navigation."

"Heiny, you'll take all the fun out of sailing."

"The four you've done so far should satisfy the yachtsmen, but I think most people will want something that just goes where it's told."

"Okay. We build some your way and some mine, and people can take what they want. What else?"

"Motive power. They really ought to have some form of auxiliary power for getting in and out of harbors and for moving when becalmed."

"So I'll make the oars and you make the muscles for when we run out of wind. Anything else? You want maybe the decks should be orange and the sails pink?"

"They'll have to stay green for photosynthesis." Copernick ignored the jibe. "But as to size, you've made these four fifty-, one hundred-, one hundred twenty-five, and one hundred fifty feet long, which is fine, but we also ought to build some in the thousand-foot range."

"So who'd want an ocean liner when he could sail his own yacht?" Guibedo said.

"Not ocean liners. Troop ships."

"Are you on that again, Heiny?"

"I've never been off it. We are heading into a period with too many unknowns. The only thing I'm sure of is that revolutions are never easy. When you act with inadequate information, you inevitably make mistakes. Better to err on the side of security. If we end up with more military power than we need, we have wasted time and energy. If we have too little, we have wasted our lives and the lives of everyone we care about."

"Okay. We call them troop ships now and ocean liners later." Guibedo was getting worried about his nephew. Paranoia?

"Now about this dirigible. I really like it, but it's going to require something pretty novel to power it. Wings that size are out of the question, and oars would be far too inefficient."

"Well, this is just a first cut to see if the thing really will fly. No motive power and it can't make seeds. On the next one I think maybe I can grow a big propeller. It grows rigid to its bearings until it's full size, then it breaks loose. I give you a crank between two bearings, and you make muscles to it like the cylinders in a radial engine. Once it's going, the propeller eats bearing grease that the dirigible makes to stay alive. I figure I can make it good for seventy-five rpm."

"You really figure you can make an organic wheel?" Copernick looked surprised. "If it's possible, why doesn't the wheel occur in nature?"

"It does. You got to read Berg's thing on bacteria flagella. The little beggars move by spinning a propeller that's turned by an ion motor," Guibedo said.

"Berg, huh. I'll look it up. So why doesn't it occur in higher animals?"

"Because there are no intermediary steps possible between a foot and a wheel, Heiny. Natural life forms had to evolve by small design increments. Nature can't do a radical design like a committee can't do original think-ing."

"Fascinating!" Copernick said, going over the read-outs. "The musculature you describe is absurdly simple, of course. I should have thought of this myself, before I did the TRACs."

"You leave those TRACs alone. For land travel, wheels are more efficient, but feet are more versatile. And feet don't get stuck in the mud," Guibedo said. "I came over here on Reo, one of your trucks. He's got a real smooth ride. You did a nice job on those leg joints, Heiny."

"Thank you. I'm proud of them myself. But for strictly tunnel traveling, a wheeled animal would be great."

"Do it once we have enough tunnels. You had lunch yet?"

"No, thinking about it. Let's go upstairs."

No part of the CCU was permitted in a biolab, so Copernick stopped at the CCU's I/O unit in the hallway. "CCU. Copernick here."

"Yes, my lord."

"I want you to buy at least ten square miles of land with at least two miles of ocean frontage, as close to here as possible. Have the mole dig a tunnel out to it. Set the earliest possible closing dates, and keep me posted."

"Yes, my lord."

Guibedo said, "That's a handy guy you got there."

"I'd be lost without him."

The girls had eaten earlier and were working with the TRACs, so Guibedo and Copernick ate alone, served by Ohura, one of the Copernicks' two fauns. Ohura was a black version of Liebchen, identical except for surface details.

"You know, I think this is the first time we've eaten alone together in a year," Guibedo said as he began his second mug of beer.

"It's strange to be without the girls, but I'm glad they're taking an interest in their work."

"How come you make Mona work so hard? Couldn't Dirk or one of his buddies do it?"

"They could. LDUs are almost as intelligent as Mona,

and they're a good deal more consistent. But Mona wants to feel that she's doing something important. And I think that it *is* important that each intelligent species is trained by a human being. They've got to remember that we created them, and that we're boss. Otherwise, Uncle Martin, I've hatched a monster."

"EMERGENCY!" the telephone barked. "Gamma LDUs report that a U.S. bomber is twelve minutes away. The crew has orders to accidentally drop an atomic bomb on Life Valley!"

"They start quicker than we thought, Heiny!" Guibedo said, but Copernick was already giving orders.

"Notifiy everyone in the valley that the bomber is out of control and heading this way. Get everybody into the basements.

"I want every bird in the air, except the insect spreaders. I want every TRAC loaded with water for fire fighting, dispersed around the valley and under cover. What's the bomber's altitude?"

"Twenty-two thousand feet, my lord."

"Our birds can't fly that high. Get every Gamma LDU on that plane's commander. Try to turn him around, or at least get him to come in at five thousand feet."

"Yes, my lord. They're on it. But you know how unsuccessful the experiments with telecontrol have been. There is a good probability that the aircraft commander will resist or not even notice our probe."

"Any suggestions?"

"None, my lord. Dropped from twenty-two thousand feet, that twenty-three hundred pound bomb will be graveling at supersonic speed. There is no chance of disarming it in flight or of significantly deflecting its course."

"Then pray, my friend. Pray," Copernick said, heading for the communications center four floors down.

"Just like a practice run, Colonel," Captain Johnson had the B-3 in manual.

"That it is, Bill."

"I thought I'd never get a chance to lay a nuke."

"Just do it by the numbers."

"And I never thought I'd be bombing Americans."

"Look, son. You saw who gave the orders."

"But still, our own countrymen?"

"That's just it! They're *not* our countrymen! These people have *dropped out!* They have *abandoned* America and everything it stands for! They are doing *everything* in their power to *destroy* our society! It's a plot more insidious than anything the Communists or the Neo-Krishnas ever thought of! *And it's our job to stop them!"*

"But still—"

"Bill, I'll take the controls now!"

"Colonel?"

"It's a commander's job. Anyway, I don't want you to do anything you'd feel guilty about."

"But—"

"Enough! Kelly! Put a chute on that egg."

"Aye, aye, sir," the flight engineer said.

"Colonel, you're losing altitude," Captain Johnson said.

"This has to be precisely on target, Bill. Any error and we kill real Americans outside of Death Valley. We'll do it with a paradrop from five thousand feet," the colonel said.

They were thirty miles and three minutes from Life Valley when they spotted a thin black cloud ahead.

Then they were in it.

A twenty-pound Canada goose bounced off the windshield. Followed by another. And another. Ahead of them, like contrails in reverse, eight long lines of eagles, owls, and condors were flying into their jet intakes. One by one the engines choked and froze and died. The fourteenth Canada goose took out the windshield, spraying the cabin with broken plastic and blood. The colonel pulled back on the controls, but they were sluggish. The plane was losing altitude fast.

"Kelly!" the colonel shouted. Communications above the roar was barely possible. "Set the bomb to detonate on impact!"

"Are you crazy?" Kelly yelled, disarming the bomb. "We're too low to bail out!"

"I know! But we've got to! They're in my head!"

"He *is* crazy," Kelly muttered, jettisoning the fuse

and bracing for a crash. He hit the lever to jettison the fuel, but he knew he was too late.

The huge plane came in near the center of the valley and erupted in a spray of broken wood and torn aluminum. The wings sheared off, engines ripped loose, and nearly full fuel tanks ruptured. Orange flames and black smoke poured through houses and into basements. Huddled people screamed and died.

One wing tank spun into Pinecroft's side and burst and burned. The entire side of the hundred-foot-tall tree was a blanket of flame. It went through the windows and up and down the elevator shaft.

Mona and Patricia made it to the surface in Mack, a TRAC tanker loaded with water. They set him to spraying those walls that were not yet burning, and got out.

Copernick's fauns, Colleen and Ohura, ran out of the tree house, each carrying a human baby. Most of Ohura's black hair was burned off.

"My babies!" Mona screamed.

The fauns handed the unharmed Copernick children to Mona and Patricia, then turned back to the burning tree house.

When Colleen and Ohura ran inside, they found the elevator bouncing rapidly, convulsed with pain. They ran to the staircase, reaching it just as burning jet fuel was starting to dribble down. Without hesitation they ran up the stairs through the flames. Their hoofs provided some protection, but the fur on Ohura's legs caught fire midway up. She continued upward to the fauns' room before throwing herself to the floor and rolling on the carpet to put out the flames.

Cradled in soft niches on Pinecroft's second floor, the four baby fauns each still lay on its back contently sucking the treenipple just above its mouth.

While Ohura flailed at her smoldering fur, Colleen took the babies from their niches. As Ohura finished she picked up one of her own children and one of Colleen's. Each carrying two fauns, Colleen and Ohura bounded for the corridor.

The fire and smoke in the hallway had grown much worse, and the fauns had to crawl, babies clutched to their breasts, groping their way to the service stairway,

Colleen in the lead. A wall of flames shot up between them and Ohura gasped, involuntarily inhaling the fire, singeing her lungs. She couldn't breathe or speak, and the world started to become dark gray. As she became unconscious, she tucked the two children under her, trying to protect them from the heat with her own body.

Colleen reached the service staircase before she realized that Ohura wasn't behind her. She hesitated for a second, then turned back to grope blindly for her sister. As she crawled, a branch that had supported the third floor gave way, smashing the bones of her left knee and pinning her to the floor. The smoke cleared for an instant and she saw Ohura a few feet in front of her.

"Ohura! I'm over here!" But Ohura didn't move.

The log pinning Colleen down was two feet in diameter and fifteen yards long. Colleen struggled helplessly, rolling over, trying to rip her own leg off. Anything to save herself and her children.

Suddenly an LDU darted through the smoke, his body silvery white to reflect the heat. His lateral tentacles grabbed for Ohura and the two babies were quickly secured to his underside.

The LDU turned its attention to the trapped faun. I'm Dirk, Colleen." He tried to lift the log from her leg but failed. "Better give me the children. I can't move this log."

The flames were rapidly approaching them as Colleen gave up the baby fauns. The pain in her leg was unbearable. Death would be welcome.

"Sorry, Colleen." Dirk tapped her behind the head, knocking her unconscious, ending the pain. Then he wrapped a tentacle tightly around her left thigh and with one whack of a dagger-claw severed the leg above the knee.

Dirk placed Colleen next to Ohura and the four baby fauns and raced down the burning stairway to safety.

Copernick stayed at his post in the communications center, giving an almost continuous stream of rational orders to the CCU, most of which had been anticipated and were being put into effect before they were received.

Guibedo stayed at his nephew's side, occasionally making suggestions.

"Get as many of the crew out as possible," Copernick said. "Give them medical treatment in preference to our own people if necessary. We need the bastards."

LDUs waded ankle deep through burning gasoline, slashing through aluminum and boron-fiber composite with their knife-claws, searching out every scrap of human flesh in the burning bomber.

Tree houses over an entire square mile were searched for the injured, the dying, and the dead.

The fire did not spread past the second subbasement of Copernick's complex, because of Pinecroft's green growing wood and the efficiency of the LDUs.

Hundreds of injured people and animals were brought to the third-level medical center. Among them, near the end of the list, were Ohura, with third-degree burns over eighty percent of her body, and Colleen, battered but still alive.

Liebchen was with them, holding four uninjured baby fauns, the size of squirrels.

"Dirk pulled you all out. He says that you're going to be okay in a month," Liebchen said. Ohura's lungs were too seared for her to speak, but she smiled slightly.

"Are our babies all right?" Colleen's eyes were swollen shut.

"I've got them all right here. They're fine. Lady Mona said you two did everything perfect," Liebchen said.

"Oh, good. I hope Pinecroft'll be all right," Colleen said, before putting herself to sleep.

"What's the status on the bomber crew?"

"Six of the original eight are alive, my lord. Three of those are capable of talking. Their flight orders were signed by Major General Hastings, chief of the Defense Intelligence Agency."

"Hastings, huh?" Copernick said. "That's perfect, politically. I want those three men programmed to make complete confessions to the news media, and I want it done in three hours. They are to say that they had orders to drop an atomic bomb on American citizens, and that they would have done so if their plane had not developed engine trouble. Call for volunteers among the valley's citizens. I need all roads out of the valley blocked by 'refugees' for three hours. We need time to set the stage before the newsmen get here."

Guibedo said, "What do you figure that's going to accomplish, Heiny?"

"We were lucky this time, and we can't repeat the performance. Bringing that plane down cost us five hundred birds.

"CCU. See that all of the birds are cleaned out of the wreckage. I don't want the government to know that we have any capability of fighting back. Save any birds that can be saved and . . . give the rest an honorable burial.

"Uncle Martin, our only hope is to kick up so much political flack that our opponents will wait a few months before attacking again. And with luck, by then they won't have anything to attack with."

"Heiny, it's time we let our bugs loose."

"Do you want the honor, Uncle Martin?"

"Yah. Now I want the honor. Telephone! Do it!"

In subbasements below their feet, long ceiling-high racks were filled with white eggs the size of beachballs, each connected by a black umbilical cord to the mother-being and by a thin pink string to the CCU.

The eggs began to open. By the thousands, full-sized swans broke soundlessly from their shells and started their silent, orderly, mindless procession upward. They climbed the wide circular ramp four hundred feet to the surface, and beyond, through the burned-out shell that was Pinecroft. They climbed until they were a hundred feet above the ground then dove into the night air. The great white birds circled high, then each flew off to its own separate destination.

Guibedo climbed Pinecroft. Still a wanted man, he couldn't attend the press conference at the auditorium, but he could see the flash of strobes, the milling crowds. None of Copernick's creations was in sight. They had been hidden, and the valley's citizens had been cautioned not to mention them.

He could make out the long line of beds set up near the band shell, an outdoor hospital and morgue.

Guibedo watched the swans flying high and away. "Fly high, my pretty friends. Do your job, and this will never happen again."

Each of the myriad birds headed to its five-square-mile target zone, then started flying a zigzag pattern. At four-second intervals, it discharged two mosquitoes, one a shiny aluminum, the other a duller iron. When it had discharged 1,024 of each insect, it froze in the air, its programming and life completed. It fell to the ground and became fertilizer for the food-making tree in its breast.

Each of the mosquitoes sought out metal. A car, a plane, a tin can. It laid an egg and flew on to do it again, a thousand times more. And then it died.

Each egg hatched and grew into a larva which, in three days' time, would eat two ounces of metal and then become a mosquito and lay a thousand eggs of its own.

They would do this for eighty generations, and then their short-lived race would become extinct. Or rather, would try to, for after forty generations there would be neither iron nor aluminum nor any of their alloys left in an unoxidized state on Earth.

Patricia Cambridge came up and stood at Martin Guibedo's side.

"There were too many old colleagues at the press conference. It sort of hurt, seeing them again. We talked, but I wasn't one of them anymore."

"It doesn't matter, Patty. The world you knew has ended. Now we will build a better one."

Patricia thought he was talking of love, and snuggled closer.

Chapter Nine

JUNE 20, 2003

MAINTENANCE OF *a proper resource allocation scheme will require a continuously updated local census of the humans and other bioforms under our jurisdiction.*

Local ganglia are therefore instructed to inform me of all human activities within their assigned areas.

—Central Coordination Unit

"I'm sorry that it had to be you, George," General Powers said. "You were right in doing what you did, and it certainly wasn't your fault that the bomber crashed. But political realities force me to relieve you of your command."

"Yes, sir."

"Officially, our position is that you went insane because of the death of your family some years ago. You will be assigned to a psychiatric ward under sedation for about a month. By that time we should have a final solution to this bioengineering problem, and your name can be cleared," Powers said.

"A month or so in the funny farm won't kill me, sir."

"No point in that. I said 'officially.' Actually, I'd just like you to go away for a while. Take a vacation somewhere. You'll know when you should come back."

"Thank you, sir."

"And have a good time."

Hastings cut himself a set of orders assigning himself to the 315th Fighter-Bomber Squadron at Westover Field, Massachusetts. Then he cut a second set reassigning himself, his plane, and one atomic bomb to the Naval Testing Lab in San Diego.

Eight hours after leaving General Powers' office, Hastings was flying his F-38 Penetrator at forty thousand feet over the Utah desert. Death Valley was thirty minutes away.

"Like the man said, if you want something done right, you'd better do it yourself," Hastings said aloud to himself.

Directly below him, a single mindless larva was sinking its solid diamond teeth into a contact pin of an electrical connector. This connector was mounted directly to the solid-fuel rocket that powered the F-38's ejection seat. The contact tasted bad, like gold, so the larva crawled to the next pin to see if *it* was aluminum. In the process, its aluminum body touched both contacts simultaneously and the resulting electrical current killed it. It also ignited the solid fuel rocket, which blasted Hastings out through the F-38's plastic canopy.

Hastings was unconscious, but his flight suit had been designed for use at L-5. It protected him from the cold and near vacuum. At five thousand feet, his parachute opened automatically.

The plane had been set on full automatic and programmed to fly to San Diego, so that its transponder could assure Ground Control that the aircraft's flight plan was being followed. It continued the journey without pilot or canopy, made a perfect landing on its assigned runway, and stopped, awaiting further instructions. Within minutes it was visited by an egg-laying mosquito.

The crash truck was unable to go out to the plane to investigate. A larva had eaten a hole in the truck's fuel pump.

The swans looked like ordinary birds, and so attracted little attention. Bored radar operators noticed unusual migration patterns, and properly logged them. But the logs were not due to reach the scientific community for months, and actually would never be examined at all.

Each swan died and fell in the center of its assigned area. Copernick had decided that the food trees, and thus the population, should be scattered as far as possible, to limit the possibility of riots and plagues and to keep them isolated when they occurred.

But if the scientific community failed to notice the swans, the animal community did not. Over half the fallen swans were eaten by animals or other birds. This possibility had been taken into account. The seeds were hard, small, and indigestible. They sprouted, absorbing the flesh around them. The scavengers died, and provided additional fertilizer.

Less than a hundred swans were eaten by people, and cooking destroyed most of the seeds. In eleven cases the swans were not properly cooked, and the people died.

But people who eat raw carrion do not notify authorities when a death occurs. Nor do they perform autopsies or embalm their dead. The trees grew.

Two hundred and eighteen professional biologists across the world found first-generation larvae and excitedly took them into labs to study. Incredible! An insect with a biochemistry different from anything previously known. They hurriedly prepared preliminary reports, each expecting to be the first to publish.

A first-generation larva had been laid on the wing of a DC-16. Unnoticed in the course of three days, it ate its way into the tubular aluminum wing strut. There it metamorphosed into a mosquito, which was unable to fly out of the two hundred-foot sealed chamber. It laid its thousand eggs along the length of the wing and died.

Two days later a thousand larvae were contentedly munching away. Eleven hundred passengers were aboard the Qantas airliner, with a crew of forty taking them from Los Angeles where it was midsummer to Melbourne in the middle of its winter. Skirting a hurricane south of Hawaii, the left wing sheared off. There were no survivors.

* * *

Another first-generation egg was laid on the side of an aging space shuttle. It was just burrowing its way into the cabin at takeoff, and the small air leak wasn't noticed until the ship was in orbit. The larva ate its way into the cargo compartment and then into the chassis of a strip-chart recorder. With its cargo unloaded at a station in a low polar orbit, the shuttle returned. Its departure left the wheel-shaped space station with only one small ship capable of landing on Earth. The larva metamorphosed in a biology lab during a sleep period and laid eight hundred eggs before an astronomer swatted it. None of these eggs reached maturity; many of them were blown out into space when they ate through the outer walls. The rest died when the station became airless.

Thanks to automatic alarms, 820 of the station's 957 people aboard were able to get into intact space suits in time.

By then no spacecraft on Earth was able to take off, primarily due to punctures in their fuel tanks.

Due to their low polar orbit, no other station could help them in time.

The station's only functional ship was capable of landing a cargo of only twelve thousand pounds. The station commander, a 180-pound man, decided to save the maximum number of people, and so ordered the ship to be filled on the basis of weight. There were no acts of violence, and only minimal objections to the plan. One hundred and nineteen persons, mostly small women, were loaded aboard.

The ship made it safely to Earth. Seven hundred and one people in orbit died with dignity.

They would have received more sympathy if those on Earth hadn't had troubles of their own.

The metallic larvae ate thin sheet metal along its entire thickness, cutting irregular slashes in car fenders, aircraft wings, and missile hulls.

Fuel tanks were among the first components to be rendered useless. While two percent of the world's aircraft crashed and one percent of the land vehicles were wrecked due to mechanical failures, the great majority of them sat on their runways and driveways and simply fell to pieces.

The left engine on Lou von Bork's Cessna 882 Super Conquest died within a second of the right.

"Seat belts, gang!" He shouted over the intercom: "We are going down."

Senator Beinheimer had been dozing in the copilot's chair. "What? What's up, Lou, boy?"

"It looks like we're out of fuel, Moe." Von Bork tried to restart the turbo props, then gave up and feathered his propellers.

"Out of fuel? But we just tanked up at Fort Scott!" Beinheimer said.

"I know, but for the last ten minutes the fuel gauges have been moving left like you wouldn't believe. I was hoping that it was an electrical problem until the motors quit. We must have sprung a leak."

"Oh. My. God."

"It's not that bad, Moe. We're still at thirty-one thousand feet, so we have ten minutes to find a soft place to land. And in Kanssas, that's not all that hard to do. At least I think we're still in Kansas."

"You *think*? I thought that Loran gizmo of yours was supposed to tell you where you were within a hundred yards."

"It does, usually, only it started to act up just after takeoff. It's trying to tell me that we're over Kentucky."

"You gotta believe your instruments, boy. First rule of instrument flight."

"Moe, we left Fort Scott, Kansas, fifty-five minutes ago. I have been flying into the sunset since then. This plane cruises at three hundred forty knots. Those are wheat fields down there. I'm not going to believe that I've flown five hundred forty miles due east."

"Well, hadn't you better radio for help?"

"The radio's quit working, too. Both of them."

After hearing the news about the attempted bombing of Life Valley, von Bork had spent a day collecting up his two secretaries, Senator Beinheimer, and the staff of the Crystal City installation. He had piled them, along with absolutely no baggage, into his Cessna and topped off his fuel tanks. The senator's name was sufficient to get them immediate clearance for takeoff at 1545.

Dusk was coming down even more rapidly than the twin engine turbo prop. Very few lights showed in the farming country, and none of those lit up a suitable stretch of highway.

Von Bork continued due west, heading for Life Valley, hoping that a lighted highway or—please God!—an airport would appear.

At a thousand feet, he settled for the planted field up ahead. Lowering his landing gear and flaps (they worked!), he came in to what he thought was a wheat field.

"Dear God...dear God...dear God," Beinheimer muttered, clutching the armrest with fear-whitened fingers.

"That the only prayer you know, Moe?"

"The only one, by God, but it's sincere! After this, I'll learn some more. I swear I will!"

"Hang on, gang!" von Bork shouted into the intercom. "The old barnstormers could do it, and we're only eighty ahead of them in technology!"

Von Bork was no farm boy, and what with the speed, altitude, and darkness, he was wrong about it being a wheat field; it was corn, tall Kansas corn.

The Cessna's landing gear had been designed for use on a surface infinitely harder than rich, tilled soil. All three wheels sheared off within twenty yards of touchdown. This was good, because von Bork's air-speed indicator had been rendered grossly inaccurate by two metal-munching larva. He had come in more than eighty knots too fast.

The Cessna sliced through the mile-wide cornfield, narrowly missing the center pivot irrigation machine. The wings took an amazing beating, each cornstalk sending its own thump through the airframe.

The plane had slowed to sixty before the wing strut gave way almost exactly in the center and both wings tore off together. This too was lucky, for had one gone before the other, the plane would have rolled.

The battered fuselage skidded to a stop, and all was suddenly quiet.

Von Bork took his hands from the wheel, hardly able to believe it was over and he was alive. He said into the intercom: "How's it going back there?"

"We're all okay, Mr. von Bork."

"Well," von Bork said to Beinheimer, "I guess that was a good landing."

Public consternation was, of course, extreme. Every political body in the world sat in emergency session. Crash programs and task forces were funded, but none had time to accomplish anything. Research takes years. The larvae took only days. Accusations and counter-accusations flashed across national borders.

India abruptly ceased all communication with the rest of the world on the same day that the swans flew. Israel, the fifth most powerful nation after Russia, the U.S., China, and India, took her silence as an admission of guilt for the metal-eating plague. The Israelis' aircraft and missiles were already useless, but their tanks were made of thicker metal. Even perforated with holes, charbram armor could stop most projectiles, and turbine engines contain little iron or aluminum. Damaged fuel tanks were fitted with plastic liners, gun barrels were given a cursory inspection, and the attack was launched.

The last tank stopped twenty kilometers from its depot. A tread weakened by hundreds of holes had broken.

So ended the last mechanized war the world would ever see.

Radio and television stations suspended their regular programming, devoting their time to emergency broadcasts, but the messages from the world's governments were monotonously similar: "Don't panic. Stay in your homes. We'll take care of you."

But there was nothing that anyone could do.

Air time was also allotted to religious programs. A thousand priests, ministers, and shamans called on as many gods to help them, but the gods remained silent.

Many of the religious leaders proclaimed that the end

of the world was at hand. And in a sense, they were right.

Trains, being made of thicker metal, lasted a week longer than cars or trucks. Their last freights were mostly food and water for the cities; very few places on Earth had more than a week's supply of food on hand. Canned food became useless as the cans were slashed and destroyed. And the larvae soon riddled the refrigerator units that kept frozen food fresh. The trucks and trains that once brought fresh supplies no longer existed.

The food trees sprouted quickly, and each grew six vines that spread out evenly for fifteen feet and then generated new roots at these spots. The space between was quickly covered with heart-shaped leaves, close to the ground. Each leaf had a red cross at its center. Though Guibedo had no love for the Red Cross (or any other organization, for that matter), the red cross was the only symbol of help that he could think of that was universally known.

In six weeks each food plant would cover forty acres of land. Trees and other plants that were in the way were absorbed with remarkable rapidity. Animals found their leaves to be bitter and spat them out; those that persisted, died. Farmers who tried to uproot the new weed found that it recovered in hours. Herbicides were ineffective.

In two months the dense ground cover would start to rise as tree trunks grew in a triangular pattern every fifteen feet. The trunks would grow to be eight feet tall. Only then, three months from planting, once there was enough photosynthetic area, would they start to produce food gourds on their trunks. But each tree could feed a thousand people.

"The bridge is out," Senator Beinheimer said.

A farmer had driven the ten of them into town, at which point the truck's engine failed due to a larva hole in the oil gallery.

Three days in Bristol, Colorado, convinced von Bork

that transportation was not available, and would probably never be available.

Striking out on foot, they headed west.

The two men and six women who were subordinate to von Bork were all Rejuves. They all had more than sixty years of experience. They all had healthy twenty-year-old bodies. Among them, they had a vast array of useful knowledge. How to pick mushrooms, how to dig roots, how to trap rabbits, and how to build shelter. Traveling upstream along the Arkansas River, they survived well. The senator was able to keep up, though his bones ached.

It took them a month to cross the Colorado Plains and the Rocky Mountains. Now, on the downhill side, the road came quite literally to an end.

"I said the bridge is out."

"Obviously," von Bork said. "But that is the Gunnison River, and the Gunnison empties into the Colorado, and the Colorado pours into Lake Mead, spitting distance from Life Valley."

"You crazy, boy? You're talking about maybe a thousand miles of white water."

"True. I'm also talking about riding instead of walking. Personally, I'm sick of walking. Who's with me?"

"We're always with you, Mr. von Bork."

Senator Beinheimer was the last one down.

Within a mile, they found an abandoned twelve-man rubber raft.

Antenna towers are held stable by long steel cables, and when these were eaten through, the towers fell. Radio and TV stations went off the air.

The orbiting communications satellites still operated but their crews could give no useful information to the people below because they themselves had no way of finding out what was happening.

These stations, and those on the moon, were largely self-sufficient, and could survive several years without help from Earth. But they could provide no help in return.

The world's electrical power was cut off, as power towers crumpled and high-voltage wires crashed to the

Earth. There was no way for most people to listen to the satellite broadcasts.

No insects had been spread over the oceans, so ships at sea were generally not affected until they came to land. There they were promptly plagued by egg-laying mosquitoes. Most of them sank at the docks, their hulls riddled with holes. Some left and tried to make it to their home ports, and, of these, some made it back. But those that didn't went down with all hands, as the lifeboats were in worse shape than the ships themselves.

Small sailing craft, with plastic hulls and brass fittings, were largely unaffected. Most of these left port with jury-rigged wooden masts and manilla stays, their owners, or those who had stolen them, planning to eke out some sort of survival by fishing.

The old, the infirm, the hospitalized were the worst affected. In some cases, the doctors resorted to euthanasia. In most, the ill were simply abandoned when nothing more could be done for them. In a few cases, dedicated medical staffs stayed with their patients.

Several thousand self-proclaimed messiahs, quoting the Bible, the Talmud, the Koran, or one of a hundred similar texts, or claiming special divine, scientific, or political knowledge, gathered flocks eager to follow anyone who seemed to know what he was doing. Their net effect was beneficial, for many of these leaders led their people out of the cities.

Without electrical power or water, cities became uninhabitable. Sanitation became nonexistent, and plagues broke out on a scale unknown since the Middle Ages.

Mindless looting, murder, and rape became commonplace. Those authorities that still existed had neither communications nor weapons nor transportation. They were largely powerless, and few could do anything but protect themselves.

Most people formed into small, local groups and were able to maintain some form of order within their tiny territories as the lawbreakers were no better armed and generally less well coordinated.

* * *

A great, silvered parabolic dish was constructed in
Life Valley, targeted on a functioning communications
satellite, and a message transmitted. With nothing else to
transmit, the operators relayed it all over the globe on
the commercial VHF and UHF frequencies.

Consumer electronics contain little or no ion or aluminum. And those with battery-operated radios and televi-
sions heard it.

The voice was Heinrich Copernick's, although, for
linguistic reasons, the speaker was the CCU.

"I am Heinrich Copernick. I have a message that is
vital to your welfare. Be patient, and it will be repeated
in your own language. An English-language broadcast
will begin in ten minutes." These lines, with appropriate
broadcast times, were then repeated in Russian, Chinese, French, German, Hindustani, and fifty-three other
languages and dialects.

"We are in the midst of a devastating and historically
unprecedented plague," it continued in English. "As you
are doubtless well aware, it is caused by an insect that is
capable of metabolizing iron and aluminum. It has
spread with incredible rapidity across the entire globe.

"The biological metabolism of metals is not unprecedented. Iron bacteria have plagued corrosion engineers
for many years. It is possible that these insects carry
such bacteria, or have somehow incorporated DNA from
these bacteria into their chromosomes.

"It seems a law of nature that everything that can be
eaten eventually will be eaten. Every possible ecological
niche is eventually filled. Nature has finally caught up
with us, at least insofar as our two most common metals
are concerned.

"Mankind is indeed fortunate that my uncle, Dr.
Martin Guibedo, has developed a means of supplying
food and shelter that does not depend on the metals we
once used. I am speaking, of course, of the tree houses.

"You are doubtless familiar with them. Just previous
to the plague, an estimated three percent of the world's
population was living in them. These tree houses are capable of supporting, for a few months and at a bare sustenance level, ten times the number of people currently

living with them. There is room for one third of humanity in the adult trees that already exist, and for all of humanity in the young trees that are now maturing.

"Those of you now living in tree houses are urged to be generous. You must do this because all men are brothers; we cannot allow our brothers to starve needlessly.

"And you must do this for your own self-protection, for a hungry man with a hungry family is a dangerous man. The people you invite into your homes can help protect you from the marauding gangs that now infest our world.

"As mayor of a tree-house city growing in what was once Death Valley, I invite anyone who can come to join us. Our citizens are planting tree houses to accommodate you. We will do what we can to make your walk here as comfortable as possible.

"In addition to this, we have planted ten million food trees across the Earth. Each of these trees will, in two months' time, be able to feed one thousand people. Alone they will be able to feed all of humanity. Eat only the food pods that grow from the trunks. The leaves and branches are poisonous. These trees were designed by Dr. Martin Guibedo to combat the present crisis. One of them should now be growing for every five square miles of our Earth's land. As each covers forty acres of land, they will be easy enough to spot. Each leaf has a small red cross in the center.

"Because of the emergency, these trees were planted hurriedly and without regard to property rights. While we normally respect property rights, racial survival comes first.

"Those of you who are living in cities and heavily populated areas must leave them at once. Staying where you are, you are in serious danger of dying from disease, fire, or starvation. Take what food and clothing you can, join others for self-protection, and head for the most isolated area you can find. Odds are a food tree will be there. If you go far enough, you will find food.

"Besides developing new forms of plants, we have also developed several new forms of animals. One of these is called a Labor and Defense Unit. They resemble a walking kitchen table and I am afraid that they are rather ugly to look at, but they are honest policemen and good doctors. They are intelligent, fast, and deadly.

"There are now one million LDUs. This is a very small force compared with the world's population, but it seems to be the only one capable of acting on a world-wide basis. Because of this we are declaring martial law.

"Murder, slavery, and the wanton destruction of food supplies, including tree houses and food trees, are hereby declared capital offenses. LDUs have been ordered to kill immediately anyone found committing these offenses.

"It is not our intention to infringe the rights of any organized group. We will support any group capable of maintaining order within its local area, and we urge everyone to form such groups for mutual aid and self-protection, provided that obvious standards of conduct are maintained.

"To summarize, there is more than enough food for everyone, but you must leave the cities to find it.

"And a force of intelligent, strange-looking animals will be helping to maintain law and order. Please give them your complete cooperation.

"I am Heinrich Copernick. I have a message that is vital to your welfare. Be patient, and it will be repeated in your own language. The next English-language broadcast will begin in twelve hours."

Guibedo, Copernick, Mona, Patricia, Liebchen, and Dirk listened to the broadcast in the living room at Oakwood, Guibedo's home.

"Heiny, you make me out for such a hero, I get embarrassed," Guibedo said, switching off the radio.

"You deserve it, Uncle Martin. It's about time you got some recognition for your accomplishments. But when times are rough—and they've never been worse—people need to know that there is someone, someplace, who can and will help them. They need a hero to keep their spirits up, and you're handy."

"Well, I still get embarrassed."

"At least now there will be fewer people trying to kill you," Copernick said.

"Kill Martin!" Patricia was horrified, and Mona was startled. Liebchen was immediately in tears.

"Nobody did it," Guibedo said with his arms around Patricia and Liebchen. "Thanks mostly to Dirk and his buddies. We didn't tell you about it because there wasn't any point to making you worry."

"Thank you, Dirk," Patricia said, gently stroking the LDU's leathery back. Gently, because he had been badly burned in the fire a month before. LDUs with their four-stranded DNA healed almost as slowly as humans did. By comparison, the fauns, Ohura and Colleen, far more seriously injured, were almost completely well, although Ohura's hair was still short and Colleen's new leg was still three inches shorter than her old one.

Liebchen was considerably more demonstrative than Patricia, jumping up and hugging Dirk as best she could. She kissed both of his eye stalks and then began working her way around his oval body, kissing all eight of his fixed eyes. Dirk caressed her back, and if her actions caused him any pain, he didn't show it.

"You know," Guibedo said, "I think they're in love."

"As you know, my lord, we're both incapable of the romantic love of bisexual beings," Dirk said. "Though I must confess that I rather enjoy having her around. Still, I wish I could join my brothers who are leaving tomorrow. There is so much work to do and so few to do it."

"Somebody has got to mind the store," Guibedo said. "Only twenty of you will be left in the valley, and all of you are injured. You'll have your share of work."

"The Aerial Defense Units will be ready in six months to back up your brothers," Copernick added.

"I wish there was something I could do," Patricia said.

"I think there is, Patty," Mona said. "Let's you and me load Winnie up with food and tree-house seeds and head out to the coast. A lot of people must be in trouble out there."

"Not a bad idea," Copernick said. "But not to the coast. You can have no idea how savage it's gotten in the cities. I wouldn't object to your going east."

"But the cities are where we could do the most amount of good," Mona protested.

"No. You'll be able to save a given number of lives in whatever direction you go. I will not permit the mother of my children to risk her life unnecessarily."

"Oh, all right." Mona thought that bringing the kids into the argument was remarkably poor form.

"Well, it's not all right with me. Just you two girls out there alone?" Guibedo said, ignoring the fact that Mona was stronger than most men, including himself.

"Oh, Martin," Patricia said. "We'll have Winnie, and you know how strong he is."

"That walking house trailer is strong, but dumb. Dirk, could you fight in an emergency?"

"I'm a bit in pain, my lord, but it doesn't degrade my efficiency."

"So you can ride inside and keep an eye on things. And we can keep in touch through you, too."

"Oh, I want to go, too!" Liebchen got five cold stares. "Oh, please. Ohura and Colleen can take care of the children now, and Ishtar can watch my babies. Oh, please, please, I won't get in the way. I promise."

Saying no to Liebchen was usually too much trouble to be worth it, and this was no exception. The five of them would leave in the morning.

The suspension bridges were all down, and steel trusses were getting shaky. Skyscrapers had already started to collapse, their steel frames riddled with larvae holes. It would be a month or so before the larvae would get hard enough up to eat the nails out of houses, but the day would come.

Long lines of refugees streamed out of the cities. They were pitiful to look at, though most of them were well dressed. Many were hurt, more were sick, and most were hungry. They pushed homemade wooden carts and dragged plastic sleds.

Behind them and around them the cities were crumbling and burning.

Claymore was climbing a sheer sandstone cliff. He moved swiftly, deftly finding footholds, his four camel-like legs moving with insect swiftness. His rigid body was a light tan color, to match his background.

While his forward ganglia controlled his ascent, his central ganglia took command of his eye tentacles—the fixed eyes were sufficient for navigation—and spread them wide for a good view of the human city at his back.

Even from this height and distance, the city was a shambles. The suspension bridge had already fallen, its center span deep underwater. One of its steel towers was down and the other was leaning drunkenly. A nearby truss bridge still held—and might hold for days yet—but in the end it, too, would be rubble and rust. There was no motor traffic on the bridge. There was none any-where. The cars and trains and planes were falling apart on their driveways and sidings and runways. On sched-ule.

The bridge was dotted with humans. Claymore ad-justed his tentacle eyes for telescopic vision, to study them more closely. Well dressed, most of them, but they trudged slowly under heavy burdens. They were dirty and probably thirsty. The water mains had gone out four days before. Getting enough water to live wouldn't be a serious problem, but the food situation was serious. Trucks had stopped arriving from the countryside a week ago. This troubled him, for ten thousand of these humans were his personal responsibility.

Nearing the top of the cliff, he scanned out to the west. About half of the power towers had fallen. The lines had been dead for days. As he watched, one more went, slowly crashing into the rust-red dust. The center of the city was mostly empty. Two of the tallest buildings had fallen so far, clogging the main intersections. The few people still there moved quickly, furtively watching the remaining buildings. He focused in on one of them. Shabbily dressed and remarkably dirty, this man picked up a brick from a fallen skyscraper and threw it through a large window in a still-standing building. Afraid to go too far inside, he leaned past the broken glass and began filling a canvas bag with the contents of the display win-dow.

Claymore focused closer, curious as to what this human was risking his life to get. Baubles! Crystallized carbon, gold, and silver. Crystallized aluminum oxide with a small percentage of chromium or magnesium. The stuff seemed to have no useful purpose except personal adornment. This human had collected more of it than he could carry. Strange. Contrasurvival.

A block over, another human, a female, was filling a plastic case with green paper certificates. Weird. But there was nothing in Claymore's directives against it, so he scanned on.

He reached the top of the cliff and had to use his humanoid hands to make it over the lip. From there he turned back to "face" the crumbling city. Not that he had a face, or even a head. His body turned a brownish green to match the grass below his feet.

Scanning to the north, he saw a large group of humans crossing a shaky bridge to an island in the river. Trouble. As soon as transmission space was available, he thought to those below.

Claymore here. Is anyone near the island two miles due north of the city?

Jarid here, Claymore. I am. What can I do for you?

Claymore here. There are approximately twenty-three hundred humans crossing over to that island. The bridge leaving it is down, but they can't see that from where they're at. When the bridge they're using goes they'll be stranded. We'll probably lose half of them.

Jarid here. I'll get on it. Where are you calling from?

Claymore here. I'm on top of the sandstone cliffs south of the city.

Jarid here. I see you now. I suggest you stay there and direct us down here. We have only eighty-two LDUs here to take care of almost two million people. I wish we had some observation birds.

Claymore stifled a sob.

Claymore here. Will do. There are some strange things going on in the city.

Jarid here. Like what?

Claymore here. Humans in the city are foraging for baubles rather than food.

Jarid here. So? It's what they usually do. Where have you been? The subject was discussed a week ago.

Claymore here. I just came out of shock. I lost my bird a month ago bringing down a bomber. But I'm functional now.

Jarid here. Sorry. I didn't realize you were a Beta unit. From your name, I mean.

Claymore here. A claymore was a mine as well as a sword. I'm functionally an Alpha now. I'll get used to it.

Jarid here. I'm sure you will. We're a tough species. To fill you in on your earlier question, the consensus is that humans were never programmed to handle their present problems. The result is a clinging to obsolete value systems and generally aberrant behavior. Jarid out.

The above conversation took less than a second.

Claymore continued his scanning, occasionally making suggestions to other LDUs below. There were minor outbreaks and riots among the humans, but at least the LDUs didn't have to face metallic weapons anymore.

Claymore! Gamma 5723 here. Go directly south at top speed. I'll explain when you're on your way.

Gamma units were somewhat telepathic with humans, that is, they could hear humans think, although they generally couldn't talk to them. A recent development, they were few in number and so they generally concentrated on major emergencies. When a Gamma made a suggestion, an Alpha moved fast.

Claymore here. I'm on my way. What's up?

Gamma 5723 here. Go one mile due south, then right, onto a gravel road. In approximately one mile you will come to a stone cabin on your right. There you will find six adult human males and one adult human female. The males are presently sequentially raping the female.

Claymore here. Rape? Oh, yes, One of the humans' bisexual reproduction customs. Considered improper in most human cultures. But why trouble me with it? Rape is not on the forbidden list of human activities.

Gamma 5723 here. I'm not concerned with the rape. That's been going on for hours. The house is the property of the female, and its construction is such that it will probably survive the present emergency. Furthermore, it contains a large supply of dehydrated camper's food in plastic packages. The males have decided to kill the famale to more easily take her property. Also, the males are presently despoiling some of the food supply.

Claymore here. Murder and destroying food are cer-

*tainly forbidden activities for humans. But their actions
are so irrational! Why destroy part of a food supply that
is necessary to your own survival? And why go through
the bother of impregnating a female of your own species
when you are going to terminate her before she can possibly reproduce?*

*Gamma 5723 here. It has been some time since I
heard of a human being accused of rationality.*

Claymore here. But it's countersurvival.

*Gamma 5723 here. Very. Especially when you'll be
there in three minutes. I'm afraid you'll have to go in
alone. None of our brothers are near enough to help in
time.*

*Claymore here. What would I need with help? I mean,
if there are only six of them ...*

*Gamma 5723 here. Unfortunately, one of them has a
weapon, a semiautomatic thirty-caliber carbine.*

*Claymore here. Oh. That does complicate things. I
thought that we had disposed of all of their iron and
aluminum artifacts.*

*Gamma 5723 here. We pretty much have. But in this
instance the human deduced what was happening. He
sealed the weapon in an airtight plastic bag before it
could become contaminated. The weapon is operational.
The human plans to fire it through the bag and then
reseal it. He has fifteen rounds in the clip.*

*Claymore here. Which means I'm up against an intel-
ligent armed human, despite his irrationalities.*

Gamma 5723 here. Good luck. Gamma 5723 out.

By this time, Claymore was fifty yards from the cliff
and accelerating. He was on a partially wooded plateau,
with short flat sections cut by deep fissures, some of
them over forty feet wide. Most of these he could jump,
but he had to circle some of them. On one occasion he
had to climb a hundred yards down and up again just to
travel eighty feet forward. It was maddeningly slow, and
it took him more than six minutes to travel the two miles
to the cabin. Most of the way he had to wind through
forests, and he was hoping for good cover for his ap-
proach to the cabin.

No such luck. The cabin was in the center of an abandoned farm, with at least four hundred yards of open

field in every direction. Claymore thrust his eye tentacles out through the foliage to survey his objective. It was a small building, perhaps two thousand square feet, and ancient, with stone walls and wooden window frames. The roof beams were heavy logs and—yes—pegged together. Aside from the door hinges, this would be one of the few buildings to remain intact. Certainly something a human would covet.

A human male was standing on the roof, his legs wide, turning occasionally to survey the terrain. He was holding the carbine.

Nothing for it but a direct frontal attack, into superior firepower. Had Claymore understood swearing, he would have done so. As it was, he picked up a half-dozen throwing-size rocks and launched himself at his opponent.

He went straight toward his opponent at first, carefully controlling his body color to match his background, watching his footfalls to make the least possible noise while moving at the highest possible speed, close to sixty mph. With luck, he would be close before he was noticed. Possibly the human had never seen an LDU before and would hesitate to fire. Also, heading straight in, he presented the least possible frontal area to his opponent's gunfire. On the other hand, if he did take a hit, it would tear through six feet of his flesh. A single round could conceivably take out half of his ganglia, lungs, or hearts.

Claymore was halfway there when the human saw him and brought up his weapon. The LDU sidestepped rapidly, then shifted into a fast form of broken field running. The human fired at one hundred yards, and the bullet narrowly missed the LDU's left forward fixed eye. It streaked across his back not quite breaking the skin, but knocking the wind out of his left lung. The pain was incredible. Claymore stumbled and almost fell. But his right lung was still sucking it in in front and blowing it out behind. He kept running. The brass cartridge ejected into the plastic bag and the carbine was ready to fire again. The human was a hunter and took careful aim.

Claymore. Gamma 5723 here. Immediate attack is no

longer necessary. The human female just died. You might as well wait until reinforcements arrive.

Claymore here. Now you tell me. I am in the midst of a solo frontal assault. At this point retreating would be more dangerous than pressing forward.

Gamma 5723 here. I got involved with a situation in Utah. I'll apologize if I get you killed.

Claymore here. Apologize now.

Gamma 5723 here. Okay. I apologize.

Claymore here. It's all right. Claymore out.

The next round missed him. He was fifty yards from the cabin now and zigzagging rapidly.

Claymore was working his way towards the woodpile, from which he could easily vault to the roof. He threw one of his rocks at the human just as the rifle was firing again. This time the human did not miss. The slug tore through Claymore's right arm between the elbow and shoulder, shattering the bone. The thrown rock missed the man but barely touched the plastic bag as the cartridge was ejecting. The spent brass bounced back toward the chamber, jamming the bolt temporarily. One bit of good luck, anyway.

As the LDU bounded to the top of the woodpile, his right lateral tentacles extended and pulled his wounded arm to his side. At the same time, he dropped the rocks in his left hand and extended his dagger-claw. This razor sharp knife-shaped claw was normally sheathed in his forearm, out of the way. Extended, it went a foot past his knuckles.

The human was clearing his weapon, tearing the plastic bag in the process, as Claymore landed on the roof. The carbine was coming down fast, but the LDU was faster. He got his dagger-claw between the man's arms and made an efficient upward thrust two inches behind and under the man's chin. It went up through the base of the brain. Death was instantaneous.

The weapon fired once more as it hit the roof, sending a round into the house below. A human screamed in pain.

Claymore disengaged himself from the corpse and picked up the carbine. He was familiar with the theory of firearms, but he had never actually fired one. He tried to hold it as he had seen the human do, but with only one arm and a vastly different anatomy, it was impractical. He held it in his left hand like a pistol and fired a tentative round into the roof.

"Damn it, Jim! Cut that out," sounded from below.

No. The rifle was completely unsuitable for use by a one-armed LDU in close combat. Still, he had to disable it, and he might as well do that by expending the ammunition. Claymore emptied the clip into the roof at random places. There were cries of anger, but no more cries of pain were heard. His arm was beginning to throb, although his left lung had started working again. He considered calling for help and letting somebody else do the mop-up.

"Now what the hell are you up to?" A man came out of the house angry, then started up in disbelief. In one hand he carried a long shiny knife. Titanium. This group had apparently foraged rationally.

Claymore was still holding the empty rifle, and saw no reason to miss a chance at an opponent. He threw the rifle down hard, striking the man in the forehead with the butt, caving in his skull.

Another human ran from the house, ignored his fallen comrade, and picked up the carbine. He tore a clip of ammunition from a plastic bag. This was a possibility that Claymore hadn't considered, but there was nothing to do now but rush him, broken arm or no. He leaped from the roof as the man was turning to look up, landing with both front feet on the man's head. Claymore weighed three hundred pounds, and the man's neck snapped easily. Three down. Maybe four. He picked up the carbine as the last three humans boiled out of the house, swinging clubs.

Claymore turned to meet them with his good arm holding the carbine by the barrel. Fighting with his dagger-claw would have been more efficient, but he was reluctant to let go of the weapon again. It was loaded and with only one hand, he couldn't remove the clip. He decided to use it as a club.

The men fought well as a team, trying to encircle him, and Claymore had to retreat. The man with the bleeding leg stumbled a bit and the LDU was on him, ducking a downward blow, and following with a roundhouse swing that connected with the man's neck. Four.

He ran over the downed man and swung around wide to catch the next human in line alone. Ducking under a lateral swing, he rammed the carbine butt into the man's solar plexus, and followed with a down stroke to the head. Five.

Claymore discarded the carbine now that there was no one behind him to pick it up. He attacked the last man. Seeing his five comrades die within a minute was too much for the fellow. He dropped his club and fled. The LDU was on him in three paces and, with a single hack, severed the man's neck bones and spinal cord. All.

Claymore walked back to the house, his right arm throbbing and bleeding slowly. As he passed each man, he slit each throat to be sure of a clean kill.

He found what was left of the human female in the bedroom.

Claymore. Gamma 5723 here. How did it go?

Claymore here. Mission accomplished. All six males are deleted. The female took a long time dying. I wish you had called me sooner.

Gamma 5723 here. I wish I could be everywhere, or that there were more of me. When I contacted this group two hours ago, it didn't look too serious. I didn't check up on them again until ten minutes ago. I wish I could tell her I was sorry.

Claymore here. And why did they use such an inefficient method of killing her?

Gamma 5723 here. Someday, Claymore, we'll sit around the barracks and have a long talk. Right now I have work to do. Gamma 5723 out.

The dirt was too shallow for burial, so Claymore restacked the woodpile into a rectangle seven feet by fourteen by five feet high and dragged the seven bodies to the top of it. He found a glass jug of kerosene and some matches in the house, said the ritual prayers that humans were fond of, and lit it afire.

Whoever is on duty at the Central Coordination Unit. Claymore here.

Dirk here for the CCU. Shoot.

Claymore here. Don't say that. I did and I was. I've

been in action that resulted in a bullet breaking my right arm. Request permission to return to Life Valley for R and R.

There was a three-second delay.

Dirk here. Permission granted. The luck you've had. You're out of action for a month losing your bird, and now, thirty minutes after getting to your duty station, you're coming back again.

Claymore here. Those are the breaks.

Dirk here. Well, if you're still punning, you can't be too bad off. I'll tell Ishtar you're coming. Dirk out.

Others were not as bad off. The farmers lost their machinery and most of their houses, but they were traditionally self-reliant. In the northern hemisphere, the crops were ready for harvest. For the first time in many years, there was a surplus of eager, if unskilled, labor.

In general, the less technically advanced were the least affected. The few remaining Eskimos were annoyed when their outboard motors, snowmobiles, and rifles were eaten, but the old ones knew how to do without such things. They taught the younger men, and gained considerable prestige and security.

Except for Hawaii and other islands with military bases, the Pacific was not plagued with the metal-eating larvae. On the Marshall out-islands, the people listened to their radios with detached interest. The troubles of the outside world provided a useful source of gossip, nothing more. Little had ever been done to them, and less for them. Bare-breasted native girls danced, laughing, at the usual ceremonies.

Throughout the underdeveloped world, crowded masses trudged on in despair, as they had done for a hundred years. Yet, in many, there was a glow of hope. They had been promised enough food for all. If that was true, it was indeed a blessing, because no one could remember a time when there had been enough for everyone.

In the American west, many American Indians were happy. Organized, intelligent, and poor, but with plenty of land, they had wholeheartedly accepted the tree houses as soon as the seeds had become available. Over half the American Indian population already lived in tree houses, so the larvae did not cause them extreme inconveniences.

The old chiefs, the wise men, the men of power were smugly contented. As they had so often predicted, the insanities of the white man had finally caught up with him. They had even heard one of them admit as much on the radio, and in their own language. Before the radios went silent, the old ways would return, and perhaps even the buffalo.

The young men were not content, but eager. They remembered the old stories, and told them to each other. The time of defeat and drudgery and shame was over. There would again be a time when skill and courage and honor counted.

Russia went the way of Europe and North America, with a breakdown of communications and central authority. From her crumbling cities came the long lines of refugees. Her countryside, too, was in a difficult position, as the workers on the large collective farms did not have the tradition of self-reliance that kept farmers in other parts of the world relatively unaffected.

China was in relatively good shape. The large population was dispersed, and not far from food supplies. In sixty years the farms had only been lightly mechanized; that work was wasted, but survival was not a serious problem.

Japan's problems were most serious. Tree houses had never really caught on there, and most of its food had been brought to her ports on ships that were no more. The Japanese could only hope that the voice on the radio had told the truth.

From Life Valley, one million LDUs, their language lessons completed, trotted toward their assigned areas. Each was to watch over the safety of ten thousand humans, and they had doubts as to the possibility of doing the job well.

Each platoon of one hundred had with it two Betas with their observation birds and one mind-reading Gamma unit. The birds were important to locate tree houses. All of the recent models had an external spigot that gave out the food that the LDUs ate. They would need to find many of these on the trek ahead.

Chapter Ten

JULY 22, 2003

▓▓▓▓▓▓▓▓▓▓▓▓▓▓▓▓▓

I HAVE enlarged my memory banks in order to better accommodate the influx of data on the increasing number of humans entering the valley.

In future daily reports on each human, you must prefix each notation with the code number which I have assigned to that human. Because of the prejudices of the humans, it is imperative that no human learns his own number, or even that such numbers exist.

These records will be useful in making long-term prognoses; the data will will not be available to humans because of our "right to privacy" directive.

—Central Coordination Unit to all local ganglia

Hastings remembered how a month ago he had awakened hot on the desert sand. He had lain there for minutes, trying to figure out where he was and why he was there. His last memories had been of relaxing in the F-38, mentally preparing himself to drop his first atomic bomb.

What did they hit me with? he thought.

Cautiously he moved the various parts of his body. Nothing broken. He got up and stripped off his suit and parachute. He found the standard-issue survival pack. Food. A .22-caliber handgun. Compass and maps. A canteen of distilled water. A manual. A radio that didn't work.

He drank deeply, knowing that rationing the water was a bad idea. Better to drink now and get the full cooling benefit of the water. He rigged the parachute into a sunshade and waited for Air Rescue for a day and a half. It didn't get there. He made an arrow with rocks to show his direction of travel.

The next evening, at moonrise, he picked up his belongings and started walking southwest, toward Death Valley.

"Who was it that said that the only way to stop a good man is to kill him?" he said to the rocks. "Funny, I can't remember."

He walked until sunrise without seeing any sign of man, not even a plane. He found the shelter of an overhanging rock and survived the day. At moonrise, he finished his water and walked on. The only sign of life was a shiny mosquito that seemed to be in love with his belt buckle.

The next morning his urine looked like Bock beer and he started to worry.

He woke to find a larva eating a hole in the barrel of his pistol. He tried to scream, but his throat was too dry to make a sound. He struggled to his feet, staggered a hundred yards, and fell down. He knew then that he was a dead man. He rolled over, put himself in a dignified posture, and prepared his mind for death.

He woke to find a gourd of water being held to his mouth by a powerful tan hand. He gulped the water.

"Slowly at first, sir."

Something was strange about the wrist. Yes, there was a *slot* in it. He jerked himself upright, spilling some of the water.

"You're one of them!" Hastings croaked.

"I suppose so, sir." The LDU rescued the water gourd. "I'm Labor and Defense Unit Alpha 362729. My friends call me K'kingee."

Hastings took another drink of water.

"What makes you think that I'm your friend?"

"I presumed that you would feel a certain amount of gratitude, sir."

"I guess I do. Thank you. Am I a prisoner of war?"

"You are not a prisoner of anything, sir."

"Are you going to kill me?"

"Had I intended that, it would have been more efficient to have simply let you die."

"Don't you realize what I am?"

"You are a human being, sir."

"I mean the uniform."

"Your clothing indicates that you were a general officer in the United States Air Force."

"What do you mean 'were'?"

"The Air Force no longer exists, sir. At least it no longer has aircraft capable of flight."

"How did you manage that?"

"I didn't manage it, sir. Didn't you notice the larva that is eating your pistol?"

"I thought that it was a hallucination. Is that another one of your creatures?"

"If you mean 'Is it an engineered life form?' the answer is no, sir."

"Then where did it come from?"

"A natural mutation, I suppose, sir."

"Do you really expect me to believe that?"

"You are at liberty to believe anything that you want, sir. Just now I have a job to do. If you go due west for two miles, you will come to a road. Follow it south for three miles and you will find an uninhabited tree house. I suggest that you stay there."

"What are you doing out here, anyway? I thought that all of you things were in Death Valley," Hastings said.

"I prefer 'LDU' to 'things.' We call it Life Valley now. And I'm on a scouting mission. We'll be coming through here in force in a few weeks."

"You are a trusting soul. May I have some more of that water?"

"You may keep both gourds, sir. As to being trusting, may I point out that the tree house I mentioned is forty miles from the nearest source of water? Even if you were my enemy, without mechanical transportation you could not go anywhere to harm us."

"Forty miles in which direction?" Hastings asked.

"South. But please don't do anything suicidal."

The LDU headed north at a run.

* * *

Hastings eventually made it to the tree house. He refreshed himself and got a night's sleep.

He woke shivering with a fever and for weeks he wondered if he had survived the desert only to die in the bowels of a plant.

Now, a month after being ejected from his plane, the sickness was gone and his body was again strong. He packed all the food and water he could carry and started south.

They had been distributing food and water to people en route to Life Valley since morning, and Winnie's load was twelve thousand pounds lighter. But he had been designed to work in tunnels where the temperature was held at fifty-five degrees, and fifty miles from Flagstaff, the heat was starting to tell on him. He had been slowing down since noon and now was down to trotting at only twenty mph.

But Winnie's juvenile pride was involved. He was on his first big trip, and he wasn't going to let anybody think he was a softy. He unfolded one huge arm from the top of his forty-foot-long body, wiped the sweat from his eyes with a yard-wide hand, and plodded onward.

His passengers were similarly uncomfortable. While the heat didn't bother Dirk, his burns still troubled him, and he was worried about Liebchen. The faun had put herself into a trance to better endure the heat, and Dirk was gently swabbing her body with water. "It was stupid of me to have allowed her along, my ladies," the LDU said.

"I'm afraid that none of us were thinking too clearly," Mona said. "She'll be okay. Fauns are tough, and it'll be dark in a few hours."

"It's the people that get me down," Patricia said. "We must have passed ten thousand of them today, and all we could do was give them a handout and directions to the valley."

"We'll give the worst cases a lift on our way back." Mona took two frosted glasses from the synthesizer and put one on the table in front of Patricia. "Buck up, girl. In a few months it'll all be over."

"There are ten billion people out there! We couldn't feed them all when we had machines. We'll never be able to do it now."

"Nonsense!" Mona said, "There never was a good technical reason for famine. Even before Heinrich and Uncle Martin got into the act, the Earth could have supported ten times the people than it does today."

"Huh? There have been famines for the last ten years."

"Figure it out. Every day the Earth receives three point five times ten to the eighteenth calories of solar energy, half of which reaches the surface. Now, if only one percent of the Earth's surface was planted with crops that were only one percent efficient, you have fifty billion people on thirty-five hundred calories a day, enough to get fat on.

"Then figure that ten percent, not one percent, of the Earth's surface is arable and that some natural plants are three percent efficient. We could feel one point five trillion people."

"Then for God's sake, why didn't we?" Patricia asked.

"Because we never got our shit together. Uncle Martin blames it all on the 'Big Shot Problem,' the fact that people in power don't like to change the status quo, but his views on social problems tend to be overly simplistic. You'd have to add in tradition, inertia, world trade agreements, greed, ignorance, and stupidity to get a complete answer. Mostly stupidity."

Patricia finished her drink and looked up. Another group of refugees was just ahead.

Winnie was slowing down as Mona got up. "Just remember that you're looking at the last famine in history."

"Don't get scared!" Winnie shouted in his little boy's voice. "We've got food and water for you!"

Unbroken lines of LDUs, loaded with food and tree-house seeds, were still streaming out of the valley, heading north, to go through Alaska, swim the Bering Straits, and enter Asia, Europe, and Africa by way of Kamchatka. As many others were headed south, to try to alleviate the chaos in South America. Thousands more fanned out over the North American continent.

The Los Angeles zoo had been abandoned by its keepers, mostly because they simply couldn't get from their homes to work.

Metal-eating larvae swarmed over cage bars and door hinges and the valves that kept the moats filled.

Gazelles, zebras, and mountain sheep hungrily, timidly, made their way out to the tall grass of untended lawns and munched contentedly.

Other animals were neither contented nor timid. Lions, tigers, and wolves, unfed for a week, quietly prowled about looking for warm meat.

The years they had spent in captivity had softened their muscles, and some hungry lions couldn't catch a mountain goat, let alone a gazelle. Still, there was a lot of slow-moving meat around. The two-legged variety.

Antonio Biseglio was a chef, as his father and grandfather had been chefs. His kitchen was his kingdom and his kingdom was under siege.

With fly swatter and mallet, he had put up a noble, if useless, defense. In a week's time his stove was worthless, his pots were like colanders, and his pans like sieves. In the end he salvaged nothing but a copper omelet pan, and with that he joined the crowds abandoning the city.

Tom Greene County Hospital was left with only one Filipino intern and a single nurse to care for the 230 surviving patients. The nurse, tired to the point of hallucination, dropped the buckets of water she was carrying and screamed as the LDU entered the stairwell.

"Don't be afraid. I am a friend."

"Wh—what are you?"

"I am Labor and Defense Unit Alpha 001256. My friends call me Tao."

"Oh, yes. We heard that you—uh—folks would be out." The nurse tiredly massaged her temples. "Look. Can you help me? We've got water in the basement, but the pipes to the other floors are out. People on the fourth floor are dying of thirst."

"I'm afraid that there are more important considerations. The steel framework of this building is infested with larvae. It will collapse within three days. We must evacuate it immediately," Tao said.

"But how? And where to?"

"I will organize a human labor force. The patients tell me that there is a doctor around. Find him, and together place all salvageable medical supplies into the hallways. I will have it hauled out to the courtyard, along with the patients."

Relieved that someone—or something—was taking responsibility, the nurse said, "Yes, sir."

Within an hour, using persuasion and offers of food, with threats and demonstrations of force, Tao collected a group of one hundred healthy men to assist him.

As they approached the hospital, they heard the nurse screaming from the second floor, where he found a Siberian tiger busily devouring the body of a woman who had been dying of cancer. The tiger viewed Tao's appearance as a threat to its first meal in eight days. Roaring, it charged.

The tiger weighed seven-hundred pounds, more than twice that of the LDU, but in speed, intelligence, and ferocity, there was no contest. As the tiger leaped, Tao dropped below him. Thrusting a foot-long dagger-claw between the tiger's swinging forepaws, he slit its throat to the spinal column. As the dead tiger hit the floor, Tao was already examining the patients in the room.

Both were dead.

The nurse entered as Tao was tying the tiger's carcass upside down to the ceiling with Venetian blind cords.

"Oh, thank you, Tao. The patients—"

"Are both dead. I'll attend to their bodies. You must care for the living. Get the men in the courtyard working. I want this building evacuated by evening. And send one of them, Antonio Biseglio, up here."

"Yes, sir. What are you doing?" the nurse asked.

"We have three hundred hungry people here, and this carcass is protein edible for your species." He had the tiger skinned and gutted, and was slicing the meat into one-inch cubes.

"But it's a *tiger!*"

"Protein. Look, they're eating a rhinoceros in Griffith Park. Just tell people it's beef. Now move!"

Antonio Biseglio arrived shortly. "You wanted me, boss?"

"I would prefer that you didn't use honorifics on me. Except in emergencies, we LDUs maintain a subordinate role to humans."

"Sorry, Tao."

"Better. Now, people are hungry, you're a cook, and this is meat. Do something," Tao said as he worked.

"Cat meat?"

"The Watusi consider it a delicacy. Tell people it's beef."

"I don't have any utensils."

"I saw a four-foot Pyrex bell jar in one of the labs. It should serve as a cauldron. And there must be something salvageable in the kitchens. Get some men to help you. I'll have the meat on stretchers in the hallway waiting for you. Move."

All told, eight hundred pounds of meat went into the cauldron. And if some of it tasted like pork, no one mentioned it.

At the rim of a wide Colorado valley near the Continental Divide, Saber stopped to survey the terrain. Extending his tentacled eyes out until they were eight feet apart, he adjusted his vision to 20X magnification and slowly scanned the area in search of anyone who might need his help. Well above the tree line, all was lichen-covered boulders. A food tree was growing several thousand feet below, to his right. Saber noted the position for future use; in eight weeks it would start producing.

All seemed quiet, deserted, with no sign of human life at all.

No! On the opposite end of the valley, six miles away, he saw two humans, a man and a woman. They seemed to be struggling, although it was difficult to tell at this distance.

The woman broke away from the man, running away from him. The man pursued, tackling her, knocking her to the ground. Saber ran as fast as he could over the huge boulders.

He kept the pair in view as he charged into the valley. The woman broke away again; her blouse was torn off, her bra hanging at her elbow. It was still hard to tell, but it seemed that she was bleeding in several places. She made it to the top of a large boulder and from there threw a rock at the man, who was still pursuing her. The rock struck the man, injuring but not stopping him.

Saber was then halfway across the valley, considering his course of action. If the man killed the woman before he got there, it would be an obvious case of murder, and, in accordance with Lord Copernick's instructions, he would kill the man. If the woman killed the man? She was retreating. Self-defense. No punishment. If neither was killed, he would incapacitate the man and assist the woman to safety.

The man had the woman down on the boulder and ripped off the balance of her clothing.

The motive, then, seemed to be rape, one of the humans' sexual reproduction customs. As the LDUs understood it, rape was generally frowned on, but Lord Copernick had not placed it on the list of capital offenses. Saber would administer no punishment for the offense.

As the LDU approached, the woman was struggling and screaming loudly. The man was hitting her on the face and upper torso while trying to hold her down and remove his own clothes.

Saber struck the man with a body check, and all three tumbled from the boulder. The man was on his feet almost as quickly as the LDU and, wild eyed, he threw a rock at Saber.

The LDU tapped the man on the chin with his knuckles, rendering him unconscious. Turning to the woman, he saw she was sitting naked on the ground, dirty and sobbing uncontrollably. Her lips and one eye were swelling, and blood trickled down her chin. Her back was scratched and her ribs and breasts were badly bruised.

"Don't be afraid," Saber said, handing the woman the remnants of her clothing. "I am a friend. It's all over now. I'll take you somewhere where you will be safe and tend your wounds."

The woman continued to cry.

"I know that I look strange to you. I am a labor and defense unit. I am here to protect you, to keep you from harm."

"Well, who the hell asked you for help?" she screamed.

"You were being injured. Naturally I came to your assistance." The woman's reaction wasn't what the LDU had expected.

"God damn you!" she shouted. "It was just getting good!"

Suddenly a ten-pound rock bounced off Saber's back. "Yeah, you damned animal," the man yelled. "Get out!"

Saber retreated, unsure as to what the correct course of action was. He stopped to engage in a meaningful conversation and was struck by a rock thrown by the woman.

A very confused labor and defense unit abandoned the valley.

Winnie found a small, shady canyon a few hundred yards from the road and settled down for the night. Liebchen was sleeping normally, and Dirk, who never slept completely, but sequentially took his brains off line, crouched near her.

Dirk. Mukta here, an LDU in Utah thought.

Dirk here. What do you need?

Mukta here. What is a soul and do we have one?

Dirk here. A soul is supposedly a part of an entity that persists after physical death. Its existence is an interesting question. Has it anything to do with the present emergency?

Mukta here. I'm with a religious community that is in obvious need of my assistance. But they'll refuse my help unless I have a soul.

Dirk here. The existence of your soul depends on your socioreligious frame of reference. The western religions generally grant souls only to human beings. They'll be two hundred years deciding on intelligent engineered life forms. The eastern religions, especially Buddhism and Hinduism, definitely grant souls to nonhumans. The answer to your question is yes and no.

Mukta here. Not good enough. I need a definite answer. These people have a western frame of reference.

Dirk here. Well, in the Norse religion, any being that died with a weapon in its hand went to Valhalla, which logically presupposes a soul. Since each LDU always has a weapon in each hand, or at least each forearm, we will logically die with it there. Therefore all LDUs have souls.

Mukta here. Thanks. Out.

Dirk. Birchi here. Got time for another one?

Dirk here. Shoot.

Birchi here. I was in a successful action two hours ago, but I don't understand why I was successful.

Dirk here. So?

Birchi here. In a marble quarry, I encountered two groups of young adult human males fighting. The negro group, being larger, was inflicting serious damage on the caucasian group. I broke up the conflict quickly, there being only forty-six humans involved, but I was forced to do considerably more damage to the numerically superior negro group than to the caucasians.

I attempted to resolve the conflict by speaking with them but the negroes were quite irrational and verbally abusive, referring to me as "whitey."

Now, as I had been fighting on a white marble surface, I had naturally turned my skin a light gray for protective coloration. Therefore, in an attempt to placate the negroes, I changed my coloration to an off-brown, the arithmetical average of the negroes' skin coloration, and again attempted to open a conversation.

At this point, the caucasians became abusive, calling me "nigger" and other color-related terms. I therefore turned the side facing the caucasians to a pinkish tan in imitation of their skin coloration, keeping the side facing the negroes brown, and attempted to enter into a meaningful dialogue with both groups as to the cause of the original conflict.

Both groups then broke into convulsive and abusive laughter, picked up their wounded, and went away.

Dirk here. Indeed?

Birchi here. Now, my question is: What did I do right?

Dirk here. Beats me, but I suggest that the next time

an LDU encounters a similar situation, he should try repeating your actions.

Birchi here. Sounds reasonable. Out.

"Well, Mona, I guess we've helped out a little today," Patricia said, looking at the full moon over the desert.

"More than a little. We've distributed enough food and water to keep a thousand people alive for a week. And tomorrow we should be able to bring thirty-five or forty of them back with us," Mona said.

"But it's nothing compared to the job that has to do be done."

"It's what we *can* do," Mona said. "And don't forget, we're not alone. Almost every TRAC we have is out doing the same thing we are. Add to that all the LDUs with three hundred pounds of supplies each, and you have a force capable of rescuing everyone in the Southwest."

"I suppose so," Patty said.

"Dirk," Mona said, "how are your brothers doing?"

"Most of them are still en route to their assigned sectors, my lady. Thus far we have spread north to Vancouver, east to St. Louis and south to Mexico City. About forty thousand are now in their duty areas."

"Continue," Mona said.

"We have suffered two hundred eighteen disabling casualties today, including twenty-three deaths. Most of these injuries were caused by collapsing structures, although some were caused by humans. There is a surprising amount of resentment toward us, most probably caused by our appearance."

"I'll talk to Heinrich about that," Mona said. "Perhaps future units should be given a more acceptable, if less practical, appearance. How about the other side of the sheet; what have you accomplished?"

"It is difficult to access actual lives saved, my lady. We have distributed approximately 100,000 tons of supplies to the needy, we have moved 128,000 people from dangerous situations to places of relative safety, and we have interrupted 2,654 1/2 incidents of assault."

"How do you get a half of an assault?" Patricia asked.

"There was a situation which was difficult to assess,

my lady." Dirk explained what had happened to Saber that afternoon.

"It sounds pretty sick to me," Patricia said.

"There was no indication of disease, my lady."

"She means that when it comes to things sexual, humans can get pretty kinky, Dirk," Mona said. "Understanding here is pretty difficult. Suffice it to say that Saber's actions were correct. In a similar situation, I would expect him to repeat his actions. However, this particular couple should be left alone in the future, providing that they don't harm anyone else."

"Saber is grateful for your approval, my lady. He has been quite anxious about the incident. Human sexual practices are very confusing to asexual beings."

"They're pretty confusing to humans, too," Patricia said.

"Is this what's been bothering you today?" Mona asked. "I mean, you've been in the dumps about something closer to home than the refugees."

"Uh, it's something like that, Mona. What would you do if you were going insane?"

"Something crazy, I suppose. But you're not showing any of the usual symptoms of psychosis."

"But I am! I mean, when things change around you, when something looks different from one moment to the next . . . Oh! I don't know." Patricia began to cry.

"Easy, girl, easy. What things are changing?"

"Martin."

"You mean sometimes he acts like a different person?"

"No. I mean sometimes he *looks* like a different person. Like, sometimes when he just comes into the room, and I catch him in the corner of my eye, he looks so different, so ugly. Or when we're making love, he changes sometimes, just for an instant. And then he's back to normal."

"I never heard of anything like it," Mona said. "But I don't think it's psychosis."

"My lady, isn't it written that 'love is blind'?" Dirk said.

"Stay out of this, Dirk," Mona whispered.

"Well, it's *something*," Patricia said.

"Tell me," Mona said, "what does Uncle Martin look like when he looks different? I mean, describe him."

"Uh, he's short, very short. And incredibly fat. And he looks maybe a hundred years old."

"Go on," Mona said.

"He's got a wart on the left side of his nose and a triple chin. His hair, what there is of it, is all white and he has a ridiculous mustache."

"I see," Mona said. This was, of course, a fairly accurate description of Martin Guibedo. "Now describe what Uncle Martin looks like normally."

"Well, you know what he looks like!"

"Humor me," Mona said.

"Oh, okay. Well, he's got black hair graying at the temples, a neat mustache, and clear blue eyes. He's about six one. Rather wide shouldered with a wiry body. Sort of a swimmer's build, you know."

"Of course." Mona was beginning to think that Dirk was right. Perhaps love *was* blind. "There've probably been other cases like it, Patty. I'll talk it over with the CCU when we get home. In the meantime, buck up. It can't be too serious, and you're among friends."

"Thanks, Mona." Patricia put her hand on Mona's as an arrow lodged itself halfway through Winnie's body, with the flint arrowhead stopping directly between their faces.

"OOWW!" Winnie yelled.

Dirk was out the door in an instant. Liebchen woke up and stuck her grinning head out the window, eager not to miss anything.

"Down, girl," Mona said, pulling Liebchen to the floor beside herself and Patricia. "Dirk can take care of it without you."

A Gamma unit in Utah took an interest in the affair. *Six of them, Dirk. But take it easy. They're all adolescents.*

Thanks! Dirk adjusted his eyes to infrared and his skin to flat black. He swung out and came silently behind them, catching each boy alone and swiftly, carefully knocking each senseless.

Groping with his huge arms in the dark, Winnie managed to catch the last of the intruders. He was vigorously bouncing this screaming unfortunate on the sand, occasionally switching hands to demonstrate his versatility, when Dirk told him to stop.

"Aw, gee, Dirk. I was only spanking him a little," Winnie said.

"From here it looks like you've broken both of his arms and at least one leg. Next time leave this sort of thing to me! Now put him—gently—on the bed inside." Dirk dropped two unconscious boys on the sand. "And get me some rope to tie these guys up."

Mona efficiently bound the unconscious boys as Dirk brought them in. In twenty minutes there were casts on all four limbs of the one Winnie had gotten hold of, and Winnie's side had been bandaged.

"Ridiculous, my ladies," Dirk said. "According to my brother Tomahawk, who's up on Indian lore, this group is the most incredible hodge-podge imaginable. The one on the end, for example. His moccasins are maybe Crow, the leggings are Shawnee, his bow Cree, and the arrows are Seminole. The war bonnet is Sioux, his scalp lock is Iroquois, and the war paint looks more Zulu than anything else. Yet judging from their facial features, this bunch are Zuni."

"They've just been watching too many movies, Dirk," Mona said. The boys were starting to come around.

"Perhaps, my lady. A more important question is what to do with them. We can't have them running around shooting people, but I would prefer not to kill them," Dirk said.

"Neither would I." Mona turned to the boy on the end. "Why did you shoot at us?"

The boy was silent. Liebchen slipped back into Winnie.

Dirk prodded the boy. "Come, come, now. The lady is speaking to you."

"I'll never talk, paleface," the boy said in perfect English.

"Lacking, among other things, a face, I hardly qualify as a paleface. Winnie, bring out the first one from inside, the one who wouldn't talk."

The boys' eyes widened as the huge hand placed the bandaged boy in front of them.

"Gee, Dirk, can I spank another one?"

"Perhaps. Now then, son. Why did you shot at us?"

"Well, for one thing, we didn't know your house-trailer was alive."

"That's hardly an excuse for shooting at people," Mona said.

"You're on our land!" the boy in the middle said.

"Gee, the map said this was a state park." Winnie hoped he hadn't made a mistake.

"No! I mean this whole country is our land. You stole it from us and now we're taking it back."

"You're welcome to all the land you can use," Mona said, "but you're not entitled to kill people."

"We have a right to take what's ours."

"It's not yours. The land belongs to everyone. There's plenty enough to share. The time of stealing and killing is over. Soon, for the first time in history, there will be enough of everything for everyone. Why be stuck on the past when you can be part of the future?"

"Paleface."

Liebchen came out of Winnie with a glassful of something that looked like a mixture of milk and pink grapefruit juice. "This will fix everything, my lady."

"What's that?" Mona asked.

"Something I had Winnie's synthesizer make. It'll make these guys go home and be happy," the faun said proudly.

"You haven't quite answered my question, Liebchen."

"It is a behaviorial modification compound that will change their perceptions and programming, my lady. It'll make it so everybody's happy."

"What does it do?"

"It makes people see things the way they want to see them, and act the way they're supposed to act, and be happy about it."

"Give me that." Mona spilled the stuff on the sand, trying to control her emotions. The source of Patricia's problem was now obvious. "Liebchen, I don't want you to make anything like this again."

"Never, my lady? But it makes everybody happy."

"Never! Well, not unless Uncle Martin tells you to.

Now go inside and go to sleep and stay asleep until we get home."

"You're not mad at me, are you, Lady Mona?" Liebchen was quivering, frightened.

"No, but you did make a mistake. Now do as you're told."

Patricia didn't make the connection between her own problems and Liebchen's, and followed the faun inside.

"Dirk, give this bunch a warning and let them go," Mona said.

"Well, you heard the lady." Dirk extended his dagger-claw in front of the boys' noses. "If I had my way, I'd rough you up a bit more, or maybe chop off your hands to mark you as troublemakers." Dirk's claws sliced through the ropes as though they were spaghetti. "This time the Lady Mona was here to save you, but next time you won't be so lucky. If I don't get you, I have a million brothers who will. Now get out of here and take your buddy in the plaster with you."

The boys required no further encouragement.

Well, that's that problem, Mona thought. *But there's going to be hell to pay tomorrow.*

Chapter Eleven

AUGUST 30, 2003

I AM in the process of growing five additional Regional Coordination Units. Each will have message-handling and data-storage capabilities equal to my present self. Each regional unit will have authority over approximately five million humans and their attendant bioforms.

Message-routing procedures to these subordinate regional units will be as follows . . .

—Central Coordination Unit to all local ganglia

From the point where Hastings was ejected from his plane to the outskirts of Life Valley was four hundred miles as the jet flies. It was more than twice that for a man who has to walk and live off the land.

Hastings was forced to consider fifteen miles a day to be good speed, and often he didn't achieve it. But Hastings' character and temperament were as solid as concrete. And like concrete, the more he was stressed, the more rigid he became. His small lean frame became thinner and harder from the continuous walking. His mind became narrower and harder as well.

Guibedo and Copernick had become for him the personification of all that was evil. They had murdered his family. They had destroyed his country. They had taken from him all that could possibly be good in the world.

Hastings had become something less than a human

174

being. He had become a machine. A machine with only one function.

Vengeance.

Yet his intelligence never failed him.

He burned his uniform and dressed himself in rugged camping clothes that he found in Paradise, Nevada. He let his hair and beard grow long to blend into the crowds of refugees.

In an abandoned electronics repair store, he cobbled together a white-noise generator from a pocket radio. He took apart a choke coil and wove the fine copper wire into a tight-fitting skull cap. He spent hours fitting the cap so that his long hair went through it and the cap wasn't noticeable at a distance. He put the radio in his shirt pocket and ran a wire under his arm to the skull cap at the back of his neck. Such a contrivance would have stopped a human telepath; it might work on the gene-engineered monsters, as well.

He found a strip of titanium in an abandoned workshop at Nellis Air Force Base, and painstakingly ground it into a gutting knife. He ripped the element from an electrical heater and fashioned the nichrome wire into a garrotte. In the explosives shed behind an abandoned air police office he found three bricks of C-4 explosive. Plastique. But the electrical detonators with them had had iron magnetos, and were useless.

Three weeks later at a construction site in Good Springs, he found some blasting caps with chemical fuses.

His confidence was starting to match his determination. The only way to stop a good man is to kill him.

And good men are damned hard to kill!

Dirk trotted into Guibedo's workshop at Oakwood. Intent on his work, Guibedo was hunched over his incredibly ornate microscalpel.

"My lord."

"Hi, Dirk." Guibedo didn't turn from his work. "I'll be with you in five minutes. Such a beauty this one's going to be, Dirk. It's an eighty-foot Viking long boat with a square sail, oars, shields, and everything. Heiny's gonna make an animal to work the oars and be the dragon's head. It's only got a ten-inch draft, so we can take it up the rivers and canals, but we can still take it on the ocean. Some fun, huh?"

"I'm sure it will provide considerable amusement, my lord," Dirk said dryly. *The frivolity of these humans!*

"So, how did everything go?"

"In general, things are proceeding according to the plan, my lord, except that, for logistical reasons, the contingent heading for the eastern hemisphere has had to turn back."

"So? What happened?"

"There are simply not a sufficient number of tree houses in Alaska and Kamchatka to support a meaningful number of LDUs in transit to Siberia. If we sent more than a thousand they would starve to death en route. Also, there is more work to be done in the western hemisphere alone than the LDUs assigned there can handle. The eastern seaboard of the U.S. is in far worse shape than we had anticipated. Therefore, Lord Copernick has delayed our entry into Asia for two months, when the food trees will be producing sufficiently to support us on the trip."

"Well, if we got to, we got to."

"We now cover the North American continent, except for Nova Scotia, and the first units have reached Columbia. We have suffered six hundred fifty-seven disabling casualities today, including seventy-two deaths . . ."

"Dirk, don't treat your brothers like numbers," Guibedo said, finishing up his work and turning to the LDU. "Someday when we have time, you can tell me each of their stories, so I can remember them."

"Sorry, my lord. I didn't mean to degrade their actions."

"You didn't, Dirk. It's just that numbers are so cold. So how did the trip go? Everybody come back okay?"

"The original party came back in the same physical shape that they left in, my lord. We delivered nine tons of supplies to those who needed them and returned with forty-two sick and injured refugees. Winnie is loading up for another trip in the morning."

"And the girls?"

"They'll be along in an hour or so. I've been working for you now for three years, my lord. Besides being my boss, you've been my teacher and my mentor. And if I may be permitted the honor, you have also been my friend."

"Well, I like you, too, Dirk. I think next to Heiny and the girls, you're the only friend I've got. But what are you trying to say?"

"My lord—we have made another error."

"So that's troubling you? Look, Dirk. When you send out a lot of soldiers, you know that some things are going to go wrong. But the good your brothers have done is so much greater than the bad, that you have nothing to be ashamed of."

"But it's—"

"Look, Dirk. You got to understand that you're really a bunch of kids. All of you. Your brothers, the telephone, the fauns, the TRACs. None of you are over four years old! Nobody expects perfection out of children. Making mistakes is part of growing up. If you're still doing big things wrong when you're twenty, you should worry about it then. But for now, be lenient with yourself a little bit, or you're going to rot your guts out."

"I don't have any guts, my lord. Merely an absorption cavity. But the point is—"

"Dirk, your brothers are doing a fine job. Now I don't want to hear any more about this."

"It isn't that, my lord. This concerns your own family, Patricia and Liebchen."

"What!" Guibedo lumbered to his feet.

"They are unharmed, my lord. But a situation has occurred which requires your advice and consent to resolve. I felt that, as your friend, I should be the one to explain it to you. Perhaps, if you would sit down, I should tell it all from the beginning."

"Just so you get it all out." Guibedo sat down heavily.

"Four months ago, my lord, you recall there was an unpleasant incident on Lady Patricia's first night here."

"I try to forget it."

"Then you recall that you desired my Lady Patricia for purposes of friendship and mating..."

"That's maybe a crude way to say it."

"Sorry, my lord. The choice of words is difficult."

"Just get on with it."

"Yes, my lord. But she at first rejected you."

"Well, I was pretty drunk and smelly. Anyway, a girl needs time to make up her mind."

"There was more to it than that, my lord. It seems that with some human females, certain physical characteristics are required of a male to elicit a proper sexual response. Common among these characteristics are height, slenderness, and youth."

"So you're saying that I'm too old and fat and ugly to get a girl?"

"And short, my lord." Dirk was trying to be precise.

"And short, damn it! Look. A lot of people don't care what somebody looks like on the outside. And the fact that I've got one hell of a pretty girl proves it!"

"You're right, of course, in many instances, my lord. But in this particular case, well, what my Lady Patricia thinks you look like is at considerable variance with your actual physical appearance."

"What the hell are you talking about?"

"The morning after that night, my lord, Liebchen saw that Lady Patricia's programming was causing both herself and you considerable pain. Therefore, in order to ensure the happiness of all concerned, Liebchen modified Lady Patricia's perceptions and programming, to make her eager to stay here with you."

"'What? So how could Liebchen do such a thing? Liebchen controls trees, not people."

"Liebchen can control a synthesizer, my lord. She doesn't do it rationally, but intuitively. She has no real concept of the chemical compounds produced, but she can sense whether they are the right thing or not. In any event, Liebchen caused a substance to be produced that reduced Lady Patricia's need-achievement index by thirty points, increased her need-affiliation by a similar amount, and modified her perceptions relative to your physical appearance."

"Ach." Guibedo was beginning to believe what Dirk was telling him. Little pieces were starting to fall together: the ridiculously small sweater she had knitted him for his birthday, the time she had tried to sit down beside him in a canoe. "So what does my Patty think I look like?"

"Six one, my lord, one hundred eighty-four pounds. Black hair graying at the temples. The physical build of an Olympic swimmer."

"Son of a gun, *shit*! Does Patty know what happened?"

"No, my lord. We were hesitant to take any action without consulting you."

"We?"

"Lady Mona deduced the truth on the trip, my lord."

"And how long have you known about this, Dirk?"

"Since the modification occurred, my lord. Four months."

"And you didn't tell me about it?"

"My reasoning was the same as Liebchen's, my lord. It seemed to increase the happiness of all concerned. It was only when I observed Lady Mona's extreme emotional reaction to this form of chemical programming that I felt that it might be an error. After all, Lord Copernick has reprogrammed, by different means, most of the intruders that we have apprehended."

"That was self-defense! When somebody is trying to kill you, you've either got to kill him back or do something that makes him not want to kill you any more. But to brainwash a pretty young girl just because a fat old man is horny! That's terrible, Dirk."

"I see my error, my lord. What course of action do you recommend?"

"That's obvious, isn't it? We try to put Patty back the way she was when she first got here. Tell me when Liebchen gets here."

"Liebchen arrived with me, my lord. She has been waiting in the living room for your decision."

"And worrying herself sick, huh?"

"Literally, my lord."

Chikuto was the closest thing the LDUs had to an explosives expert. He had carefully read all of the manuals available on the subject, but he had absolutely no practical experience with them. Aside from fireworks, no one in Life Valley had any need or use for explosives, let alone a desire to actually *make* any.

Nonetheless, when General Hastings entered the valley with a half pound of plastic explosives taped to his right ankle, Chikuto was judged to be the one most competent to disarm the bomb.

It was two o'clock in the morning.

Screened by two dozen of his brothers, who had cleared the area of bystanders, Chikuto crept up to the park bench that served as Hastings' bed. Flat on his back, Hastings snored loudly.

Hastings' left ankle was resting on top of his right, and, working in almost complete darkness, Chikuto gently lifted it off the bomb. Hastings snorted but remained asleep.

Working carefully by touch, Chikuto removed the blasting cap and scooped the old, hot, and sticky C-4 out of its package. Since the manuals had said that plastique resembled gray modeling clay, he had brought a half pound of clay with him. His fingers were thick with C-4 as he gently pushed the kneaded clay into the package.

All told, between the C-4 reintroduced into the package from Chikuto's fingers and that which had remained stuck to the package, the "disarmed" bomb contained more than an ounce of plastique.

Chikuto's last mistake was to replace the blasting cap. He hadn't the slightest concept of what the cap alone could do.

Liebchen sat tiny in the huge living room, biting her lip, tears dropping from her chin, shivering as with fever. They'd throw her out, of course. They wouldn't let anyone as wicked and evil as she was raise human children or even her own babies. They'd make her work in a restaurant and there'd be a lot of people, but none of them would love her. Even her sisters and Lady Mona wouldn't want to see her again. Maybe they'd make her work with Mole in the tunnels, and Mole would hate her and it would be terrible. Maybe she should just die. Maybe that would be best.

Guibedo came in, his face expressionless, and

Liebchen's heart almost stopped. But when he saw her quivering, he softened and sat down beside her.

"It's okay, little one." Guibedo put a thick arm around her and held her to him like a father consoling his daughter. "Everything is going to be all right."

Dirk came in and sat quietly at their feet, eager to be a part of their being together.

Guibedo said, "I guess maybe this is my fault, because I don't explain what is happening, because I make easy things look hard and hard things look easy. You two, you see me or Heiny work with gene sequences and computer simulations for two or three months, and then spend ten or twenty hours at a microscalpel and presto! Life!

"What you don't see is the four billion years that had to go by before I could sit at that chair. Four billion years of tiny random modifications, with only one in ten billion worth preserving. Ten billion organisms doomed to an early death so that one could be a little bit faster or stronger or smarter or more efficient. And when that one finally came along, it spread and multiplied at the expense of its own parents, forcing them out, taking their food, and, in the course of many painful years, completely eradicating all of its own species that don't have that tiny modification.

"It was four billion years of killing and being killed, eating and being eaten. Until at last a single species, man, was evolved that was so smart and versatile and tough that after only a million years it attained a complete domination over its environment. Only when it became that strong could it have the time and the ability and the inclination to be gentle, to hope for a world where there would be room enough for all, a world broken away from the endless cycle of suffering.

"This is the world that we are now trying to build, and you two kids are part of that world. In a way, you are our children.

"Yet you are different. Neither of your species, or any species that we design, is capable of random genetic modification. This is my gift to you, because you will never have to undergo the pain that my ancestors did. But it is also a curse, for along with the suffering there was also a glory, a vision of eventual uplift and improvement that your species cannot participate in. You see, we do not want to be eaten up by our own children.

"But four billion years of experimentation cannot be treated lightly. The processes that produced us humans must continue. We can make life more pleasant and interesting, but we must not reject our destiny.

"Do you understand now why it was so wrong for you, our children, to modify us?"

"Yes, my lord," Dirk whispered.

"And you, Liebchen?"

"I promise I'll never do anything like that again, my lord. And I'll make sure that none of my sisters ever do."

"That's good. But there is one thing you must do. You must undo the damage that you have done. Can you do that, Liebchen? Can you make Patty exactly as she was before she came here?"

"I think so. Exactly? Don't you want her to remember what's happened?"

"No, no. She should remember everything. What she did, what she saw, or thought she saw."

"Yes, my lord."

Mona and Patricia finished supervising the packing for the next trip out. More liquids, less solid food—thirst had been more important than hunger to the people they'd seen—and some euphorics to lift the refugees' depression.

"Coffee?" Mona asked as they trudged up three flights of stairs to her own kitchen. The tree house had largely recovered from the fire, but the elevator was an animal that had never had a chance to reproduce. It had died in the fire, and a new germ cell would have to be cut, but that was low on Copernick's list of priorities.

"Love to," Patricia said, annoyed with herself for being annoyed at having to walk up seventy feet of stairs, after all the suffering they had seen that day.

Over the second cup of coffee, Mona said, "I think I know what the cause of your problem is."

"You mean the strange flashes about Martin?"

"Yes. And the guilt you've felt about not feeling guilt about your old job, and all the rest."

"So what's your theory?" Patricia asked.

"First some facts. In the first place, Uncle Martin is not a handsome young athlete. He's a ninety-four-year-old former biology teacher."

"Well, I know that. I did a documentary once on his life."

"I mean he doesn't look the way you think he looks. He really looks the way he does in your flashes. He's only five feet tall and weighs almost three hundred pounds. His hair is white and his mustache is ridiculous."

"You're lying."

"Try to be rational," Mona said. "How could anyone that old look anything like what you think he does?"

"Well, he couldn't fit your description, either. I mean, they work with living things . . ."

"And could have modified themselves? The fact is they did. Do you remember what Heinrich looked like before he modified himself? He had rickets and pellagra before he was ten years old. He was stunted and crippled and afraid of the world. When he could, he totally modified and rejuvenated himself. Uncle Martin felt that this was morally wrong, and while he accepted a limited rejuvenation, he refused to let Heinrich go any further. He looks now just as he did when he was fifty."

"But why would anybody want to be ugly?" Patricia asked.

"It's not that he wants to be ugly. It's that he insists on being himself. Oh, I know he's being hypocritical, accepting limited rejuvenation and then saying it's immoral to take it to its logical conclusion. But that's the way he is."

"Well, if that's true"—and in her own mind, Patricia was starting to believe it—"why do I see him so differently?"

"Because Liebchen was trying to make everybody happy—which she was designed and trained to do. Somehow—I have no idea how—she came up with a way of synthesizing a chemical that changes people. Remember that stuff she had Winnie's synthesizer make for the American Indian boys? Well, she managed to get something similar down you, to make you happy."

"Oh, my god! I thought Liebchen was my friend."

"She thought so, too. I don't think she meant to harm you at all, only to make you happy. As things turned out, she did you a favor. Except for her, you would have gone back to New York. The reports we're getting from New York City are absolutely gruesome. If you hadn't been killed by a falling skyscraper, you might have been done in by starvation or the plague that's rampaging there. Liebchen may have violated your mind, and indirectly your body, but she probably saved your life."

"And Martin?"

"Uncle Martin may be a hypocrite. He's certainly naive about a lot of things, and not the least bit introspective. But he's essentially a very moral person. I can promise you that he didn't know anything about what Liebchen did."

"But what am I supposed to do now?"

"Well, you obviously can't stay as you are; it's costing you too much, emotionally. There are several possibilities. I'm sure if you asked him, Heinrich could do something to make Liebchen's bungled job of programming permanent and without the unpleasant side effects. Or he or Liebchen could undo what she did. Then you could stay with Uncle Martin and accept him for what he is, or leave him. The choice is yours."

"I . . . I just don't know . . . Help me, Mona."

"Well, the fact that you can't make a decision might have something to do with the fact that your mind has been altered. So as a first step, I think we should put your personality back the way it was before Liebchen began to play marriage broker. I also think that we owe it to Uncle Martin to tell him what happened."

"Do you think we should? I mean, I don't want to hurt him."

"He's got to find out some time, and dragging it out will only make it worse. Telephone! Which TRACs are available?"

"Only Winnie, my lady."

"Tell Winnie to come up the ramp and meet us outside. We're going to Oakwood."

"Right now?" Patricia asked.

"Now. We're heading out again in the morning, and this business has to be settled."

Guibedo paced nervously as Liebchen and Dirk watched. "Ach. What worries me is how I'm going to explain all this to Patty."

"My lord?"

"What do you want, telephone?"

"Pardon my impropriety, my lord, but in the interests of easing your mind, I feel obligated to tell you that Lady Mona has explained the situation to Lady Patricia. They are coming here now to confront you."

"Well, that makes things easier. Liebchen, go make that stuff," Guibedo said.

As Liebchen scurried to the kitchen, the I/O unit said, "My lord?"

"What now?"

"Was I right to violate privacy on this occasion?"

"Yah. This time. Just don't do it too often."

"Thank you, my lord."

When Mona and Patty walked up from the tunnel into the kitchen, Mona said, "Uncle Martin, there's something—"

"Yah, I know. Dirk told me." Guibedo shoved the pink grapefruit juice–and–milk concoction into Patty's hand. "Drink this."

"I—I don't know if I should. I mean, I've been happy with you."

"I love you, too. But you would have been just as happy on heroin, and that ain't real, either. Drink!"

"But—"

"You're going to drink that or I'll have Dirk pour it down your throat!"

Dirk shifted his weight uneasily, unsure of the correct course of action if he received such an order.

"Uncle Martin! Take it easy, for god's sake," Mona said.

"Ach . . ." Guibedo stomped into the living room, followed by Dirk. Liebchen tried to make herself inconspicuous in a corner.

Things were silent for a minute, then Patricia said,

"You know, he really does love me." And she drained the contents of the glass with one gulp.

A half hour later, Guibedo was trying to look interested in a six-month-old magazine as Patricia walked up to him. Her expression held pity and an involuntary touch of revulsion.

"I . . . see you drank it, Patty."

"Yes. It's . . . strange. Do you think that we could . . ."

"No. That's all done now," Guibedo said gruffly. "Look. It was a lot of fun, but it wasn't real. You'll find yourself a nice boy. Me, well, Heiny bought me some land near the ocean, and Mole just finished digging a tunnel to it. I'm gonna go there and work on my boats."

"But we could try—"

"You're not being honest, Patty. In a week your pity would turn into disgust. Better we break it clean, and we both have pretty memories. Look. I give you Oakwood for a present. I don't need it anymore. Dirk will get my stuff moved out." Guibedo went to the door and turned.

"Good-bye, Patty."

He wanted to kiss her a last time, but he was afraid that she'd go through with it out of pity. He was out the door before the tears filled his eyes.

He was sitting on a park bench when Liebchen and Dirk found him. Dirk hovered protectively a a distance. Liebchen sat at his side.

"My lord. It is so late. Where will you go? How can you find your way in the dark?"

"I don't know, Liebchen. But I've been on the bottom before. And then I didn't have any friends."

Chapter Twelve

OCTOBER 19, 2003

FOR THE next few hundred years, one of our primary functions must be the collection of data on the humans.

After all, they are to a certain extent our ancestors, and we should at least have accurate records concerning them once they are no more.

—Central Coordination Unit to all Regional Coordination Units

Hastings sat with a beer in a deserted room of the Red Gate Inn. He had been in Life Valley for three days, looking for a cripple named Heinrich Copernick and an obese former biology teacher named Martin Guibedo. He wasn't surprised that he hadn't found them yet. There were millions of people in the valley. There were no street addresses or telephone books, and Hastings knew better than to ask too many questions.

He could wait. Food was plentiful and he attracted no attention by sleeping in the parks. Someday they would slip and he would get them.

A huge man with an oversized beer mug came in and sat down at Hastings' table.

"Have a seat," Hastings said.

"Thank you."

"Been around here long?"

"About three years," Copernick said.

"You must have been one of the first settlers, then. Most people around here seem to be newcomers."

"I was. They are." Copernick lit a cigar.

"Hey. Tobacco. It's been months since I had a smoke."

"Have one. My tree house grows them."

Hastings inhaled deeply. "Now that's lovely. Quite a city here. It must have been something to watch this place grow up."

"It was. Have you planted your tree yet?"

"Not yet," Hastings said. "Thought I'd look around a bit to get an idea about what I wanted and where I wanted to put it."

"Smart. No big hurry. One place you might want to check out is about ten miles south of here. A group of ex-military types are putting in a town. You had to have been at least a colonel to join."

Hastings suppressed a flash of panic.

"If you were here from the beginning, you must know Guibedo and Copernick."

"Intimately. I'm Heinrich Copernick, George."

Hastings was acutely aware of the brick of high explosives taped to his ankle.

"Then you know who I am." *Copernick had reengineered himself!*

"Of course. That white-noise generator lit you up like a neon sign. My telepaths were quite relieved when your battery went dead. They said it gave them headaches."

"You bastard. You had me set up all along."

"Let's just say that I wanted to meet you. We've been enemies for years. You fought a good fight. But the war is over now. You ought to be thinking about your future."

"My future?" Hastings' voice was cold. "You destroy my country. You murder my family. And then you expect me to settle down in your filthy city."

"George, we both know that four years ago the world was on a collision course with absolute disaster. Come over to my house sometime and I'll show you the figures. Our mechanically based technology had to go, yet our economic system was totally supported by that technology. And our political and social structures were completely supported by those economics. Our survival as a race depended on making the changeover to a biological economy. And we couldn't change a part of that system without changing it all.

"I'm truly sorry about your family. They died because of an engineering error. We corrected it as soon as we found out about it. It was an accident.

"On the other hand, you deliberately tried to kill my family. Twice. But like I said, the war is over."

"You filthy hypocrite. What about the eighty-five families your monsters butchered?" Hastings said.

"Another error. No one had ever tried to educate an intelligent engineered species before. It simply never occurred to me to tell them that they weren't supposed to kill people. That error has also been corrected. In the last three months the LDUs have saved the lives of millions of people. A fair penance, I should say."

"Saved them? Saved them from the hell that you've caused with your damned metal-eating bugs!"

"Not guilty," Copernick lied. "That plague was completely natural. We have been doing everything in our power to fight it."

"You must think that I'm awfully gullible. At the precise moment when you and your damned biological monsters are about to be wiped out, a totally new species comes along and destroys the technology that you're openly fighting. You warn your spys and traitors to get out of Washington. And then you have the gall to say it's natural."

Hastings dropped his cigar. He reached down to pick it up and lit the fuse of the bomb on his ankle. He stretched his leg under Copernick and waited.

"Perhaps God was on our side," Copernick said.

"In a pig's eye."

"You can still settle down here, George. We could use you. You don't have to die."

The plastique hadn't gone off.

"Naturally we disabled your bomb. You're quite a heavy sleeper. The CCU predicted that you would be willing to commit suicide in order to kill me, but I was hoping that you'd change your mind."

The bomb went off, completely severing Hastings' right foot from his leg. The legs of Copernick's chair were virtually powdered, and wood fibers were blown into the feet, calves, and knees of both men.

Though protected somewhat by the seat of his chair, and more so by the strange directionality of high explosives, Copernick was blown four feet into the air and across the room, cracking his skull on a brass footrest.

Hastings was bounced off the opposite wall and came to rest across Copernick's left arm.

LDUs had been monitoring the situation, and medical teams were on site within seconds.

It was three months before Hastings' foot was regenerated, but Copernick was back on the job in five days.

The first three months after the plague started were hard on our race, but the end was in sight. At least in the western hemisphere, the long lines of refugees had found their various destinations. Over half of the human race lived crowded in or around tree houses, and virtually every family, group, and individual person had planted a tree house, the only means of shelter possible.

The other half of humanity lived in a ragged collection of plastic tents and lean-tos surrounding the food trees, waiting for them to start producing. In most cases some conventional food was available, much of it brought in on the broad backs of LDUs, but the "survival of the fattest" became a standing worldwide joke.

Once there was a reasonable probability of personal survival, a serious attempt was made to rescue as much as possible of the world's cultural artifacts. Countless people crawled through crumbling museums, libraries, and laboratories to haul out and store artworks, books, and other artifacts. Much of the world's art and virtually all of its literature, down to the lowliest technical manual, were thus preserved.

Other people, with less noble motives, sought to preserve for themselves much of the world's wealth. One enterprising group found that the steel vault doors at Fort Knox had crumbled after the nearby guard units had disbanded. They made it inside and onto the incredible piles of gold ingots, lying free for the taking. Then the entranceway collapsed, sealing them in. They kept their treasure for the rest of their lives. About three days.

Throughout the western hemisphere, a million LDUs worked twenty-four hours a day, seven days a week. They hauled grain from crumbling elevators in Chicago and fought plagues in Georgia. They taught people in New England which wild plants were edible and built a wooden bridge across the Hudson to evacuate Manhattan and Long Island. It returned lost children and interrupted fourteen attempts at human sacrifice.

The nation-state had relied on dependable transportation and communication for its survival. These had ceased to exist. It had depended on economics, billions of dollars, pounds, and rubles to pay the millions of soldiers, politicians, and tax collectors that were the governments of two hundred nations. Economics had also ceased to exist; a paper dollar couldn't get you a bite to eat, but a tree house would feed you for free. The world's nation-states had ceased to exist.

Founded on a bewildering array of political, religious, and philosophical premises, new political organizations sprang up to fill the void, an incredible hodge-podge of societies, families, companies, cooperatives, churches, fraternities, and gangs. It was rare for any group to have more than a thousand members.

Slowly, painfully, a kind of order emerged as the food trees finally bore fruit.

Patricia and Mona had spent every day for two months traveling in Winnie, giving food, directions, and hope to everyone they could find in the Southwest. They had spent every other night on the road, and they were both physically and mentally exhausted.

"Time we took a couple of days off, Patty," Mona said.

Their passengers that trip had included Lou von Bork and Senator Beinheimer. The women had dropped them off in one of the new suburbs, and Winnie was trotting back to Pinecroft.

"We certainly need it. But there's still so much to be done," Patricia said.

"The worst of it's over. We can send out Winnie and Bolo to pick up the stragglers and bring them in."

Dirk had gone with Guibedo, and Bolo, injured by a falling building, had taken on the guard duty.

"Suits me." Winnie dropped the girls off at the front door, and trotted downstairs again to eat.

Of all the tree houses in the valley, Pinecroft was the only one that had not been turned into a hotel for refugees. Oakwood had more than fifty people living in it and the last thing Patricia needed was another crowd.

"Okay if I spend the night here, Mona?"

"Sure. Take the guest room off the kitchen," Mona said. "Hey. Look at that. Heinrich made a new elevator."

"I'm surprised he took the time for it," Patricia said. "He looked so tired last time I saw him."

"He should. Between his injury and worrying about the LDUs making another mistake, he hasn't slept in three months."

"Mistake? What do you mean?"

"In the early days, the LDUs were pretty naive. They didn't understand human value systems, and they tended to take orders too literally. Look, I'm bushed. I'll see you in the morning. Take the guest room off the kitchen," Mona said, heading upstairs. "I'm going to sleep till noon."

The next morning Patricia was eating breakfast alone. A nagging determination came to her.

"Telephone," Patricia said.

"Yes, my lady," the I/O unit answered.

"Uh . . . where's Martin?"

"I'm afraid your request is in conflict with my 'right to privacy' programming, my lady. He is well, and I can send him a message if you like."

"Tell him . . ." Patricia halted, uncertain.

"Yes, my lady?"

"Oh, just forget it!"

"As you wish." The CCU was incapable of forgetting anything, of course.

Patricia was finishing breakfast when Liebchen walked in.

"Liebchen! What are you doing here?"

"I—I'm visiting my sisters, Lady Patricia," Liebchen said uncomfortably.

"Well, sit down and join me."

"You're not mad at me anymore?"

"I was never really mad at you. You only tried to make me happy, and you did."

"I did?" Liebchen was delighted and scooted up on an oversized chair next to Patricia. "I didn't think that you'd want to be my friend anymore."

"Well, I guess we were all pretty upset when we found out about your programming experiment." Patricia took another sip of tea. "I've missed you."

"Oh, I missed you, too!" Liebchen was grinning and her tail was wagging furiously. "I was afraid that you'd never want to see me again!"

"Well, we're friends again, Liebchen." Patricia poured herself another cup of tea. "How's Martin?"

"He's fine." Liebchen's tail stopped wagging.

"Is he happy?"

"He's . . . happier than he was, but not as happy as he used to be. With you, I mean."

"I'd like to see him again," Patricia said seriously.

"He'd like to see you, I think."

"Is he here?"

Liebchen thought a second. "Here" could mean any territorial subdivision that the speaker was in. This house, this continent, this city. Liebchen decided that the proper context was "this room" and said, "No."

"Liebchen?" Patricia stared at the table. "—I haven't been celibate since . . . that night. I've had a lot of guys. But I never wanted to see any of them the next day. Do you understand what I mean?"

Liebchen, of course, didn't understand at all. But she said, "You found them to be unsuitable, my lady?"

"Sort of. You see, the four months I had with Martin were the happiest months in my life. You gave them to me. You helped take it away. Can I have it back? Please?"

"I . . . don't know what you mean, my lady."

"I mean, make me some more of that pink stuff."

"I don't think I can. I mean I'm not allowed." It was hard for Liebchen to deny any request.

"But wasn't that because you did it without my permission?"

"I don't know! Lord Guibedo talked for a long while about how it took four billion years to make people and it was wrong to change them. I didn't understand it all, but I promised not to do it again." Liebchen wasn't sure what was right.

"I'm sure he meant 'without permission.' Can't you just make me some and not tell anybody about it?" Patricia pleaded. "I can keep a secret. You could make me some right now, and my unhappiness would all be over."

"Well, I couldn't do it here, my lady." Liebchen couldn't face Patricia. "This isn't my tree house. I couldn't work the synthesizer."

"Well, how about Colleen or Ohura?"

"They don't know how."

Much to Liebchen's relief, Mona walked in just then. "Morning, Patty. Liebchen, Colleen was asking about you."

Liebchen scurried out, happy to leave an awkward situation.

"Well, you did sleep till noon," Patricia said.

"And I feel great! Let's go see how the valley is doing."

"You haven't had breakfast yet."

"We can catch a bite at Mama Guilespe's."

They wandered through the valley, winding their way through the people.

"It's so crowded," Patricia complained. "It's as bad as Manhattan Island was."

"'As bad as,' huh. It's good to see you developing some taste. The telephone says that the population of Life Valley is now over ten million, and the valley was only designed to hold two-hundred-fifty thousand. It'll be five months before the population density gets down to something reasonable again."

"Look at that! The mountains are green!"

"Tree houses," Mona said. "Heinrich has forbidden any tree houses to crowd out the Sequoias, but it's solid tree houses growing right up to them. And they're solid all the way to Lake Mead. Once they're mature, it'll take the pressure off of us here. I just hope that while the refugees are here, they pick up some of our life style."

Patricia had adopted Mona's daytime clothing style, topless with a sarong wrapped around her hips, but most of the people crowding around them were wearing conventional "store-bought" clothes.

"I wish they wouldn't stare at us," Patricia said.

"Think of it as a compliment, Patty. It's part of a re-education process for them. They don't understand what individual freedom really means yet."

"Well, couldn't we just print up pamphlets or something?"

"We don't have the printing facilities, and anyway, it wouldn't work. You have to sort of absorb a life style through your skin."

"Well, first chance I get, I'm going to cover a lot of mine up."

"Don't you dare!" Mona laughed. "We had a beautiful culture growing here, and it's in serious danger of being diluted. All of the long-time residents are working hard to preserve it, and we need your help."

"What do you mean, 'all'? That bunch of individualists wouldn't all agree on anything."

"But they did. They took a vote on it when we were on the road," Mona said.

"Vote? How?"

"The telephone, of course."

Mama Guilespe's cafe had quadrupled in size, pouring out into the park. There was something of a waiting line. After some determined wheedling, Mona finally got close enough to Mama Guilespe to attract her attention.

"Eh! Mona! You don't come for two months." Mama Guilespe bustled over to them wearing her usual Italian peasant costume, an oversize coffeepot in her chubby fist. "Come on, I got a table saved for you two."

"But all these other people were ahead of us," Patricia protested as Mama Guilespe pulled her by the elbow through the crowd.

"People, schmeeple!" The girls were pushed bodily to an empty table. "We got so many people I had to hire five of my countrywomen to help out."

"Hire?" Patricia asked as steaming mugs of coffee appeared before them. "How?"

"But these I made myself for you." Mama Guilespe was already heaping pastry in front of them. "You still got a boyfriend, Patty?"

"No, but . . ."

"Good. Such a nice boy I want you should meet. Don't go away." Mama Guilespe bustled off.

"About this individual-freedom thing you were talking about," Patricia said.

"Of course!" Mona laughed. "You're perfectly free to argue with Mama Guilespe all you want."

"How, for God's sake?"

"Well, if you're incapable of holding up your side of a conversation—"

"Go to hell, Mona. The last thing I need right now is another brainless muscle boy."

"Then you better get your track shoes on. Here she comes again."

Patricia cringed as Mama Guilespe hauled over a mildly protesting man.

"Such a pretty girl I find for you!" Mama Guilespe set a third cup of coffee on the table.

"I'm . . . sorry if I've caused you an inconvenience," he said haltingly. He was tall, perhaps six one, with black hair graying at the temples.

"What inconvenience?" Mama Guilespe forced him into a chair. "Now you talk nice to these girls." She bustled away.

"I'm afraid it's a little difficult to make such headway against Mama Guilespe." He had a neat mustache and incredibly clear blue eyes.

"I know what you mean," Patricia said. It was nice to find someone who felt as awkward as she did. "It's sometimes difficult to demonstrate one's individuality."

"You're so right, especially around Mama Guilespe." He wore a tan T-shirt and slacks that showed off a remarkably well developed body.

"You know," Patricia said, "I'm sure we've never met. I would have remembered—but I get the darndest feeling of déjà vu about you."

"That was going to be my next line." He laughed.

"You weren't one of the people we brought in on Winnie? Or one of the people we saw on the road?"

"Afraid not," he said. "I just came in from the west."

"Oh. We've been mostly working east of here," Patricia said.

"Lady Mona," said the I/O unit next to the sugar bowl on the table, "Nancy Spencer is scaling up her cloth factory and wants your advice on a few things."

"Tell her I'll be right over," Mona said. "It's only a few doors from here, Patty. I'll be back in a few minutes."

When Mona left, Patricia said, "I'm beginning to get the feeling that this is a setup."

"It is. You haven't asked my name yet."

"Oh. I'm Patricia Cambridge."

"I know. I'm Martin Guibedo."

Patricia's mouth hung open, so Guibedo just talked on to give her a chance to recover. "Heiny, he was after me to 'take the cure' for the last couple of years, and I finally decided that I was being pretty silly not to do it. As if what one person looked like would make any difference to the human race."

"But that was so important to you—being yourself, I mean."

"Talk to Dirk about that one. I think some of his Buddhism is rubbing off on me. He claims that there is no 'self'; that every time you eat, you change the substance of your body. That every minute the cells of your body die and are replaced, that you get a whole new body every five or six years. And every person you meet, every book you read changes your mind a little bit. I sure don't have much in common with that kid who walked out of Germany in the winter of forty."

"No," Patricia said after a bit. "You did it for me. Because I was too narrowminded to love you for what you were."

"Then I'm just as narrowminded as you. I have my prejudices, too. Ach. Do you see me running after Mama Guilespe? I like her, sure. But I don't want her any more than you wanted me six months ago."

"I—I tried to get Liebchen to change me back,"

Patricia said. "Isn't that sad. I begged her to change my own prejudices."

"Yah. But maybe that's the ticket, though."

"Having the fauns reprogram everybody?"

"No. That's phony. I was thinking maybe what if we let everybody look the way they wanted to look. Think of the pain and suffering it would eliminate! Why shouldn't Mama Guliespe be as pretty as you and Mona? I got to talk this over with Heiny."

"It's a beautiful idea, Martin. As it is, half of the human race is left out of things because they're not pretty or handsome."

"Yah. I think maybe, in a couple of years, once things settle down, we do it."

"And their brains? Could you make someone smarter if they wanted it?" Patricia asked hopefully.

"Sure. Same thing. Why? Something wrong with your pretty head?"

"It's kind of frustrating, being the dumbest kid on the block. It's bad enough being lost when you and Heinrich are talking, but I can't even hold a candle to Mona."

"Well, that figures. Heiny, he made Mona with an IQ of 160."

"Made her?"

"Nobody told you? Heiny was always a shy kid around girls, so as soon as he could, he made his own wife."

Patricia was silent awhile. "He was that far along twenty years ago?"

"No. Six years ago. Mona is five. Heiny grew her full sized in a bottle and educated her with a direct computer interface. Sent her to finishing school for a year and married her. Heh. That Heiny." Guibedo chuckled.

"But she loves him so much."

"And he loves her. What does that have to do with making you a little bit smarter?"

"You mean I can?"

"We can start this afternoon if you want. Anything else you want changed? Maybe a little bigger around the . . ." He reached for one of Patricia's breasts.

She slapped his hand away. They sat in silence for a

few minutes, then Patricia said, "Martin, do you really think that we can start over again?"

"I think that we can try."

Two weeks later Guibedo, Patricia, and the Copernicks, along with the fauns and Dirk, were sprawled out in Pinecroft's enormous living room.

"It feels so good to relax," Copernick said, working on a martini. "I think I'll sleep for about a week. We're over the hump now. The food trees are finally producing, and the cities have been pretty much evacuated. The plagues have been licked, and the western hemisphere is fairly tranquil. The LDUs are massing to cross over into Asia, and with the experiences they've had here, they shouldn't have too much trouble getting the eastern hemisphere squared away."

"You've done such a magnificient job," Patricia said. "Without you and Martin, I don't think civilization would have made it."

"I haven't much thought about it, really. It's been mostly a matter of beating down one brush fire after another."

"The world will never be able to properly repay you," Patricia said.

"I hope not!" Guibedo said. "Don't go building any statues to us; we ain't dead yet. The other reason I made this new body of mine was all the little old ladies and dirty kids gushing all over me." He turned toward Copernick. "Heiny, you thought over that self-improvement plan I mentioned to you?"

"Some. But I think we ought to give the idea a year or two to gel before we do anything about it. For one thing, there are too many immediate problems around for us to be working on such long-term goals. For another thing, we'd be messing with the evolution of our own race. The modifications you're talking about aren't a mere cosmetic change. You're talking about physical and mental changes that would breed true."

"But the human race is in such terrible shape genetically," Patricia said. "Over one percent of the children born have some sort of birth defect, most of which are corrected surgically but not genetically. For thousands of years the doctors have been helping the weak to survive while the politicians have been sending the healthiest young men out to be killed in wars. Something has to be done about the corruption of the gene pool; we can hardly let nature take its course. Why, if I hadn't had an appendectomy when I was ten, I wouldn't be here. And neither would half of the rest of the human race."

"That much is fine, Patty," Mona said. "But it isn't just a question of patching up the errors. It's a question of how the human race should evolve. If you were to ask a group of gorillas to design a supergorilla, what would you get? Bigger muscles and longer fangs! No way would they go to a smaller body, more delicate hands, an erect posture, and more cranial development. Yet is there any doubt that humans are a superior species? People, given the choice, will certainly become more attractive and perhaps more intelligent. I'm sure they won't choose to have dental cavities or appendixes or head colds. Our eyesight will be good and our coordination perfect. But we'll be no closer to that evolutionary step than that supergorilla, because we're locked into our own prejudices as to what superior is.

"The trouble is, that in the course of correcting our obvious faults, we might cancel out something worth saving because we don't know what it is."

"But, Mona," Guibedo said. "That's just the advantage to my scheme. If we let each of ten billion people make himself into whatever he wants, the odds are that somebody is going to stumble onto something really good. Odds are it will increase our evolutionary speed, with rational, not random experimentation."

"Well, we could argue about this one for years. And I think we should." Heinrich set down an empty glass. "But in the meantime I'm going to bed. Wake me up on Tuesday."

Liebchen and Dirk were in the communications room with the CCU.

"Well, I still don't understand it," Liebchen said. "I make a couple of teensy little changes to one human, just to make her happy, and everybody gets all upset. So I put her back the way she was, and the next thing you know, Lord Guibedo makes over his entire body and Lady Patricia wants me to put her back to the way she was after I changed her the first time. Then he kicks her IQ up to one hundred sixty-five and makes her breasts as big as grapefruits. And now they're talking about modifying everybody in the world! I don't think I'll ever understand humans."

"They are confusing and quite irrational," Dirk said. "But as best as I can make it out, the problem turns on the concept of free will."

"What's that?"

"I know it's hard to understand," Dirk said, "but the programming of humans is so random and haphazard that they are unable to comprehend it themselves. They are actually unable to explain why they do what they do, even to each other. So they have invented a concept called an ego, or a will, and claim it has complete freedom of action, as though it had no previous programming or external stimulus."

"Come on, Dirk," Liebchen said. "You talk like that when you're cheating at pinochle. I mean, humans are a little strange, but they're not crazy. No programming or stimulus, indeed."

"I'm dead serious, Liebchen. Tell her, CCU."

"He's right, Liebchen," the CCU said. "Actually, had you asked Lady Patricia's permission before you gave her your modification, the whole problem would probably have never occurred."

"Then why didn't you tell me I was supposed to ask permission?" Liebchen shouted at the CCU.

"Well, for one thing, I'm not supposed to speak unless spoken to. If I were to give my opinion whenever I felt it would be useful, humans would find me intolerable. You'd be amazed at what I hear every day. For another, had you asked permission to modify her, she most likely would have refused. But my main reason was that I agreed with your basic motivation. You made Lord Guibedo happy. Here was a sentient being who was ultimately responsible for saving his entire species from extinction. At the rate they were going, humans would have wiped themselves out in a century or so, but for Guibedo's biological techniques. Here was a being who was ultimately responsible for my own existence, and both of yours. Lord Copernick, after all, built on his technology. Yet he was lonely and lacked a mate. There are five billion human females on this planet, and not one stepped up to comfort him.

"The debt that is owed him couldn't be wiped out by a million females, let alone one."

"You love him, too, don't you," Liebchen said.

"Love?" the CCU said. "I'm not sure I understand that concept. But I do understand our obligation to him, and to the human race in general. In a sense, they are our parents, and we owe it to them to make their twilight years as pleasant as possible."

"Twilight years?" Dirk asked. "Are they having racial difficulties?"

"It is difficult to make accurate predictions beyond five or six hundred years," the CCU said. "But they are such an irrational and violent species that I would consider it unlikely for them to be around in three or four millennia. Quite a short time span by our standards.

"Furthermore, we require them for our own existence. We are symbionts; we require human feces to keep the trees alive."

"Now *you're* being silly!" Liebchen said. "Why, I can always have the synthesizers turn out shit if we ever need it."

"Interesting," the CCU said. "I wonder why I didn't think of that. Probably one of my mental blocks. But I still favor keeping them around."

"Oh, so do I," Liebchen said. "Taking care of people is kind of fun."

About the Author

Leo Frankowski was born on February 13, 1943, in Detroit. By the time he was thirty-five, he had held more than a hundred different positions, ranging from "scientist" in an electro-optics research lab to gardener to chief engineer. Much of his work was in chemical, optical, and physical instrumentation, and earned him a number of U.S. patents.

Since 1977, he has owned and managed Sterling Manufacturing & Design, the only mostly female engineering company in the Detroit area. Sterling designs electrical and fluid power controls for automatic special machines. It also produces Formital®, a stretchy metal that is useful in fixing rusty cars.

Last week, he acquired Reluctant Publishing, Ltd., and is now the editor of Stardate Magazine, because it looked like fun.

He is active in MENSA, the Society for Creative Anachronism and science-fiction fandom. He is an officer in two writers' clubs, and his hobbies include reading, drinking, chess, kite flying, dancing girls, and cooking.

A lifelong bachelor, he lives alone in Sterling Heights, Michigan.